Tales of the Fish Patrol

&

The Red One

Jack London

Tales of the Fish Patrol & The Red One

ISBN: 978-1-64799-428-0

CONTENTS

TALES OF THE FISH PATROL

THE RED ONE

TALES OF THE FISH PATROL

I

WHITE AND YELLOW

San Francisco Bay is so large that often its storms are more disastrous to ocean-going craft than is the ocean itself in its violent moments. The waters of the bay contain all manner of fish, wherefore its surface is ploughed by the keels of all manner of fishing boats manned by all manner of fishermen. To protect the fish from this motley floating population many wise laws have been passed, and there is a fish patrol to see that these laws are enforced. Exciting times are the lot of the fish patrol: in its history more than one dead patrolman has marked defeat, and more often dead fishermen across their illegal nets have marked success.

Wildest among the fisher-folk may be accounted the Chinese shrimp-catchers. It is the habit of the shrimp to crawl along the bottom in vast armies till it reaches fresh water, when it turns about and crawls back again to the salt. And where the tide ebbs and flows, the Chinese sink great bag-nets to the bottom, with gaping mouths, into which the shrimp crawls and from which it is transferred to the boiling-pot. This in itself would not be bad, were it not for the small mesh of the nets, so small that the tiniest fishes, little new-hatched things not a quarter of an inch long, cannot pass through. The beautiful beaches of Points Pedro and Pablo, where are the shrimp-catchers villages, are made fearful by the stench from myriads of decaying fish, and against this wasteful destruction it has ever been the duty of the fish patrol to act.

When I was a youngster of sixteen, a good sloop-sailor and all-round bay-waterman, my sloop, the Reindeer, was chartered by the Fish Commission, and I became for the time being a deputy patrolman. After a deal of work among the Greek fishermen of the Upper Bay and rivers, where knives flashed at the beginning of trouble and men permitted themselves to be made prisoners only after a revolver was thrust in their faces, we hailed with delight an expedition to the Lower Bay against the Chinese shrimp-catchers.

1

There were six of us, in two boats, and to avoid suspicion we ran down after dark and dropped anchor under a projecting bluff of land known as Point Pinole. As the east paled with the first light of dawn we got under way again, and hauled close on the land breeze as we slanted across the bay toward Point Pedro. The morning mists curled and clung to the water so that we could see nothing, but we busied ourselves driving the chill from our bodies with hot coffee. Also we had to devote ourselves to the miserable task of bailing, for in some incomprehensible way the Reindeer had sprung a generous leak. Half the night had been spent in overhauling the ballast and exploring the seams, but the labor had been without avail. The water still poured in, and perforce we doubled up in the cockpit and tossed it out again.

After coffee, three of the men withdrew to the other boat, a Columbia River salmon boat, leaving three of us in the Reindeer. Then the two craft proceeded in company till the sun showed over the eastern skyline. Its fiery rays dispelled the clinging vapors, and there, before our eyes, like a picture, lay the shrimp fleet, spread out in a great half-moon, the tips of the crescent fully three miles apart, and each junk moored fast to the buoy of a shrimp-net. But there was no stir, no sign of life.

The situation dawned upon us. While waiting for slack water, in which to lift their heavy nets from the bed of the bay, the Chinese had all gone to sleep below. We were elated, and our plan of battle was swiftly formed.

"Throw each of your two men on to a junk," whispered Le Grant to me from the salmon boat. "And you make fast to a third yourself. We'll do the same, and there's no reason in the world why we shouldn't capture six junks at the least."

Then we separated. I put the Reindeer about on the other tack, ran up under the lee of a junk, shivered the mainsail into the wind and lost headway, and forged past the stern of the junk so slowly and so near that one of the patrolmen stepped lightly aboard. Then I kept off, filled the mainsail, and bore away for a second junk.

Up to this time there had been no noise, but from the first junk captured by the salmon boat an uproar now broke forth. There was shrill Oriental yelling, a pistol shot, and more yelling.

"It's all up. They're warning the others," said George, the remaining patrolman, as he stood beside me in the cockpit.

By this time we were in the thick of the fleet, and the alarm was spreading with incredible swiftness. The decks were beginning to swarm with half-awakened and half-naked Chinese. Cries and yells of warning and anger were flying over the quiet water, and somewhere a conch shell was being blown with great success. To the

2

right of us I saw the captain of a junk chop away his mooring line with an axe and spring to help his crew at the hoisting of the huge, outlandish lug-sail. But to the left the first heads were popping up from below on another junk, and I rounded up the Reindeer alongside long enough for George to spring aboard.

The whole fleet was now under way. In addition to the sails they had gotten out long sweeps, and the bay was being ploughed in every direction by the fleeing junks. I was now alone in the Reindeer, seeking feverishly to capture a third prize. The first junk I took after was a clean miss, for it trimmed its sheets and shot away surprisingly into the wind. By fully half a point it outpointed the Reindeer, and I began to feel respect for the clumsy craft. Realizing the hopelessness of the pursuit, I filled away, threw out the main-sheet, and drove down before the wind upon the junks to leeward, where I had them at a disadvantage.

The one I had selected wavered indecisively before me, and, as I swung wide to make the boarding gentle, filled suddenly and darted away, the swart Mongols shouting a wild rhythm as they bent to the sweeps. But I had been ready for this. I luffed suddenly. Putting the tiller hard down, and holding it down with my body, I brought the main-sheet in, hand over hand, on the run, so as to retain all possible striking force. The two starboard sweeps of the junk were crumpled up, and then the two boats came together with a crash. The Reindeer's bowsprit, like a monstrous hand, reached over and ripped out the junk's chunky mast and towering sail.

This was met by a curdling yell of rage. A big Chinaman, remarkably evil-looking, with his head swathed in a yellow silk handkerchief and face badly pock-marked, planted a pike-pole on the Reindeer's bow and began to shove the entangled boats apart. Pausing long enough to let go the jib halyards, and just as the Reindeer cleared and began to drift astern, I leaped aboard the junk with a line and made fast. He of the yellow handkerchief and pock-marked face came toward me threateningly, but I put my hand into my hip pocket, and he hesitated. I was unarmed, but the Chinese have learned to be fastidiously careful of American hip pockets, and it was upon this that I depended to keep him and his savage crew at a distance.

I ordered him to drop the anchor at the junk's bow, to which he replied, "No sabbe." The crew responded in like fashion, and though I made my meaning plain by signs, they refused to understand. Realizing the inexpediency of discussing the matter, I went forward myself, overran the line, and let the anchor go.

"Now get aboard, four of you," I said in a loud voice, indicating with my fingers that four of them were to go with me and the fifth was to remain by the junk. The Yellow Handkerchief hesitated; but I repeated the order fiercely (much more fiercely than I felt), at the same time sending my hand to my hip. Again the Yellow Handkerchief was overawed, and with surly looks he led three of his men aboard the Reindeer. I cast off at once, and, leaving the jib down, steered a course for George's junk. Here it was easier, for there were two of us, and George had a pistol to fall back on if it came to the worst. And here, as with my junk, four Chinese were transferred to the sloop and one left behind to take care of things.

Four more were added to our passenger list from the third junk. By this time the salmon boat had collected its twelve prisoners and came alongside, badly overloaded. To make matters worse, as it was a small boat, the patrolmen were so jammed in with their prisoners that they would have little chance in case of trouble.

"You'll have to help us out," said Le Grant.

I looked over my prisoners, who had crowded into the cabin and on top of it. "I can take three," I answered.

"Make it four," he suggested, "and I'll take Bill with me." (Bill was the third patrolman.) "We haven't elbow room here, and in case of a scuffle one white to every two of them will be just about the right proportion."

The exchange was made, and the salmon boat got up its spritsail and headed down the bay toward the marshes off San Rafael. I ran up the jib and followed with the Reindeer. San Rafael, where we were to turn our catch over to the authorities, communicated with the bay by way of a long and tortuous slough, or marshland creek, which could be navigated only when the tide was in. Slack water had come, and, as the ebb was commencing, there was need for hurry if we cared to escape waiting half a day for the next tide.

But the land breeze had begun to die away with the rising sun, and now came only in failing puffs. The salmon boat got out its oars and soon left us far astern. Some of the Chinese stood in the forward part of the cockpit, near the cabin doors, and once, as I leaned over the cockpit rail to flatten down the jib-sheet a bit, I felt some one brush against my hip pocket. I made no sign, but out of the corner of my eye I saw that the Yellow Handkerchief had discovered the emptiness of the pocket which had hitherto overawed him.

To make matters serious, during all the excitement of boarding the junks the Reindeer had not been bailed, and the water was beginning to slush over the cockpit floor. The shrimp-catchers pointed at it and looked to me questioningly.

"Yes," I said. "Bime by, allee same dlown, velly quick, you no bail now. Sabbe?"

4

No, they did not "sabbe," or at least they shook their heads to that effect, though they chattered most comprehendingly to one another in their own lingo. I pulled up three or four of the bottom boards, got a couple of buckets from a locker, and by unmistakable sign-language invited them to fall to. But they laughed, and some crowded into the cabin and some climbed up on top.

Their laughter was not good laughter. There was a hint of menace in it, a maliciousness which their black looks verified. The Yellow Handkerchief, since his discovery of my empty pocket, had become most insolent in his bearing, and he wormed about among the other prisoners, talking to them with great earnestness.

Swallowing my chagrin, I stepped down into the cockpit and began throwing out the water. But hardly had I begun, when the boom swung overhead, the mainsail filled with a jerk, and the Reindeer heeled over. The day wind was springing up. George was the veriest of landlubbers, so I was forced to give over bailing and take the tiller. The wind was blowing directly off Point Pedro and the high mountains behind, and because of this was squally and uncertain, half the time bellying the canvas out, and the other half flapping it idly.

George was about the most all-round helpless man I had ever met. Among his other disabilities, he was a consumptive, and I knew that if he attempted to bail, it might bring on a hemorrhage. Yet the rising water warned me that something must be done. Again I ordered the shrimp-catchers to lend a hand with the buckets. They laughed defiantly, and those inside the cabin, the water up to their ankles, shouted back and forth with those on top.

"You'd better get out your gun and make them bail," I said to George.

But he shook his head and showed all too plainly that he was afraid. The Chinese could see the funk he was in as well as I could, and their insolence became insufferable. Those in the cabin broke into the food lockers, and those above scrambled down and joined them in a feast on our crackers and canned goods.

"What do we care?" George said weakly.

I was fuming with helpless anger. "If they get out of hand, it will be too late to care. The best thing you can do is to get them in check right now."

The water was rising higher and higher, and the gusts, forerunners of a steady breeze, were growing stiffer and stiffer. And between the gusts, the prisoners, having gotten away with a week's grub, took to crowding first to one side and then to the other till the Reindeer rocked like a cockle-shell. Yellow Handkerchief approached me, and, pointing out his village on the Point Pedro beach, gave me to understand that if I turned the Reindeer in that direction and put them ashore, they, in turn, would go to bailing. By now the water in the cabin was up to the bunks, and the bed-clothes were sopping. It was a foot deep on the cockpit floor. Nevertheless I refused, and I could see by George's face that he was disappointed.

"If you don't show some nerve, they'll rush us and throw us overboard," I said to him. "Better give me your revolver, if you want to be safe."

"The safest thing to do," he chattered cravenly, "is to put them ashore. I, for one, don't want to be drowned for the sake of a handful of dirty Chinamen."

"And I, for another, don't care to give in to a handful of dirty Chinamen to escape drowning," I answered hotly.

"You'll sink the Reindeer under us all at this rate," he whined. "And what good that'll do I can't see."

"Every man to his taste," I retorted.

He made no reply, but I could see he was trembling pitifully. Between the threatening Chinese and the rising water he was beside himself with fright; and, more than the Chinese and the water, I feared him and what his fright might impel him to do. I could see him casting longing glances at the small skiff towing astern, so in the next calm I hauled the skiff alongside. As I did so his eyes brightened with hope; but before he could guess my intention, I stove the frail bottom through with a hand-axe, and the skiff filled to its gunwales.

"It's sink or float together," I said. "And if you'll give me your revolver, I'll have the Reindeer bailed out in a jiffy."

"They're too many for us," he whimpered. "We can't fight them all."

I turned my back on him in disgust. The salmon boat had long since passed from sight behind a little archipelago known as the Marin Islands, so no help could be looked for from that quarter. Yellow Handkerchief came up to me in a familiar manner, the water in the cockpit slushing against his legs. I did not like his looks. I felt that beneath the pleasant smile he was trying to put on his face there was an ill purpose. I ordered him back, and so sharply that he obeyed.

"Now keep your distance," I commanded, "and don't you come closer!"

"Wha' fo'?" he demanded indignantly. "I t'ink-um talkee talkee heap good."

"Talkee talkee," I answered bitterly, for I knew now that he had understood all that passed between George and me. "What for talkee talkee? You no sabbe talkee talkee."

He grinned in a sickly fashion. "Yep, I sabbe velly much. I honest Chinaman."

"All right," I answered. "You sabbe talkee talkee, then you bail water plenty plenty. After that we talkee talkee."

He shook his head, at the same time pointing over his shoulder to his comrades. "No can do. Velly bad Chinamen, heap velly bad. I t'ink-um—"

"Stand back!" I shouted, for I had noticed his hand disappear beneath his blouse and his body prepare for a spring.

Disconcerted, he went back into the cabin, to hold a council, apparently, from the way the jabbering broke forth. The Reindeer was very deep in the water, and her movements had grown quite loggy. In a rough sea she would have inevitably swamped; but the wind, when it did blow, was off the land, and scarcely a ripple disturbed the surface of the bay.

"I think you'd better head for the beach," George said abruptly, in a manner that told me his fear had forced him to make up his mind to some course of action.

"I think not," I answered shortly.

"I command you," he said in a bullying tone.

"I was commanded to bring these prisoners into San Rafael," was my reply.

Our voices were raised, and the sound of the altercation brought the Chinese out of the cabin.

"Now will you head for the beach?"

This from George, and I found myself looking into the muzzle of his revolver—of the revolver he dared to use on me, but was too cowardly to use on the prisoners.

My brain seemed smitten with a dazzling brightness. The whole situation, in all its bearings, was focussed sharply before me— the shame of losing the prisoners, the worthlessness and cowardice of George, the meeting with Le Grant and the other patrol-men and the lame explanation; and then there was the fight I had fought so hard, victory wrenched from me just as I thought I had it within my grasp. And out of the tail of my eye I could see the Chinese crowding together by the cabin doors and leering triumphantly. It would never do.

I threw my hand up and my head down. The first act elevated the muzzle, and the second removed my head from the path of the bullet which went whistling past. One hand closed on George's wrist, the other on the revolver. Yellow Handkerchief and his gang sprang toward me. It was now or never. Putting all my strength into a sudden effort, I swung George's body forward to meet them. Then I pulled back with equal suddenness, ripping the revolver out of his fingers and jerking him off his feet. He fell against Yellow Handkerchief's knees, who stumbled over him, and the pair wallowed in the bailing hole where the cockpit floor was torn open. The next instant I was covering them with my revolver, and the wild shrimp-catchers were cowering and cringing away.

But I swiftly discovered that there was all the difference in the world between shooting men who are attacking and men who are doing nothing more than simply refusing to obey. For obey they would not when I ordered them into the bailing hole. I threatened them with the revolver, but they sat stolidly in the flooded cabin and on the roof and would not move.

Fifteen minutes passed, the Reindeer sinking deeper and deeper, her mainsail flapping in the calm. But from off the Point Pedro shore I saw a dark line form on the water and travel toward us. It was the steady breeze I had been expecting so long. I called to the Chinese and pointed it out. They hailed it with exclamations. Then I pointed to the sail and to the water in the Reindeer, and indicated by signs that when the wind reached the sail, what of the water aboard we would capsize. But they jeered defiantly, for they knew it was in my power to luff the helm and let go the main-sheet, so as to spill the wind and escape damage.

But my mind was made up. I hauled in the main-sheet a foot or two, took a turn with it, and bracing my feet, put my back against the tiller. This left me one hand for the sheet and one for the revolver. The dark line drew nearer, and I could see them looking from me to it and back again with an apprehension they could not successfully conceal. My brain and will and endurance were pitted against theirs, and the problem was which could stand the strain of imminent death the longer and not give in.

Then the wind struck us. The mainsheet tautened with a brisk rattling of the blocks, the boom uplifted, the sail bellied out, and the Reindeer heeled over—over, and over, till the lee-rail went under, the deck went under, the cabin windows went under, and the bay began to pour in over the cockpit rail. So violently had she heeled over, that the men in the cabin had been thrown on top of one another into the lee bunk, where they squirmed and twisted and were washed about, those underneath being perilously near to drowning.

The wind freshened a bit, and the Reindeer went over farther than ever. For the moment I thought she was gone, and I knew that another puff like that and she surely would go. While I pressed her under and debated whether I should give up or not, the Chinese cried for mercy. I think it was the sweetest sound I have ever heard. And then, and not until then, did I luff up and ease out the main-sheet. The Reindeer righted very slowly, and when she was on an even keel was so much awash that I doubted if she could be saved.

But the Chinese scrambled madly into the cockpit and fell to bailing with buckets, pots, pans, and everything they could lay hands on. It was a beautiful sight to see that water flying over the side! And when the Reindeer was high and proud on the water once more, we dashed away with the breeze on our quarter, and at the last possible moment crossed the mud flats and entered the slough.

The spirit of the Chinese was broken, and so docile did they become that ere we made San Rafael they were out with the tow-rope, Yellow Handkerchief at the head of the line. As for George, it was his last trip with the fish patrol. He did not care for that sort of thing, he explained, and he thought a clerkship ashore was good enough for him. And we thought so, too.

II

THE KING OF THE GREEKS

Big Alec had never been captured by the fish patrol. It was his boast that no man could take him alive, and it was his history that of the many men who had tried to take him dead none had succeeded. It was also history that at least two patrolmen who had tried to take him dead had died themselves. Further, no man violated the fish laws more systematically and deliberately than Big Alec.

He was called "Big Alec" because of his gigantic stature. His height was six feet three inches, and he was correspondingly broad-shouldered and deep-chested. He was splendidly muscled and hard as steel, and there were innumerable stories in circulation among the fisher-folk concerning his prodigious strength. He was as bold and dominant of spirit as he was strong of body, and because of this he was widely known by another name, that of "The King of the Greeks." The fishing population was largely composed of Greeks, and they looked up to him and obeyed him as their chief. And as their chief, he fought their fights for them, saw that they were protected, saved them from the law when they fell into its clutches, and made them stand by one another and himself in time of trouble.

In the old days, the fish patrol had attempted his capture many disastrous times and had finally given it over, so that when the word was out that he was coming to Benicia, I was most anxious to see him.

But I did not have to hunt him up. In his usual bold way, the first thing he did on arriving was to hunt us up. Charley Le Grant and I at the time were under a patrolman named Carmintel, and the three of us were on the Reindeer, preparing for a trip, when Big Alec stepped aboard. Carmintel evidently knew him, for they shook hands in recognition. Big Alec took no notice of Charley or me.

"I've come down to fish sturgeon a couple of months," he said to Carmintel.

His eyes flashed with challenge as he spoke, and we noticed the patrolman's eyes drop before him.

"That's all right, Alec," Carmintel said in a low voice. "I'll not bother you. Come on into the cabin, and we'll talk things over," he added.

When they had gone inside and shut the doors after them, Charley winked with slow deliberation at me. But I was only a

10

youngster, and new to men and the ways of some men, so I did not understand. Nor did Charley explain, though I felt there was something wrong about the business.

Leaving them to their conference, at Charley's suggestion we boarded our skiff and pulled over to the Old Steamboat Wharf, where Big Alec's ark was lying. An ark is a house-boat of small though comfortable dimensions, and is as necessary to the Upper Bay fisherman as are nets and boats. We were both curious to see Big Alec's ark, for history said that it had been the scene of more than one pitched battle, and that it was riddled with bullet-holes.

We found the holes (stopped with wooden plugs and painted over), but there were not so many as I had expected. Charley noted my look of disappointment, and laughed; and then to comfort me he gave an authentic account of one expedition which had descended upon Big Alec's floating home to capture him, alive preferably, dead if necessary. At the end of half a day's fighting, the patrolmen had drawn off in wrecked boats, with one of their number killed and three wounded. And when they returned next morning with reënforcements they found only the mooring-stakes of Big Alec's ark; the ark itself remained hidden for months in the fastnesses of the Suisun tules.

"But why was he not hanged for murder?" I demanded. "Surely the United States is powerful enough to bring such a man to justice."

"He gave himself up and stood trial," Charley answered. "It cost him fifty thousand dollars to win the case, which he did on technicalities and with the aid of the best lawyers in the state. Every Greek fisherman on the river contributed to the sum. Big Alec levied and collected the tax, for all the world like a king. The United States may be all-powerful, my lad, but the fact remains that Big Alec is a king inside the United States, with a country and subjects all his own."

"But what are you going to do about his fishing for sturgeon? He's bound to fish with a 'Chinese line.'"

Charley shrugged his shoulders. "We'll see what we will see," he said enigmatically.

Now a "Chinese line" is a cunning device invented by the people whose name it bears. By a simple system of floats, weights, and anchors, thousands of hooks, each on a separate leader, are suspended at a distance of from six inches to a foot above the bottom. The remarkable thing about such a line is the hook. It is barbless, and in place of the barb, the hook is filed long and tapering

11

to a point as sharp as that of a needle. These hooks are only a few inches apart, and when several thousand of them are suspended just above the bottom, like a fringe, for a couple of hundred fathoms, they present a formidable obstacle to the fish that travel along the bottom.

Such a fish is the sturgeon, which goes rooting along like a pig, and indeed is often called "pig-fish." Pricked by the first hook it touches, the sturgeon gives a startled leap and comes into contact with half a dozen more hooks. Then it threshes about wildly, until it receives hook after hook in its soft flesh; and the hooks, straining from many different angles, hold the luckless fish fast until it is drowned. Because no sturgeon can pass through a Chinese line, the device is called a trap in the fish laws; and because it bids fair to exterminate the sturgeon, it is branded by the fish laws as illegal. And such a line, we were confident, Big Alec intended setting, in open and flagrant violation of the law.

Several days passed after the visit of Big Alec, during which Charley and I kept a sharp watch on him. He towed his ark around the Solano Wharf and into the big bight at Turner's Shipyard. The bight we knew to be good ground for sturgeon, and there we felt sure the King of the Greeks intended to begin operations. The tide circled like a mill-race in and out of this bight, and made it possible to raise, lower, or set a Chinese line only at slack water. So between the tides Charley and I made it a point for one or the other of us to keep a lookout from the Solano Wharf.

On the fourth day I was lying in the sun behind the stringer-piece of the wharf, when I saw a skiff leave the distant shore and pull out into the bight. In an instant the glasses were at my eyes and I was following every movement of the skiff. There were two men in it, and though it was a good mile away, I made out one of them to be Big Alec; and ere the skiff returned to shore I made out enough more to know that the Greek had set his line.

"Big Alec has a Chinese line out in the bight off Turner's Shipyard," Charley Le Grant said that afternoon to Carmintel.

A fleeting expression of annoyance passed over the patrolman's face, and then he said, "Yes?" in an absent way, and that was all.

Charley bit his lip with suppressed anger and turned on his heel.

"Are you game, my lad?" he said to me later on in the evening, just as we finished washing down the Reindeer's decks and were preparing to turn in.

A lump came up in my throat, and I could only nod my head.

"Well, then," and Charley's eyes glittered in a determined way, "we've got to capture Big Alec between us, you and I, and we've got to do it in spite of Carmintel. Will you lend a hand?"

"It's a hard proposition, but we can do it," he added after a pause.

"Of course we can," I supplemented enthusiastically.

And then he said, "Of course we can," and we shook hands on it and went to bed.

But it was no easy task we had set ourselves. In order to convict a man of illegal fishing, it was necessary to catch him in the act with all the evidence of the crime about him—the hooks, the lines, the fish, and the man himself. This meant that we must take Big Alec on the open water, where he could see us coming and prepare for us one of the warm receptions for which he was noted.

"There's no getting around it," Charley said one morning. "If we can only get alongside it's an even toss, and there's nothing left for us but to try and get alongside. Come on, lad."

We were in the Columbia River salmon boat, the one we had used against the Chinese shrimp-catchers. Slack water had come, and as we dropped around the end of the Solano Wharf we saw Big Alec at work, running his line and removing the fish.

"Change places," Charley commanded, "and steer just astern of him as though you're going into the shipyard."

I took the tiller, and Charley sat down on a thwart amidships, placing his revolver handily beside him.

"If he begins to shoot," he cautioned, "get down in the bottom and steer from there, so that nothing more than your hand will be exposed."

I nodded, and we kept silent after that, the boat slipping gently through the water and Big Alec growing nearer and nearer. We could see him quite plainly, gaffing the sturgeon and throwing them into the boat while his companion ran the line and cleared the hooks as he dropped them back into the water. Nevertheless, we were five hundred yards away when the big fisherman hailed us.

"Here! You! What do you want?" he shouted.

"Keep going," Charley whispered, "just as though you didn't hear him."

The next few moments were very anxious ones. The fisherman was studying us sharply, while we were gliding up on him every second.

"You keep off if you know what's good for you!" he called out

13

suddenly, as though he had made up his mind as to who and what we were. "If you don't, I'll fix you!"

He brought a rifle to his shoulder and trained it on me.

"Now will you keep off?" he demanded.

I could hear Charley groan with disappointment. "Keep off," he whispered; "it's all up for this time."

I put up the tiller and eased the sheet, and the salmon boat ran off five or six points. Big Alec watched us till we were out of range, when he returned to his work.

"You'd better leave Big Alec alone," Carmintel said, rather sourly, to Charley that night.

"So he's been complaining to you, has he?" Charley said significantly.

Carmintel flushed painfully. "You'd better leave him alone, I tell you," he repeated. "He's a dangerous man, and it won't pay to fool with him."

"Yes," Charley answered softly; "I've heard that it pays better to leave him alone."

This was a direct thrust at Carmintel, and we could see by the expression of his face that it sank home. For it was common knowledge that Big Alec was as willing to bribe as to fight, and that of late years more than one patrolman had handled the fisherman's money.

"Do you mean to say—" Carmintel began, in a bullying tone.

But Charley cut him off shortly. "I mean to say nothing," he said. "You heard what I said, and if the cap fits, why—"

He shrugged his shoulders, and Carmintel glowered at him, speechless.

"What we want is imagination," Charley said to me one day, when we had attempted to creep upon Big Alec in the gray of dawn and had been shot at for our trouble.

And thereafter, and for many days, I cudgelled my brains trying to imagine some possible way by which two men, on an open stretch of water, could capture another who knew how to use a rifle and was never to be found without one. Regularly, every slack water, without slyness, boldly and openly in the broad day, Big Alec was to be seen running his line. And what made it particularly exasperating was the fact that every fisherman, from Benicia to Vallejo, knew that he was successfully defying us. Carmintel also bothered us, for he kept us busy among the shad-fishers of San Pablo, so that we had little time to spare on the King of the Greeks. But Charley's wife and children lived at Benicia, and we had made the place our headquarters, so that we always returned to it.

"I'll tell you what we can do," I said, after several fruitless weeks had passed; "we can wait some slack water till Big Alec has run his line and gone ashore with the fish, and then we can go out and capture the line. It will put him to time and expense to make another, and then we'll figure to capture that too. If we can't capture him, we can discourage him, you see."

Charley saw, and said it wasn't a bad idea. We watched our chance, and the next low-water slack, after Big Alec had removed the fish from the line and returned ashore, we went out in the salmon boat. We had the bearings of the line from shore marks, and we knew we would have no difficulty in locating it. The first of the flood tide was setting in, when we ran below where we thought the line was stretched and dropped over a fishing-boat anchor. Keeping a short rope to the anchor, so that it barely touched the bottom, we dragged it slowly along until it stuck and the boat fetched up hard and fast.

"We've got it," Charley cried. "Come on and lend a hand to get it in."

Together we hove up the rope till the anchor came in sight with the sturgeon line caught across one of the flukes. Scores of the murderous-looking hooks flashed into sight as we cleared the anchor, and we had just started to run along the line to the end where we could begin to lift it, when a sharp thud in the boat startled us. We looked about, but saw nothing and returned to our work. An instant later there was a similar sharp thud and the gunwale splintered between Charley's body and mine.

"That's remarkably like a bullet, lad," he said reflectively. "And it's a long shot Big Alec's making."

"And he's using smokeless powder," he concluded, after an examination of the mile-distant shore. "That's why we can't hear the report."

I looked at the shore, but could see no sign of Big Alec, who was undoubtedly hidden in some rocky nook with us at his mercy. A third bullet struck the water, glanced, passed singing over our heads, and struck the water again beyond.

"I guess we'd better get out of this," Charley remarked coolly. "What do you think, lad?"

I thought so, too, and said we didn't want the line anyway. Whereupon we cast off and hoisted the spritsail. The bullets ceased at once, and we sailed away, unpleasantly confident that Big Alec was laughing at our discomfiture.

And more than that, the next day on the fishing wharf, where we were inspecting nets, he saw fit to laugh and sneer at us, and this

15

before all the fishermen. Charley's face went black with anger; but beyond promising Big Alec that in the end he would surely land him behind the bars, he controlled himself and said nothing. The King of the Greeks made his boast that no fish patrol had ever taken him or ever could take him, and the fishermen cheered him and said it was true. They grew excited, and it looked like trouble for a while; but Big Alec asserted his kingship and quelled them.

Carmintel also laughed at Charley, and dropped sarcastic remarks, and made it hard for him. But Charley refused to be angered, though he told me in confidence that he intended to capture Big Alec if it took all the rest of his life to accomplish it.

"I don't know how I'll do it," he said, "but do it I will, as sure as I am Charley Le Grant. The idea will come to me at the right and proper time, never fear."

And at the right time it came, and most unexpectedly. Fully a month had passed, and we were constantly up and down the river, and down and up the bay, with no spare moments to devote to the particular fisherman who ran a Chinese line in the bight of Turner's Shipyard. We had called in at Selby's Smelter one afternoon, while on patrol work, when all unknown to us our opportunity happened along. It appeared in the guise of a helpless yacht loaded with seasick people, so we could hardly be expected to recognize it as the opportunity. It was a large sloop-yacht, and it was helpless inasmuch as the trade-wind was blowing half a gale and there were no capable sailors aboard.

From the wharf at Selby's we watched with careless interest the lubberly manœuvre performed of bringing the yacht to anchor, and the equally lubberly manœuvre of sending the small boat ashore. A very miserable-looking man in draggled ducks, after nearly swamping the boat in the heavy seas, passed us the painter and climbed out. He staggered about as though the wharf were rolling, and told us his troubles, which were the troubles of the yacht. The only rough-weather sailor aboard, the man on whom they all depended, had been called back to San Francisco by a telegram, and they had attempted to continue the cruise alone. The high wind and big seas of San Pablo Bay had been too much for them; all hands were sick, nobody knew anything or could do anything; and so they had run in to the smelter either to desert the yacht or to get somebody to bring it to Benicia. In short, did we know of any sailors who would bring the yacht into Benicia?

Charley looked at me. The Reindeer was lying in a snug place. We had nothing on hand in the way of patrol work till midnight. With the wind then blowing, we could sail the yacht into Benicia in a couple of hours, have several more hours ashore, and come back to the smelter on the evening train.

"All right, captain," Charley said to the disconsolate yachtsman, who smiled in sickly fashion at the title.

"I'm only the owner," he explained.

We rowed him aboard in much better style than he had come ashore, and saw for ourselves the helplessness of the passengers. There were a dozen men and women, and all of them too sick even to appear grateful at our coming. The yacht was rolling savagely, broad on, and no sooner had the owner's feet touched the deck than he collapsed and joined the others. Not one was able to bear a hand, so Charley and I between us cleared the badly tangled running gear, got up sail, and hoisted anchor.

It was a rough trip, though a swift one. The Carquinez Straits were a welter of foam and smother, and we came through them wildly before the wind, the big mainsail alternately dipping and flinging its boom skyward as we tore along. But the people did not mind. They did not mind anything. Two or three, including the owner, sprawled in the cockpit, shuddering when the yacht lifted and raced and sank dizzily into the trough, and between-whiles regarding the shore with yearning eyes. The rest were huddled on the cabin floor among the cushions. Now and again some one groaned, but for the most part they were as limp as so many dead persons.

As the bight at Turner's Shipyard opened out, Charley edged into it to get the smoother water. Benicia was in view, and we were bowling along over comparatively easy water, when a speck of a boat danced up ahead of us, directly in our course. It was low-water slack. Charley and I looked at each other. No word was spoken, but at once the yacht began a most astonishing performance, veering and yawing as though the greenest of amateurs was at the wheel. It was a sight for sailormen to see. To all appearances, a runaway yacht was careering madly over the bight, and now and again yielding a little bit to control in a desperate effort to make Benicia.

The owner forgot his seasickness long enough to look anxious. The speck of a boat grew larger and larger, till we could see Big Alec and his partner, with a turn of the sturgeon line around a cleat, resting from their labor to laugh at us. Charley pulled his sou'wester over his eyes, and I followed his example, though I could not guess the idea he evidently had in mind and intended to carry into execution.

We came foaming down abreast of the skiff, so close that we

could hear above the wind the voices of Big Alec and his mate as they shouted at us with all the scorn that professional watermen feel for amateurs, especially when amateurs are making fools of themselves.

We thundered on past the fishermen, and nothing had happened. Charley grinned at the disappointment he saw in my face, and then shouted:

"Stand by the main-sheet to jibe!"

He put the wheel hard over, and the yacht whirled around obediently. The main-sheet slacked and dipped, then shot over our heads after the boom and tautened with a crash on the traveller. The yacht heeled over almost on her beam ends, and a great wail went up from the seasick passengers as they swept across the cabin floor in a tangled mass and piled into a heap in the starboard bunks.

But we had no time for them. The yacht, completing the manoeuvre, headed into the wind with slatting canvas, and righted to an even keel. We were still plunging ahead, and directly in our path was the skiff. I saw Big Alec dive over-board and his mate leap for our bowsprit. Then came the crash as we struck the boat, and a series of grinding bumps as it passed under our bottom.

"That fixes his rifle," I heard Charley mutter, as he sprang upon the deck to look for Big Alec somewhere astern.

The wind and sea quickly stopped our forward movement, and we began to drift backward over the spot where the skiff had been. Big Alec's black head and swarthy face popped up within arm's reach; and all unsuspecting and very angry with what he took to be the clumsiness of amateur sailors, he was hauled aboard. Also he was out of breath, for he had dived deep and stayed down long to escape our keel.

The next instant, to the perplexity and consternation of the owner, Charley was on top of Big Alec in the cockpit, and I was helping bind him with gaskets. The owner was dancing excitedly about and demanding an explanation, but by that time Big Alec's partner had crawled aft from the bowsprit and was peering apprehensively over the rail into the cockpit. Charley's arm shot around his neck and the man landed on his back beside Big Alec.

"More gaskets!" Charley shouted, and I made haste to supply them.

The wrecked skiff was rolling sluggishly a short distance to windward, and I trimmed the sheets while Charley took the wheel and steered for it.

"These two men are old offenders," he explained to the angry owner; "and they are most persistent violators of the fish and game laws. You have seen them caught in the act, and you may expect to be subpœnaed as witness for the state when the trial comes off."

As he spoke he rounded alongside the skiff. It had been torn from the line, a section of which was dragging to it. He hauled in forty or fifty feet with a young sturgeon still fast in a tangle of barbless hooks, slashed that much of the line free with his knife, and tossed it into the cockpit beside the prisoners.

"And there's the evidence, Exhibit A, for the people," Charley continued. "Look it over carefully so that you may identify it in the court-room with the time and place of capture."

And then, in triumph, with no more veering and yawing, we sailed into Benicia, the King of the Greeks bound hard and fast in the cockpit, and for the first time in his life a prisoner of the fish patrol.

III

A RAID ON THE OYSTER PIRATES

Of the fish patrolmen under whom we served at various times, Charley Le Grant and I were agreed, I think, that Neil Partington was the best. He was neither dishonest nor cowardly; and while he demanded strict obedience when we were under his orders, at the same time our relations were those of easy comradeship, and he permitted us a freedom to which we were ordinarily unaccustomed, as the present story will show.

Neil's family lived in Oakland, which is on the Lower Bay, not more than six miles across the water from San Francisco. One day, while scouting among the Chinese shrimp-catchers of Point Pedro, he received word that his wife was very ill; and within the hour the Reindeer was bowling along for Oakland, with a stiff northwest breeze astern. We ran up the Oakland Estuary and came to anchor, and in the days that followed, while Neil was ashore, we tightened up the Reindeer's rigging, overhauled the ballast, scraped down, and put the sloop into thorough shape.

This done, time hung heavy on our hands. Neil's wife was dangerously ill, and the outlook was a week's lie-over, awaiting the crisis. Charley and I roamed the docks, wondering what we should do, and so came upon the oyster fleet lying at the Oakland City Wharf. In the main they were trim, natty boats, made for speed and bad weather, and we sat down on the stringer-piece of the dock to study them.

"A good catch, I guess," Charley said, pointing to the heaps of oysters, assorted in three sizes, which lay upon their decks.

Pedlers were backing their wagons to the edge of the wharf, and from the bargaining and chaffering that went on, I managed to learn the selling price of the oysters.

"That boat must have at least two hundred dollars' worth aboard," I calculated. "I wonder how long it took to get the load?"

"Three or four days," Charley answered. "Not bad wages for two men—twenty-five dollars a day apiece."

The boat we were discussing, the Ghost, lay directly beneath us. Two men composed its crew. One was a squat, broad-shouldered fellow with remarkably long and gorilla-like arms, while the other was tall and well proportioned, with clear blue eyes and a mat of straight black hair. So unusual and striking was this combination of

20

hair and eyes that Charley and I remained somewhat longer than we intended.

And it was well that we did. A stout, elderly man, with the dress and carriage of a successful merchant, came up and stood beside us, looking down upon the deck of the Ghost. He appeared angry, and the longer he looked the angrier he grew.

"Those are my oysters," he said at last. "I know they are my oysters. You raided my beds last night and robbed me of them."

The tall man and the short man on the Ghost looked up.

"Hello, Taft," the short man said, with insolent familiarity. (Among the bayfarers he had gained the nickname of "The Centipede" on account of his long arms.) "Hello, Taft," he repeated, with the same touch of insolence. "Wot 'r you growlin' about now?"

"Those are my oysters—that's what I said. You've stolen them from my beds."

"Yer mighty wise, ain't ye?" was the Centipede's sneering reply. "S'pose you can tell your oysters wherever you see 'em?"

"Now, in my experience," broke in the tall man, "oysters is oysters wherever you find 'em, an' they're pretty much alike all the Bay over, and the world over, too, for that matter. We're not wantin' to quarrel with you, Mr. Taft, but we jes' wish you wouldn't insinuate that them oysters is yours an' that we're thieves an' robbers till you can prove the goods."

"I know they're mine; I'd stake my life on it!" Mr. Taft snorted.

"Prove it," challenged the tall man, who we afterward learned was known as "The Porpoise" because of his wonderful swimming abilities.

Mr. Taft shrugged his shoulders helplessly. Of course he could not prove the oysters to be his, no matter how certain he might be.

"I'd give a thousand dollars to have you men behind the bars!" he cried. "I'll give fifty dollars a head for your arrest and conviction, all of you!"

A roar of laughter went up from the different boats, for the rest of the pirates had been listening to the discussion.

"There's more money in oysters," the Porpoise remarked dryly.

Mr. Taft turned impatiently on his heel and walked away. From out of the corner of his eye, Charley noted the way he went. Several minutes later, when he had disappeared around a corner, Charley rose lazily to his feet. I followed him, and we sauntered off in the opposite direction to that taken by Mr. Taft.

"Come on! Lively!" Charley whispered, when we passed from the view of the oyster fleet.

Our course was changed at once, and we dodged around

corners and raced up and down side-streets till Mr. Taft's generous form loomed up ahead of us.

"I'm going to interview him about that reward," Charley explained, as we rapidly overhauled the oyster-bed owner. "Neil will be delayed here for a week, and you and I might as well be doing something in the meantime. What do you say?"

"Of course, of course," Mr. Taft said, when Charley had introduced himself and explained his errand. "Those thieves are robbing me of thousands of dollars every year, and I shall be glad to break them up at any price,—yes, sir, at any price. As I said, I'll give fifty dollars a head, and call it cheap at that. They've robbed my beds, torn down my signs, terrorized my watchmen, and last year killed one of them. Couldn't prove it. All done in the blackness of night. All I had was a dead watchman and no evidence. The detectives could do nothing. Nobody has been able to do anything with those men. We have never succeeded in arresting one of them. So I say, Mr.—— What did you say your name was?"

"Le Grant," Charley answered.

"So I say, Mr. Le Grant, I am deeply obliged to you for the assistance you offer. And I shall be glad, most glad, sir, to co-operate with you in every way. My watchmen and boats are at your disposal. Come and see me at the San Francisco offices any time, or telephone at my expense. And don't be afraid of spending money. I'll foot your expenses, whatever they are, so long as they are within reason. The situation is growing desperate, and something must be done to determine whether I or that band of ruffians own those oyster beds."

"Now we'll see Neil," Charley said, when he had seen Mr. Taft upon his train to San Francisco.

Not only did Neil Partington interpose no obstacle to our adventure, but he proved to be of the greatest assistance. Charley and I knew nothing of the oyster industry, while his head was an encyclopædia of facts concerning it. Also, within an hour or so, he was able to bring to us a Greek boy of seventeen or eighteen who knew thoroughly well the ins and outs of oyster piracy.

At this point I may as well explain that we of the fish patrol were free lances in a way. While Neil Partington, who was a patrolman proper, received a regular salary, Charley and I, being merely deputies, received only what we earned—that is to say, a certain percentage of the fines imposed on convicted violators of the fish laws. Also, any rewards that chanced our way were ours. We offered to share with Partington whatever we should get from Mr. Taft, but the patrolman would not hear of it. He was only too happy, he said, to do a good turn for us, who had done so many for him.

22

We held a long council of war, and mapped out the following line of action. Our faces were unfamiliar on the Lower Bay, but as the Reindeer was well known as a fish-patrol sloop, the Greek boy, whose name was Nicholas, and I were to sail some innocent-looking craft down to Asparagus Island and join the oyster pirates' fleet. Here, according to Nicholas's description of the beds and the manner of raiding, it was possible for us to catch the pirates in the act of stealing oysters, and at the same time to get them in our power. Charley was to be on the shore, with Mr. Taft's watchmen and a posse of constables, to help us at the right time.

"I know just the boat," Neil said, at the conclusion of the discussion, "a crazy old sloop that's lying over at Tiburon. You and Nicholas can go over by the ferry, charter it for a song, and sail direct for the beds."

"Good luck be with you, boys," he said at parting, two days later. "Remember, they are dangerous men, so be careful."

Nicholas and I succeeded in chartering the sloop very cheaply; and between laughs, while getting up sail, we agreed that she was even crazier and older than she had been described. She was a big, flat-bottomed, square-sterned craft, sloop-rigged, with a sprung mast, slack rigging, dilapidated sails, and rotten running-gear, clumsy to handle and uncertain in bringing about, and she smelled vilely of coal tar, with which strange stuff she had been smeared from stem to stern and from cabin-roof to centreboard. And to cap it all, Coal Tar Maggie was printed in great white letters the whole length of either side.

It was an uneventful though laughable run from Tiburon to Asparagus Island, where we arrived in the afternoon of the following day. The oyster pirates, a fleet of a dozen sloops, were lying at anchor on what was known as the "Deserted Beds." The Coal Tar Maggie came sloshing into their midst with a light breeze astern, and they crowded on deck to see us. Nicholas and I had caught the spirit of the crazy craft, and we handled her in most lubberly fashion.

"Wot is it?" some one called.

"Name it 'n' ye kin have it!" called another.

"I swan naow, ef it ain't the old Ark itself!" mimicked the Centipede from the deck of the Ghost.

"Hey! Ahoy there, clipper ship!" another wag shouted. "Wot's yer port?"

We took no notice of the joking, but acted, after the manner of greenhorns, as though the Coal Tar Maggie required our undivided attention. I rounded her well to windward of the Ghost, and Nicholas ran for'ard to drop the anchor. To all appearances it was a bungle, the way the chain tangled and kept the anchor from reaching the bottom. And to all appearances Nicholas and I were terribly excited as we strove to clear it. At any rate, we quite deceived the pirates, who took huge delight in our predicament.

But the chain remained tangled, and amid all kinds of mocking advice we drifted down upon and fouled the Ghost, whose bowsprit poked square through our mainsail and ripped a hole in it as big as a barn door. The Centipede and the Porpoise doubled up on the cabin in paroxysms of laughter, and left us to get clear as best we could. This, with much unseamanlike performance, we succeeded in doing, and like-wise in clearing the anchor-chain, of which we let out about three hundred feet. With only ten feet of water under us, this would permit the Coal Tar Maggie to swing in a circle six hundred feet in diameter, in which circle she would be able to foul at least half the fleet.

The oyster pirates lay snugly together at short hawsers, the weather being fine, and they protested loudly at our ignorance in putting out such an unwarranted length of anchor-chain. And not only did they protest, for they made us heave it in again, all but thirty feet.

Having sufficiently impressed them with our general lubberliness, Nicholas and I went below to congratulate ourselves and to cook supper. Hardly had we finished the meal and washed the dishes, when a skiff ground against the Coal Tar Maggie's side, and heavy feet trampled on deck. Then the Centipede's brutal face appeared in the companionway, and he descended into the cabin, followed by the Porpoise. Before they could seat themselves on a bunk, another skiff came alongside, and another, and another, till the whole fleet was represented by the gathering in the cabin.

"Where'd you swipe the old tub?" asked a squat and hairy man, with cruel eyes and Mexican features.

"Didn't swipe it," Nicholas answered, meeting them on their own ground and encouraging the idea that we had stolen the Coal Tar Maggie. "And if we did, what of it?"

"Well, I don't admire your taste, that's all," sneered he of the Mexican features. "I'd rot on the beach first before I'd take a tub that couldn't get out of its own way."

"How were we to know till we tried her?" Nicholas asked, so innocently as to cause a laugh. "And how do you get the oysters?" he hurried on. "We want a load of them; that's what we came for, a load of oysters."

"What d'ye want 'em for?" demanded the Porpoise.

"Oh, to give away to our friends, of course," Nicholas retorted. "That's what you do with yours, I suppose."

This started another laugh, and as our visitors grew more genial we could see that they had not the slightest suspicion of our identity or purpose.

"Didn't I see you on the dock in Oakland the other day?" the Centipede asked suddenly of me.

"Yep," I answered boldly, taking the bull by the horns. "I was watching you fellows and figuring out whether we'd go oystering or not. It's a pretty good business, I calculate, and so we're going in for it. That is," I hastened to add, "if you fellows don't mind."

"I'll tell you one thing, which ain't two things," he replied, "and that is you'll have to hump yerself an' get a better boat. We won't stand to be disgraced by any such box as this. Understand?"

"Sure," I said. "Soon as we sell some oysters we'll outfit in style."

"And if you show yerself square an' the right sort," he went on, "why, you kin run with us. But if you don't" (here his voice became stern and menacing), "why, it'll be the sickest day of yer life. Understand?"

"Sure," I said.

After that and more warning and advice of similar nature, the conversation became general, and we learned that the beds were to be raided that very night. As they got into their boats, after an hour's stay, we were invited to join them in the raid with the assurance of "the more the merrier."

"Did you notice that short, Mexican-looking chap?" Nicholas asked, when they had departed to their various sloops. "He's Barchi, of the Sporting Life Gang, and the fellow that came with him is Skilling. They're both out now on five thousand dollars' bail."

I had heard of the Sporting Life Gang before, a crowd of hoodlums and criminals that terrorized the lower quarters of Oakland, and two-thirds of which were usually to be found in state's prison for crimes that ranged from perjury and ballot-box stuffing to murder.

"They are not regular oyster pirates," Nicholas continued. "They've just come down for the lark and to make a few dollars. But we'll have to watch out for them."

We sat in the cockpit and discussed the details of our plan till eleven o'clock had passed, when we heard the rattle of an oar in a boat from the direction of the Ghost. We hauled up our own skiff, tossed in a few sacks, and rowed over. There we found all the skiffs assembling, it being the intention to raid the beds in a body.

To my surprise, I found barely a foot of water where we had dropped anchor in ten feet. It was the big June run-out of the full moon, and as the ebb had yet an hour and a half to run, I knew that our anchorage would be dry ground before slack water.

Mr. Taft's beds were three miles away, and for a long time we rowed silently in the wake of the other boats, once in a while grounding and our oar blades constantly striking bottom. At last we came upon soft mud covered with not more than two inches of water—not enough to float the boats. But the pirates at once were over the side, and by pushing and pulling on the flat-bottomed skiffs, we moved steadily along.

The full moon was partly obscured by high-flying clouds, but the pirates went their way with the familiarity born of long practice. After half a mile of the mud, we came upon a deep channel, up which we rowed, with dead oyster shoals looming high and dry on either side. At last we reached the picking grounds. Two men, on one of the shoals, hailed us and warned us off. But the Centipede, the Porpoise, Barchi, and Skilling took the lead, and followed by the rest of us, at least thirty men in half as many boats, rowed right up to the watchmen.

"You'd better slide outa this here," Barchi said threateningly, "or we'll fill you so full of holes you wouldn't float in molasses."

The watchmen wisely retreated before so overwhelming a force, and rowed their boat along the channel toward where the shore should be. Besides, it was in the plan for them to retreat.

We hauled the noses of the boats up on the shore side of a big shoal, and all hands, with sacks, spread out and began picking. Every now and again the clouds thinned before the face of the moon, and we could see the big oysters quite distinctly. In almost no time sacks were filled and carried back to the boats, where fresh ones were obtained. Nicholas and I returned often and anxiously to the boats with our little loads, but always found some one of the pirates coming or going.

"Never mind," he said; "no hurry. As they pick farther and farther away, it will take too long to carry to the boats. Then they'll stand the full sacks on end and pick them up when the tide comes in and the skiffs will float to them."

Fully half an hour went by, and the tide had begun to flood, when this came to pass. Leaving the pirates at their work, we stole back to the boats. One by one, and noiselessly, we shoved them off and made them fast in an awkward flotilla. Just as we were shoving off the last skiff, our own, one of the men came upon us. It was Barchi. His quick eye took in the situation at a glance, and he sprang for us; but we went clear with a mighty shove, and he was left floundering in the water over his head. As soon as he got back to the shoal he raised his voice and gave the alarm.

26

We rowed with all our strength, but it was slow going with so many boats in tow. A pistol cracked from the shoal, a second, and a third; then a regular fusillade began. The bullets spat and spat all about us; but thick clouds had covered the moon, and in the dim darkness it was no more than random firing. It was only by chance that we could be hit.

"Wish we had a little steam launch," I panted.

"I'd just as soon the moon stayed hidden," Nicholas panted back.

It was slow work, but every stroke carried us farther away from the shoal and nearer the shore, till at last the shooting died down, and when the moon did come out we were too far away to be in danger. Not long afterward we answered a shoreward hail, and two Whitehall boats, each pulled by three pairs of oars, darted up to us. Charley's welcome face bent over to us, and he gripped us by the hands while he cried, "Oh, you joys! You joys! Both of you!"

When the flotilla had been landed, Nicholas and I and a watchman rowed out in one of the Whitehalls, with Charley in the stern-sheets. Two other Whitehalls followed us, and as the moon now shone brightly, we easily made out the oyster pirates on their lonely shoal. As we drew closer, they fired a rattling volley from their revolvers, and we promptly retreated beyond range.

"Lot of time," Charley said. "The flood is setting in fast, and by the time it's up to their necks there won't be any fight left in them."

So we lay on our oars and waited for the tide to do its work. This was the predicament of the pirates: because of the big run-out, the tide was now rushing back like a mill-race, and it was impossible for the strongest swimmer in the world to make against it the three miles to the sloops. Between the pirates and the shore were we, precluding escape in that direction. On the other hand, the water was rising rapidly over the shoals, and it was only a question of a few hours when it would be over their heads.

It was beautifully calm, and in the brilliant white moonlight we watched them through our night glasses and told Charley of the voyage of the Coal Tar Maggie. One o'clock came, and two o'clock, and the pirates were clustering on the highest shoal, waist-deep in water.

"Now this illustrates the value of imagination," Charley was saying. "Taft has been trying for years to get them, but he went at it with bull strength and failed. Now we used our heads...."

Just then I heard a scarcely audible gurgle of water, and holding up my hand for silence, I turned and pointed to a ripple slowly widening out in a growing circle. It was not more than fifty feet from us. We kept perfectly quiet and waited. After a minute the

27

water broke six feet away, and a black head and white shoulder showed in the moonlight. With a snort of surprise and of suddenly expelled breath, the head and shoulder went down.

We pulled ahead several strokes and drifted with the current. Four pairs of eyes searched the surface of the water, but never another ripple showed, and never another glimpse did we catch of the black head and white shoulder.

"It's the Porpoise," Nicholas said. "It would take broad daylight for us to catch him."

At a quarter to three the pirates gave their first sign of weakening. We heard cries for help, in the unmistakable voice of the Centipede, and this time, on rowing closer, we were not fired upon. The Centipede was in a truly perilous plight. Only the heads and shoulders of his fellow-marauders showed above the water as they braced themselves against the current, while his feet were off the bottom and they were supporting him.

"Now, lads," Charley said briskly, "we have got you, and you can't get away. If you cut up rough, we'll have to leave you alone and the water will finish you. But if you're good, we'll take you aboard, one man at a time, and you'll all be saved. What do you say?"

"Ay," they chorused hoarsely between their chattering teeth.

"Then one man at a time, and the short men first."

The Centipede was the first to be pulled aboard, and he came willingly, though he objected when the constable put the handcuffs on him. Barchi was next hauled in, quite meek and resigned from his soaking. When we had ten in our boat we drew back, and the second Whitehall was loaded. The third Whitehall received nine prisoners only—a catch of twenty-nine in all.

"You didn't get the Porpoise," the Centipede said exultantly, as though his escape materially diminished our success.

Charley laughed. "But we saw him just the same, a-snorting for shore like a puffing pig."

It was a mild and shivering band of pirates that we marched up the beach to the oyster house. In answer to Charley's knock, the door was flung open, and a pleasant wave of warm air rushed out upon us.

"You can dry your clothes here, lads, and get some hot coffee," Charley announced, as they filed in.

And there, sitting ruefully by the fire, with a steaming mug in his hand, was the Porpoise. With one accord Nicholas and I looked at Charley. He laughed gleefully.

"That comes of imagination," he said. "When you see a thing, you've got to see it all around, or what's the good of seeing it at all? I saw the beach, so I left a couple of constables behind to keep an eye on it. That's all."

28

IV

THE SIEGE OF THE "LANCASHIRE QUEEN"

Possibly our most exasperating experience on the fish patrol was when Charley Le Grant and I laid a two weeks' siege to a big four-masted English ship. Before we had finished with the affair, it became a pretty mathematical problem, and it was by the merest chance that we came into possession of the instrument that brought it to a successful termination.

After our raid on the oyster pirates we had returned to Oakland, where two more weeks passed before Neil Partington's wife was out of danger and on the highroad to recovery. So it was after an absence of a month, all told, that we turned the Reindeer's nose toward Benicia. When the cat's away the mice will play, and in these four weeks the fishermen had become very bold in violating the law. When we passed Point Pedro we noticed many signs of activity among the shrimp-catchers, and, well into San Pablo Bay, we observed a widely scattered fleet of Upper Bay fishing-boats hastily pulling in their nets and getting up sail.

This was suspicious enough to warrant investigation, and the first and only boat we succeeded in boarding proved to have an illegal net. The law permitted no smaller mesh for catching shad than one that measured seven and one-half inches inside the knots, while the mesh of this particular net measured only three inches. It was a flagrant breach of the rules, and the two fishermen were forthwith put under arrest. Neil Partington took one of them with him to help manage the Reindeer, while Charley and I went on ahead with the other in the captured boat.

But the shad fleet had headed over toward the Petaluma shore in wild flight, and for the rest of the run through San Pablo Bay we saw no more fishermen at all. Our prisoner, a bronzed and bearded Greek, sat sullenly on his net while we sailed his craft. It was a new Columbia River salmon boat, evidently on its first trip, and it handled splendidly. Even when Charley praised it, our prisoner refused to speak or to notice us, and we soon gave him up as a most unsociable fellow.

We ran up the Carquinez Straits and edged into the bight at Turner's Shipyard for smoother water. Here were lying several English steel sailing ships, waiting for the wheat harvest; and here, most unexpectedly, in the precise place where we had captured Big Alec, we came upon two Italians in a skiff that was loaded with a complete "Chinese" sturgeon line. The surprise was mutual, and we were on top of them before either they or we were aware. Charley had barely time to luff into the wind and run up to them. I ran forward and tossed them a line with orders to make it fast. One of the Italians took a turn with it over a cleat, while I hastened to lower our big spritsail. This accomplished, the salmon boat dropped astern, dragging heavily on the skiff.

Charley came forward to board the prize, but when I proceeded to haul alongside by means of the line, the Italians cast it off. We at once began drifting to leeward, while they got out two pairs of oars and rowed their light craft directly into the wind. This manœuvre for the moment disconcerted us, for in our large and heavily loaded boat we could not hope to catch them with the oars. But our prisoner came unexpectedly to our aid. His black eyes were flashing eagerly, and his face was flushed with suppressed excitement, as he dropped the centreboard, sprang forward with a single leap, and put up the sail.

"I've always heard that Greeks don't like Italians," Charley laughed, as he ran aft to the tiller.

And never in my experience have I seen a man so anxious for the capture of another as was our prisoner in the chase that followed. His eyes fairly snapped, and his nostrils quivered and dilated in a most extraordinary way. Charley steered while he tended the sheet; and though Charley was as quick and alert as a cat, the Greek could hardly control his impatience.

The Italians were cut off from the shore, which was fully a mile away at its nearest point. Did they attempt to make it, we could haul after them with the wind abeam, and overtake them before they had covered an eighth of the distance. But they were too wise to attempt it, contenting themselves with rowing lustily to windward along the starboard side of a big ship, the Lancashire Queen. But beyond the ship lay an open stretch of fully two miles to the shore in that direction. This, also, they dared not attempt, for we were bound to catch them before they could cover it. So, when they reached the bow of the Lancashire Queen, nothing remained but to pass around and row down her port side toward the stern, which meant rowing to leeward and giving us the advantage.

We in the salmon boat, sailing close on the wind, tacked about and crossed the ship's bow. Then Charley put up the tiller and headed down the port side of the ship, the Greek letting out the sheet and grinning with delight. The Italians were already half-way down the ship's length; but the stiff breeze at our back drove us after them far faster than they could row. Closer and closer we came, and

30

I, lying down forward, was just reaching out to grasp the skiff, when it ducked under the great stern of the Lancashire Queen.

The chase was virtually where it had begun. The Italians were rowing up the starboard side of the ship, and we were hauled close on the wind and slowly edging out from the ship as we worked to windward. Then they darted around her bow and began the row down her port side, and we tacked about, crossed her bow, and went plunging down the wind hot after them. And again, just as I was reaching for the skiff, it ducked under the ship's stern and out of danger. And so it went, around and around, the skiff each time just barely ducking into safety.

By this time the ship's crew had become aware of what was taking place, and we could see their heads in a long row as they looked at us over the bulwarks. Each time we missed the skiff at the stern, they set up a wild cheer and dashed across to the other side of the Lancashire Queen to see the chase to windward. They showered us and the Italians with jokes and advice, and made our Greek so angry that at least once on each circuit he raised his fist and shook it at them in a rage. They came to look for this, and at each display greeted it with uproarious mirth.

"Wot a circus!" cried one.

"Tork about yer marine hippodromes,—if this ain't one, I'd like to know!" affirmed another.

"Six-days-go-as-yer-please," announced a third. "Who says the dagoes won't win?"

On the next tack to windward the Greek offered to change places with Charley.

"Let-a me sail-a de boat," he demanded. "I fix-a them, I catch-a them, sure."

This was a stroke at Charley's professional pride, for pride himself he did upon his boat-sailing abilities; but he yielded the tiller to the prisoner and took his place at the sheet. Three times again we made the circuit, and the Greek found that he could get no more speed out of the salmon boat than Charley had.

"Better give it up," one of the sailors advised from above.

The Greek scowled ferociously and shook his fist in his customary fashion. In the meanwhile my mind had not been idle, and I had finally evolved an idea.

"Keep going, Charley, one time more," I said.

And as we laid out on the next tack to windward, I bent a piece of line to a small grappling hook I had seen lying in the bail-hole. The end of the line I made fast to the ring-bolt in the bow, and with the hook out of sight I waited for the next opportunity to use it. Once more they made their leeward pull down the port side of the

31

Lancashire Queen, and more once we churned down after them before the wind. Nearer and nearer we drew, and I was making believe to reach for them as before. The stern of the skiff was not six feet away, and they were laughing at me derisively as they ducked under the ship's stern. At that instant I suddenly arose and threw the grappling iron. It caught fairly and squarely on the rail of the skiff, which was jerked backward out of safety as the rope tautened and the salmon boat ploughed on.

A groan went up from the row of sailors above, which quickly changed to a cheer as one of the Italians whipped out a long sheath-knife and cut the rope. But we had drawn them out of safety, and Charley, from his place in the stern-sheets, reached over and clutched the stern of the skiff. The whole thing happened in a second of time, for the first Italian was cutting the rope and Charley was clutching the skiff, when the second Italian dealt him a rap over the head with an oar. Charley released his hold and collapsed, stunned, into the bottom of the salmon boat, and the Italians bent to their oars and escaped back under the ship's stern.

The Greek took both tiller and sheet and continued the chase around the Lancashire Queen, while I attended to Charley, on whose head a nasty lump was rapidly rising. Our sailor audience was wild with delight, and to a man encouraged the fleeing Italians. Charley sat up, with one hand on his head, and gazed about him sheepishly.

"It will never do to let them escape now," he said, at the same time drawing his revolver.

On our next circuit, he threatened the Italians with the weapon; but they rowed on stolidly, keeping splendid stroke and utterly disregarding him.

"If you don't stop, I'll shoot," Charley said menacingly.

But this had no effect, nor were they to be frightened into surrendering even when he fired several shots dangerously close to them. It was too much to expect him to shoot unarmed men, and this they knew as well as we did; so they continued to pull doggedly round and round the ship.

"We'll run them down, then!" Charley exclaimed. "We'll wear them out and wind them!"

So the chase continued. Twenty times more we ran them around the Lancashire Queen, and at last we could see that even their iron muscles were giving out. They were nearly exhausted, and it was only a matter of a few more circuits, when the game took on a new feature. On the row to windward they always gained on us, so that they were half-way down the ship's side on the row to leeward when we were passing the bow. But this last time, as we passed the bow, we saw them escaping up the ship's gangway, which had been suddenly lowered. It was an organized move on the part of the sailors, evidently countenanced by the captain; for by the time we arrived where the gangway had been, it was being hoisted up, and the skiff, slung in the ship's davits, was likewise flying aloft out of reach.

The parley that followed with the captain was short and snappy. He absolutely forbade us to board the Lancashire Queen, and as absolutely refused to give up the two men. By this time Charley was as enraged as the Greek. Not only had he been foiled in a long and ridiculous chase, but he had been knocked senseless into the bottom of his boat by the men who had escaped him.

"Knock off my head with little apples," he declared emphatically, striking the fist of one hand into the palm of the other, "if those two men ever escape me! I'll stay here to get them if it takes the rest of my natural life, and if I don't get them, then I promise you I'll live unnaturally long or until I do get them, or my name's not Charley Le Grant!"

And then began the siege of the Lancashire Queen, a siege memorable in the annals of both fishermen and fish patrol. When the Reindeer came along, after a fruitless pursuit of the shad fleet, Charley instructed Neil Partington to send out his own salmon boat, with blankets, provisions, and a fisherman's charcoal stove. By sunset this exchange of boats was made, and we said good-by to our Greek, who perforce had to go into Benicia and be locked up for his own violation of the law. After supper, Charley and I kept alternate four-hour watches till daylight. The fishermen made no attempt to escape that night, though the ship sent out a boat for scouting purposes to find if the coast were clear.

By the next day we saw that a steady siege was in order, and we perfected our plans with an eye to our own comfort. A dock, known as the Solano Wharf, which ran out from the Benicia shore, helped us in this. It happened that the Lancashire Queen, the shore at Turner's Shipyard, and the Solano Wharf were the corners of a big equilateral triangle. From ship to shore, the side of the triangle along which the Italians had to escape, was a distance equal to that from the Solano Wharf to the shore, the side of the triangle along which we had to travel to get to the shore before the Italians. But as we could sail much faster than they could row, we could permit them to travel about half their side of the triangle before we darted out along our side. If we allowed them to get more than half-way, they were certain to beat us to shore; while if we started before they were half-way, they were equally certain to beat us back to the ship.

We found that an imaginary line, drawn from the end of the

wharf to a windmill farther along the shore, cut precisely in half the line of the triangle along which the Italians must escape to reach the land. This line made it easy for us to determine how far to let them run away before we bestirred ourselves in pursuit. Day after day we would watch them through our glasses as they rowed leisurely along toward the half-way point; and as they drew close into line with the windmill, we would leap into the boat and get up sail. At sight of our preparation, they would turn and row slowly back to the Lancashire Queen, secure in the knowledge that we could not overtake them.

To guard against calms—when our salmon boat would be useless—we also had in readiness a light rowing skiff equipped with spoon-oars. But at such times, when the wind failed us, we were forced to row out from the wharf as soon as they rowed from the ship. In the night-time, on the other hand, we were compelled to patrol the immediate vicinity of the ship; which we did, Charley and I standing four-hour watches turn and turn about. The Italians, however, preferred the daytime in which to escape, and so our long night vigils were without result.

"What makes me mad," said Charley, "is our being kept from our honest beds while those rascally lawbreakers are sleeping soundly every night. But much good may it do them," he threatened. "I'll keep them on that ship till the captain charges them board, as sure as a sturgeon's not a catfish!"

It was a tantalizing problem that confronted us. As long as we were vigilant, they could not escape; and as long as they were careful, we would be unable to catch them. Charley cudgelled his brains continually, but for once his imagination failed him. It was a problem apparently without other solution than that of patience. It was a waiting game, and whichever waited the longer was bound to win. To add to our irritation, friends of the Italians established a code of signals with them from the shore, so that we never dared relax the siege for a moment. And besides this, there were always one or two suspicious-looking fishermen hanging around the Solano Wharf and keeping watch on our actions. We could do nothing but "grin and bear it," as Charley said, while it took up all our time and prevented us from doing other work.

The days went by, and there was no change in the situation. Not that no attempts were made to change it. One night friends from the shore came out in a skiff and attempted to confuse us while the two Italians escaped. That they did not succeed was due to the lack of a little oil on the ship's davits. For we were drawn back from the pursuit of the strange boat by the creaking of the davits, and arrived at the Lancashire Queen just as the Italians were lowering their skiff. Another night, fully half a dozen skiffs rowed around us in the darkness, but we held on like a leech to the side of the ship and frustrated their plan till they grew angry and showered us with abuse. Charley laughed to himself in the bottom of the boat.

"It's a good sign, lad," he said to me. "When men begin to abuse, make sure they're losing patience; and shortly after they lose patience, they lose their heads. Mark my words, if we only hold out, they'll get careless some fine day, and then we'll get them."

But they did not grow careless, and Charley confessed that this was one of the times when all signs failed. Their patience seemed equal to ours, and the second week of the siege dragged monotonously along. Then Charley's lagging imagination quickened sufficiently to suggest a ruse. Peter Boyelen, a new patrolman and one unknown to the fisher-folk, happened to arrive in Benicia, and we took him into our plan. We were as secret as possible about it, but in some unfathomable way the friends ashore got word to the beleaguered Italians to keep their eyes open.

On the night we were to put our ruse into effect, Charley and I took up our usual station in our rowing skiff alongside the Lancashire Queen. After it was thoroughly dark, Peter Boyelen came out in a crazy duck boat, the kind you can pick up and carry away under one arm. When we heard him coming along, paddling noisily, we slipped away a short distance into the darkness and rested on our oars. Opposite the gangway, having jovially hailed the anchor-watch of the Lancashire Queen and asked the direction of the Scottish Chiefs, another wheat ship, he awkwardly capsized himself. The man who was standing the anchor-watch ran down the gangway and hauled him out of the water. This was what he wanted, to get aboard the ship; and the next thing he expected was to be taken on deck and then below to warm up and dry out. But the captain inhospitably kept him perched on the lowest gangway step, shivering miserably and with his feet dangling in the water, till we, out of very pity, rowed in from the darkness and took him off. The jokes and gibes of the awakened crew sounded anything but sweet in our ears, and even the two Italians climbed up on the rail and laughed down at us long and maliciously.

"That's all right," Charley said in a low voice, which I only could hear. "I'm mighty glad it's not us that's laughing first. We'll save our laugh to the end, eh, lad?"

He clapped a hand on my shoulder as he finished, but it seemed to me that there was more determination than hope in his voice.

It would have been possible for us to secure the aid of United States marshals and board the English ship, backed by government authority. But the instructions of the Fish Commission were to the effect that the patrolmen should avoid complications, and this one, did we call on the higher powers, might well end in a pretty international tangle.

The second week of the siege drew to its close, and there was no sign of change in the situation. On the morning of the fourteenth day the change came, and it came in a guise as unexpected and startling to us as it was to the men we were striving to capture.

Charley and I, after our customary night vigil by the side of the Lancashire Queen, rowed into the Solano Wharf.

"Hello!" cried Charley, in surprise. "In the name of reason and common sense, what is that? Of all unmannerly craft did you ever see the like?"

Well might he exclaim, for there, tied up to the dock, lay the strangest-looking launch I had ever seen. Not that it could be called a launch, either, but it seemed to resemble a launch more than any other kind of boat. It was seventy feet long, but so narrow was it, and so bare of superstructure, that it appeared much smaller than it really was. It was built wholly of steel, and was painted black. Three smokestacks, a good distance apart and raking well aft, arose in single file amidships; while the bow, long and lean and sharp as a knife, plainly advertised that the boat was made for speed. Passing under the stern, we read Streak, painted in small white letters.

Charley and I were consumed with curiosity. In a few minutes we were on board and talking with an engineer who was watching the sunrise from the deck. He was quite willing to satisfy our curiosity, and in a few minutes we learned that the Streak had come in after dark from San Francisco; that this was what might be called the trial trip; and that she was the property of Silas Tate, a young mining millionaire of California, whose fad was high-speed yachts. There was some talk about turbine engines, direct application of steam, and the absence of pistons, rods, and cranks,—all of which was beyond me, for I was familiar only with sailing craft; but I did understand the last words of the engineer.

"Four thousand horse-power and forty-five miles an hour, though you wouldn't think it," he concluded proudly.

"Say it again, man! Say it again!" Charley exclaimed in an excited voice.

"Four thousand horse-power and forty-five miles an hour," the engineer repeated, grinning good-naturedly.

"Where's the owner?" was Charley's next question. "Is there any way I can speak to him?"

The engineer shook his head. "No, I'm afraid not. He's asleep, you see."

At that moment a young man in blue uniform came on deck farther aft and stood regarding the sunrise.

"There he is, that's him, that's Mr. Tate," said the engineer.

Charley walked aft and spoke to him, and while he talked earnestly the young man listened with an amused expression on his face. He must have inquired about the depth of water close in to the shore at Turner's Shipyard, for I could see Charley making gestures and explaining. A few minutes later he came back in high glee.

"Come on, lad," he said. "On to the dock with you. We've got them!"

It was our good fortune to leave the Streak when we did, for a little later one of the spy fishermen appeared. Charley and I took up our accustomed places, on the stringer-piece, a little ahead of the Streak and over our own boat, where we could comfortably watch the Lancashire Queen. Nothing occurred till about nine o'clock, when we saw the two Italians leave the ship and pull along their side of the triangle toward the shore. Charley looked as unconcerned as could be, but before they had covered a quarter of the distance, he whispered to me:

"Forty-five miles an hour...nothing can save them...they are ours!"

Slowly the two men rowed along till they were nearly in line with the windmill. This was the point where we always jumped into our salmon boat and got up the sail, and the two men, evidently expecting it, seemed surprised when we gave no sign.

When they were directly in line with the windmill, as near to the shore as to the ship, and nearer the shore than we had ever allowed them before, they grew suspicious. We followed them through the glasses, and saw them standing up in the skiff and trying to find out what we were doing. The spy fisherman, sitting beside us on the stringerpiece, was likewise puzzled. He could not understand our inactivity. The men in the skiff rowed nearer the shore, but stood up again and scanned it, as if they thought we might be in hiding there. But a man came out on the beach and waved a handkerchief to indicate that the coast was clear. That settled them. They bent to the oars to make a dash for it. Still Charley waited. Not until they had covered three-quarters of the distance from the Lancashire Queen, which left them hardly more than a quarter of a mile to gain the shore, did Charley slap me on the shoulder and cry:

"They're ours! They're ours!"

We ran the few steps to the side of the Streak and jumped aboard. Stern and bow lines were cast off in a jiffy. The Streak shot ahead and away from the wharf. The spy fisherman we had left behind on the stringer-piece pulled out a revolver and fired five shots into the air in rapid succession. The men in the skiff gave instant heed to the warning, for we could see them pulling away like mad.

But if they pulled like mad, I wonder how our progress can be described? We fairly flew. So frightful was the speed with which we displaced the water, that a wave rose up on either side our bow and foamed aft in a series of three stiff, up-standing waves, while astern a great crested billow pursued us hungrily, as though at each moment it would fall aboard and destroy us. The Streak was pulsing and vibrating and roaring like a thing alive. The wind of our progress was like a gale—a forty-five-mile gale. We could not face it and draw breath without choking and strangling. It blew the smoke straight back from the mouths of the smoke-stacks at a direct right angle to the perpendicular. In fact, we were travelling as fast as an express train. "We just streaked it," was the way Charley told it afterward, and I think his description comes nearer than any I can give.

As for the Italians in the skiff—hardly had we started, it seemed to me, when we were on top of them. Naturally, we had to slow down long before we got to them; but even then we shot past like a whirlwind and were compelled to circle back between them and the shore. They had rowed steadily, rising from the thwarts at every stroke, up to the moment we passed them, when they recognized Charley and me. That took the last bit of fight out of them. They hauled in their oars and sullenly submitted to arrest.

"Well, Charley," Neil Partington said, as we discussed it on the wharf afterward, "I fail to see where your boasted imagination came into play this time."

But Charley was true to his hobby. "Imagination?" he demanded, pointing to the Streak. "Look at that! Just look at it! If the invention of that isn't imagination, I should like to know what is."

"Of course," he added, "it's the other fellow's imagination, but it did the work all the same."

V

CHARLEY'S COUP

Perhaps our most laughable exploit on the fish patrol, and at the same time our most dangerous one, was when we rounded in, at a single haul, an even score of wrathful fishermen. Charley called it a "coup," having heard Neil Partington use the term; but I think he misunderstood the word, and thought it meant "coop," to catch, to trap. The fishermen, however, coup or coop, must have called it a Waterloo, for it was the severest stroke ever dealt them by the fish patrol, while they had invited it by open and impudent defiance of the law.

During what is called the "open season" the fishermen might catch as many salmon as their luck allowed and their boats could hold. But there was one important restriction. From sun-down Saturday night to sun-up Monday morning, they were not permitted to set a net. This was a wise provision on the part of the Fish Commission, for it was necessary to give the spawning salmon some opportunity to ascend the river and lay their eggs. And this law, with only an occasional violation, had been obediently observed by the Greek fishermen who caught salmon for the canneries and the market.

One Sunday morning, Charley received a telephone call from a friend in Collinsville, who told him that the full force of fishermen was out with its nets. Charley and I jumped into our salmon boat and started for the scene of the trouble. With a light favoring wind at our back we went through the Carquinez Straits, crossed Suisun Bay, passed the Ship Island Light, and came upon the whole fleet at work.

But first let me describe the method by which they worked. The net used is what is known as a gill-net. It has a simple diamond-shaped mesh which measures at least seven and one-half inches between the knots. From five to seven and even eight hundred feet in length, these nets are only a few feet wide. They are not stationary, but float with the current, the upper edge supported on the surface by floats, the lower edge sunk by means of leaden weights.

This arrangement keeps the net upright in the current and effectually prevents all but the smaller fish from ascending the river. The salmon, swimming near the surface, as is their custom, run their heads through these meshes, and are prevented from going on through by their larger girth of body, and from going back because of their gills, which catch in the mesh. It requires two fishermen to set such a net,—one to row the boat, while the other, standing in the stern, carefully pays out the net. When it is all out, stretching directly across the stream, the men make their boat fast to one end of the net and drift along with it.

As we came upon the fleet of law-breaking fishermen, each boat two or three hundred yards from its neighbors, and boats and nets dotting the river as far as we could see, Charley said:

"I've only one regret, lad, and that is that I haven't a thousand arms so as to be able to catch them all. As it is, we'll only be able to catch one boat, for while we are tackling that one it will be up nets and away with the rest."

As we drew closer, we observed none of the usual flurry and excitement which our appearance invariably produced. Instead, each boat lay quietly by its net, while the fishermen favored us with not the slightest attention.

"It's curious," Charley muttered. "Can it be they don't recognize us?"

I said that it was impossible, and Charley agreed; yet there was a whole fleet, manned by men who knew us only too well, and who took no more notice of us than if we were a hay scow or a pleasure yacht.

This did not continue to be the case, however, for as we bore down upon the nearest net, the men to whom it belonged detached their boat and rowed slowly toward the shore. The rest of the boats showed no sign of uneasiness.

"That's funny," was Charley's remark. "But we can confiscate the net, at any rate."

We lowered sail, picked up one end of the net, and began to heave it into the boat. But at the first heave we heard a bullet zip-zipping past us on the water, followed by the faint report of a rifle. The men who had rowed ashore were shooting at us. At the next heave a second bullet went zipping past, perilously near. Charley took a turn around a pin and sat down. There were no more shots. But as soon as he began to heave in, the shooting recommenced.

"That settles it," he said, flinging the end of the net overboard. "You fellows want it worse than we do, and you can have it."

We rowed over toward the next net, for Charley was intent on finding out whether or not we were face to face with an organized defiance. As we approached, the two fishermen proceeded to cast off from their net and row ashore, while the first two rowed back and made fast to the net we had abandoned. And at the second net we

40

were greeted by rifle shots till we desisted and went on to the third, where the manœuvre was again repeated.

Then we gave it up, completely routed, and hoisted sail and started on the long wind-ward beat back to Benicia. A number of Sundays went by, on each of which the law was persistently violated. Yet, short of an armed force of soldiers, we could do nothing. The fishermen had hit upon a new idea and were using it for all it was worth, while there seemed no way by which we could get the better of them.

About this time Neil Partington happened along from the Lower Bay, where he had been for a number of weeks. With him was Nicholas, the Greek boy who had helped us in our raid on the oyster pirates, and the pair of them took a hand. We made our arrangements carefully. It was planned that while Charley and I tackled the nets, they were to be hidden ashore so as to ambush the fishermen who landed to shoot at us.

It was a pretty plan. Even Charley said it was. But we reckoned not half so well as the Greeks. They forestalled us by ambushing Neil and Nicholas and taking them prisoners, while, as of old, bullets whistled about our ears when Charley and I attempted to take possession of the nets. When we were again beaten off, Neil Partington and Nicholas were released. They were rather shamefaced when they put in an appearance, and Charley chaffed them unmercifully. But Neil chaffed back, demanding to know why Charley's imagination had not long since overcome the difficulty.

"Just you wait; the idea'll come all right," Charley promised.

"Most probably," Neil agreed. "But I'm afraid the salmon will be exterminated first, and then there will be no need for it when it does come."

Neil Partington, highly disgusted with his adventure, departed for the Lower Bay, taking Nicholas with him, and Charley and I were left to our own resources. This meant that the Sunday fishing would be left to itself, too, until such time as Charley's idea happened along. I puzzled my head a good deal to find out some way of checkmating the Greeks, as also did Charley, and we broached a thousand expedients which on discussion proved worthless.

The fishermen, on the other hand, were in high feather, and their boasts went up and down the river to add to our discomfiture. Among all classes of them we became aware of a growing insubordination. We were beaten, and they were losing respect for us. With the loss of respect, contempt began to arise. Charley began to be spoken of as the "olda woman," and I received my rating as the "pee-wee kid." The situation was fast becoming unbearable, and we knew that we should have to deliver a stunning stroke at the Greeks in order to regain the old-time respect in which we had stood.

Then one morning the idea came. We were down on Steamboat Wharf, where the river steamers made their landings, and where we found a group of amused long-shoremen and loafers listening to the hard-luck tale of a sleepy-eyed young fellow in long sea-boots. He was a sort of amateur fisherman, he said, fishing for the local market of Berkeley. Now Berkeley was on the Lower Bay, thirty miles away. On the previous night, he said, he had set his net and dozed off to sleep in the bottom of the boat.

The next he knew it was morning, and he opened his eyes to find his boat rubbing softly against the piles of Steamboat Wharf at Benicia. Also he saw the river steamer Apache lying ahead of him, and a couple of deck-hands disentangling the shreds of his net from the paddle-wheel. In short, after he had gone to sleep, his fisherman's riding light had gone out, and the Apache had run over his net. Though torn pretty well to pieces, the net in some way still remained foul, and he had had a thirty-mile tow out of his course.

Charley nudged me with his elbow. I grasped his thought on the instant, but objected:

"We can't charter a steamboat."

"Don't intend to," he rejoined. "But let's run over to Turner's Shipyard. I've something in my mind there that may be of use to us."

And over we went to the shipyard, where Charley led the way to the Mary Rebecca, lying hauled out on the ways, where she was being cleaned and overhauled. She was a scow-schooner we both knew well, carrying a cargo of one hundred and forty tons and a spread of canvas greater than any other schooner on the bay.

"How d'ye do, Ole," Charley greeted a big blue-shirted Swede who was greasing the jaws of the main gaff with a piece of pork rind.

Ole grunted, puffed away at his pipe, and went on greasing. The captain of a bay schooner is supposed to work with his hands just as well as the men.

Ole Ericsen verified Charley's conjecture that the Mary Rebecca, as soon as launched, would run up the San Joaquin River nearly to Stockton for a load of wheat. Then Charley made his proposition, and Ole Ericsen shook his head.

"Just a hook, one good-sized hook," Charley pleaded.

"No, Ay tank not," said Ole Ericsen. "Der Mary Rebecca yust hang up on efery mud-bank with that hook. Ay don't want to lose der Mary Rebecca. She's all Ay got."

"No, no," Charley hurried to explain. "We can put the end of

42

the hook through the bottom from the outside, and fasten it on the inside with a nut. After it's done its work, why, all we have to do is to go down into the hold, unscrew the nut, and out drops the hook. Then drive a wooden peg into the hole, and the Mary Rebecca will be all right again."

Ole Ericsen was obstinate for a long time; but in the end, after we had had dinner with him, he was brought round to consent.

"Ay do it, by Yupiter!" he said, striking one huge fist into the palm of the other hand. "But yust hurry you up with der hook. Der Mary Rebecca slides into der water to-night."

It was Saturday, and Charley had need to hurry. We headed for the shipyard blacksmith shop, where, under Charley's directions, a most generously curved hook of heavy steel was made. Back we hastened to the Mary Rebecca. Aft of the great centre-board case, through what was properly her keel, a hole was bored. The end of the hook was inserted from the outside, and Charley, on the inside, screwed the nut on tightly. As it stood complete, the hook projected over a foot beneath the bottom of the schooner. Its curve was something like the curve of a sickle, but deeper.

In the late afternoon the Mary Rebecca was launched, and preparations were finished for the start up-river next morning. Charley and Ole intently studied the evening sky for signs of wind, for without a good breeze our project was doomed to failure. They agreed that there were all the signs of a stiff westerly wind—not the ordinary afternoon sea-breeze, but a half-gale, which even then was springing up.

Next morning found their predictions verified. The sun was shining brightly, but something more than a half-gale was shrieking up the Carquinez Straits, and the Mary Rebecca got under way with two reefs in her mainsail and one in her foresail. We found it quite rough in the Straits and in Suisun Bay; but as the water grew more land-locked it became calm, though without let-up in the wind.

Off Ship Island Light the reefs were shaken out, and at Charley's suggestion a big fisherman's staysail was made all ready for hoisting, and the main-topsail, bunched into a cap at the masthead, was overhauled so that it could be set on an instant's notice.

We were tearing along, wing-and-wing, before the wind, foresail to starboard and mainsail to port, as we came upon the salmon fleet. There they were, boats and nets, as on that first Sunday when they had bested us, strung out evenly over the river as far as we could see. A narrow space on the right-hand side of the channel was left clear for steam-boats, but the rest of the river was covered with the wide-stretching nets. The narrow space was our logical course, but Charley, at the wheel, steered the Mary Rebecca straight for the nets.

This did not cause any alarm among the fishermen, because up-river sailing craft are always provided with "shoes" on the ends of their keels, which permit them to slip over the nets without fouling them.

"Now she takes it!" Charley cried, as we dashed across the middle of a line of floats which marked a net. At one end of this line was a small barrel buoy, at the other the two fishermen in their boat. Buoy and boat at once began to draw together, and the fishermen to cry out, as they were jerked after us. A couple of minutes later we hooked a second net, and then a third, and in this fashion we tore straight up through the centre of the fleet.

The consternation we spread among the fishermen was tremendous. As fast as we hooked a net the two ends of it, buoy and boat, came together as they dragged out astern; and so many buoys and boats, coming together at such breakneck speed, kept the fishermen on the jump to avoid smashing into one another. Also, they shouted at us like mad to heave to into the wind, for they took it as some drunken prank on the part of scow-sailors, little dreaming that we were the fish patrol.

The drag of a single net is very heavy, and Charley and Ole Ericsen decided that even in such a wind ten nets were all the Mary Rebecca could take along with her. So when we had hooked ten nets, with ten boats containing twenty men streaming along behind us, we veered to the left out of the fleet and headed toward Collinsville.

We were all jubilant. Charley was handling the wheel as though he were steering the winning yacht home in a race. The two sailors who made up the crew of the Mary Rebecca, were grinning and joking. Ole Ericsen was rubbing his huge hands in child-like glee.

"Ay tank you fish patrol fallers never ban so lucky as when you sail with Ole Ericsen," he was saying, when a rifle cracked sharply astern, and a bullet gouged along the newly painted cabin, glanced on a nail, and sang shrilly onward into space.

This was too much for Ole Ericsen. At sight of his beloved paintwork thus defaced, he jumped up and shook his fist at the fishermen; but a second bullet smashed into the cabin not six inches from his head, and he dropped down to the deck under cover of the rail.

All the fishermen had rifles, and they now opened a general fusillade. We were all driven to cover—even Charley, who was compelled to desert the wheel. Had it not been for the heavy drag of

44

the nets, we would inevitably have broached to at the mercy of the enraged fishermen. But the nets, fastened to the bottom of the Mary Rebecca well aft, held her stern into the wind, and she continued to plough on, though somewhat erratically.

Charley, lying on the deck, could just manage to reach the lower spokes of the wheel; but while he could steer after a fashion, it was very awkward. Ole Ericsen bethought himself of a large piece of sheet steel in the empty hold. It was in fact a plate from the side of the New Jersey, a steamer which had recently been wrecked outside the Golden Gate, and in the salving of which the Mary Rebecca had taken part.

Crawling carefully along the deck, the two sailors, Ole, and myself got the heavy plate on deck and aft, where we reared it as a shield between the wheel and the fishermen. The bullets whanged and banged against it till it rang like a bull's-eye, but Charley grinned in its shelter, and coolly went on steering.

So we raced along, behind us a howling, screaming bedlam of wrathful Greeks, Collinsville ahead, and bullets spat-spatting all around us.

"Ole," Charley said in a faint voice, "I don't know what we're going to do."

Ole Ericsen, lying on his back close to the rail and grinning upward at the sky, turned over on his side and looked at him. "Ay tank we go into Collinsville yust der same," he said.

"But we can't stop," Charley groaned. "I never thought of it, but we can't stop."

A look of consternation slowly overspread Ole Ericsen's broad face. It was only too true. We had a hornet's nest on our hands, and to stop at Collinsville would be to have it about our ears.

"Every man Jack of them has a gun," one of the sailors remarked cheerfully.

"Yes, and a knife, too," the other sailor added.

It was Ole Ericsen's turn to groan. "What for a Svaidish faller like me monkey with none of my biziness, I don't know," he soliloquized.

A bullet glanced on the stern and sang off to starboard like a spiteful bee. "There's nothing to do but plump the Mary Rebecca ashore and run for it," was the verdict of the first cheerful sailor.

"And leaf der Mary Rebecca?" Ole demanded, with unspeakable horror in his voice.

"Not unless you want to," was the response. "But I don't want to be within a thousand miles of her when those fellers come aboard"—indicating the bedlam of excited Greeks towing behind.

45

We were right in at Collinsville then, and went foaming by within biscuit-toss of the wharf.

"I only hope the wind holds out," Charley said, stealing a glance at our prisoners.

"What of der wind?" Ole demanded disconsolately. "Der river will not hold out, and then...and then..."

"It's head for tall timber, and the Greeks take the hindermost," adjudged the cheerful sailor, while Ole was stuttering over what would happen when we came to the end of the river.

We had now reached a dividing of the ways. To the left was the mouth of the Sacramento River, to the right the mouth of the San Joaquin. The cheerful sailor crept forward and jibed over the foresail as Charley put the helm to starboard and we swerved to the right into the San Joaquin. The wind, from which we had been running away on an even keel, now caught us on our beam, and the Mary Rebecca was pressed down on her port side as if she were about to capsize.

Still we dashed on, and still the fishermen dashed on behind. The value of their nets was greater than the fines they would have to pay for violating the fish laws; so to cast off from their nets and escape, which they could easily do, would profit them nothing. Further, they remained by their nets instinctively, as a sailor remains by his ship. And still further, the desire for vengeance was roused, and we could depend upon it that they would follow us to the ends of the earth, if we undertook to tow them that far.

The rifle-firing had ceased, and we looked astern to see what our prisoners were doing. The boats were strung along at unequal distances apart, and we saw the four nearest ones bunching together. This was done by the boat ahead trailing a small rope astern to the one behind. When this was caught, they would cast off from their net and heave in on the line till they were brought up to the boat in front. So great was the speed at which we were travelling, however, that this was very slow work. Sometimes the men would strain to their utmost and fail to get in an inch of the rope; at other times they came ahead more rapidly.

When the four boats were near enough together for a man to pass from one to another, one Greek from each of three got into the nearest boat to us, taking his rifle with him. This made five in the foremost boat, and it was plain that their intention was to board us. This they undertook to do, by main strength and sweat, running hand over hand the float-line of a net. And though it was slow, and they stopped frequently to rest, they gradually drew nearer.

Charley smiled at their efforts, and said, "Give her the topsail, Ole."

The cap at the mainmast head was broken out, and sheet and downhaul pulled flat, amid a scattering rifle fire from the boats; and the Mary Rebecca lay over and sprang ahead faster than ever.

But the Greeks were undaunted. Unable, at the increased speed, to draw themselves nearer by means of their hands, they rigged from the blocks of their boat sail what sailors call a "watch-tackle." One of them, held by the legs by his mates, would lean far over the bow and make the tackle fast to the float-line. Then they would heave in on the tackle till the blocks were together, when the manœuvre would be repeated.

"Have to give her the staysail," Charley said.

Ole Ericsen looked at the straining Mary Rebecca and shook his head. "It will take der masts out of her," he said.

"And we'll be taken out of her if you don't," Charley replied.

Ole shot an anxious glance at his masts, another at the boat load of armed Greeks, and consented.

The five men were in the bow of the boat—a bad place when a craft is towing. I was watching the behavior of their boat as the great fisherman's staysail, far, far larger than the topsail and used only in light breezes, was broken out. As the Mary Rebecca lurched forward with a tremendous jerk, the nose of the boat ducked down into the water, and the men tumbled over one another in a wild rush into the stern to save the boat from being dragged sheer under water.

"That settles them!" Charley remarked, though he was anxiously studying the behavior of the Mary Rebecca, which was being driven under far more canvas than she was rightly able to carry.

"Next stop is Antioch!" announced the cheerful sailor, after the manner of a railway conductor. "And next comes Merryweather!"

"Come here, quick," Charley said to me.

I crawled across the deck and stood upright beside him in the shelter of the sheet steel.

"Feel in my inside pocket," he commanded, "and get my notebook. That's right. Tear out a blank page and write what I tell you."

And this is what I wrote:

Telephone to Merryweather, to the sheriff, the constable, or the judge. Tell them we are coming and to turn out the town. Arm everybody. Have them down on the wharf to meet us or we are gone gooses.

"Now make it good and fast to that marlinspike, and stand by to toss it ashore."

I did as he directed. By then we were close to Antioch. The

47

wind was shouting through our rigging, the Mary Rebecca was half over on her side and rushing ahead like an ocean greyhound. The seafaring folk of Antioch had seen us breaking out topsail and staysail, a most reckless performance in such weather, and had hurried to the wharf-ends in little groups to find out what was the matter.

Straight down the water front we boomed, Charley edging in till a man could almost leap ashore. When he gave the signal I tossed the marlinspike. It struck the planking of the wharf a resounding smash, bounced along fifteen or twenty feet, and was pounced upon by the amazed onlookers.

It all happened in a flash, for the next minute Antioch was behind and we were heeling it up the San Joaquin toward Merryweather, six miles away. The river straightened out here into its general easterly course, and we squared away before the wind, wing-and-wing once more, the foresail bellying out to starboard.

Ole Ericsen seemed sunk into a state of stolid despair. Charley and the two sailors were looking hopeful, as they had good reason to be. Merryweather was a coal-mining town, and, it being Sunday, it was reasonable to expect the men to be in town. Further, the coal-miners had never lost any love for the Greek fishermen, and were pretty certain to render us hearty assistance.

We strained our eyes for a glimpse of the town, and the first sight we caught of it gave us immense relief. The wharves were black with men. As we came closer, we could see them still arriving, stringing down the main street, guns in their hands and on the run. Charley glanced astern at the fishermen with a look of ownership in his eye which till then had been missing. The Greeks were plainly overawed by the display of armed strength and were putting their own rifles away.

We took in topsail and staysail, dropped the main peak, and as we got abreast of the principal wharf jibed the mainsail. The Mary Rebecca shot around into the wind, the captive fishermen describing a great arc behind her, and forged ahead till she lost way, when lines were flung ashore and she was made fast. This was accomplished under a hurricane of cheers from the delighted miners.

Ole Ericsen heaved a great sigh. "Ay never tank Ay see my wife never again," he confessed.

"Why, we were never in any danger," said Charley.

Ole looked at him incredulously.

"Sure, I mean it," Charley went on. "All we had to do, any time, was to let go our end—as I am going to do now, so that those Greeks can untangle their nets."

48

He went below with a monkey-wrench, unscrewed the nut, and let the hook drop off. When the Greeks had hauled their nets into their boats and made everything ship-shape, a posse of citizens took them off our hands and led them away to jail.

"Ay tank Ay ban a great big fool," said Ole Ericsen. But he changed his mind when the admiring townspeople crowded aboard to shake hands with him, and a couple of enterprising newspaper men took photographs of the Mary Rebecca and her captain.

VI

DEMETRIOS CONTOS

It must not be thought, from what I have told of the Greek fishermen, that they were altogether bad. Far from it. But they were rough men, gathered together in isolated communities and fighting with the elements for a livelihood. They lived far away from the law and its workings, did not understand it, and thought it tyranny. Especially did the fish laws seem tyrannical. And because of this, they looked upon the men of the fish patrol as their natural enemies.

We menaced their lives, or their living, which is the same thing, in many ways. We confiscated illegal traps and nets, the materials of which had cost them considerable sums and the making of which required weeks of labor. We prevented them from catching fish at many times and seasons, which was equivalent to preventing them from making as good a living as they might have made had we not been in existence. And when we captured them, they were brought into the courts of law, where heavy cash fines were collected from them. As a result, they hated us vindictively. As the dog is the natural enemy of the cat, the snake of man, so were we of the fish patrol the natural enemies of the fishermen.

But it is to show that they could act generously as well as hate bitterly that this story of Demetrios Contos is told. Demetrios Contos lived in Vallejo. Next to Big Alec, he was the largest, bravest, and most influential man among the Greeks. He had given us no trouble, and I doubt if he would ever have clashed with us had he not invested in a new salmon boat. This boat was the cause of all the trouble. He had had it built upon his own model, in which the lines of the general salmon boat were somewhat modified.

To his high elation he found his new boat very fast—in fact, faster than any other boat on the bay or rivers. Forthwith he grew proud and boastful: and, our raid with the Mary Rebecca on the Sunday salmon fishers having wrought fear in their hearts, he sent a challenge up to Benicia. One of the local fishermen conveyed it to us; it was to the effect that Demetrios Contos would sail up from Vallejo on the following Sunday, and in the plain sight of Benicia set his net and catch salmon, and that Charley Le Grant, patrolman, might come and get him if he could. Of course Charley and I had heard nothing of the new boat. Our own boat was pretty fast, and we were not afraid to have a brush with any other that happened along.

50

Sunday came. The challenge had been bruited abroad, and the fishermen and seafaring folk of Benicia turned out to a man, crowding Steamboat Wharf till it looked like the grand stand at a football match. Charley and I had been sceptical, but the fact of the crowd convinced us that there was something in Demetrios Contos's dare.

In the afternoon, when the sea-breeze had picked up in strength, his sail hove into view as he bowled along before the wind. He tacked a score of feet from the wharf, waved his hand theatrically, like a knight about to enter the lists, received a hearty cheer in return, and stood away into the Straits for a couple of hundred yards. Then he lowered sail, and, drifting the boat sidewise by means of the wind, proceeded to set his net. He did not set much of it, possibly fifty feet; yet Charley and I were thunderstruck at the man's effrontery. We did not know at the time, but we learned afterward, that the net he used was old and worthless. It could catch fish, true; but a catch of any size would have torn it to pieces.

Charley shook his head and said:

"I confess, it puzzles me. What if he has out only fifty feet? He could never get it in if we once started for him. And why does he come here anyway, flaunting his law-breaking in our faces? Right in our home town, too."

Charley's voice took on an aggrieved tone, and he continued for some minutes to inveigh against the brazenness of Demetrios Contos.

In the meantime, the man in question was lolling in the stern of his boat and watching the net floats. When a large fish is meshed in a gill-net, the floats by their agitation advertise the fact. And they evidently advertised it to Demetrios, for he pulled in about a dozen feet of net, and held aloft for a moment, before he flung it into the bottom of the boat, a big, glistening salmon. It was greeted by the audience on the wharf with round after round of cheers. This was more than Charley could stand.

"Come on, lad," he called to me; and we lost no time jumping into our salmon boat and getting up sail.

The crowd shouted warning to Demetrios, and as we darted out from the wharf we saw him slash his worthless net clear with a long knife. His sail was all ready to go up, and a moment later it fluttered in the sunshine. He ran aft, drew in the sheet, and filled on the long tack toward the Contra Costa Hills.

By this time we were not more than thirty feet astern. Charley was jubilant. He knew our boat was fast, and he knew, further, that in fine sailing few men were his equals. He was confident that we should surely catch Demetrios, and I shared his confidence. But somehow we did not seem to gain.

It was a pretty sailing breeze. We were gliding sleekly through the water, but Demetrios was slowly sliding away from us. And not only was he going faster, but he was eating into the wind a fraction of a point closer than we. This was sharply impressed upon us when he went about under the Contra Costa Hills and passed us on the other tack fully one hundred feet dead to windward.

"Whew!" Charley exclaimed. "Either that boat is a daisy, or we've got a five-gallon coal-oil can fast to our keel!"

It certainly looked it one way or the other. And by the time Demetrios made the Sonoma Hills, on the other side of the Straits, we were so hopelessly outdistanced that Charley told me to slack off the sheet, and we squared away for Benicia. The fishermen on Steamboat Wharf showered us with ridicule when we returned and tied up. Charley and I got out and walked away, feeling rather sheepish, for it is a sore stroke to one's pride when he thinks he has a good boat and knows how to sail it, and another man comes along and beats him.

Charley mooned over it for a couple of days; then word was brought to us, as before, that on the next Sunday Demetrios Contos would repeat his performance. Charley roused himself. He had our boat out of the water, cleaned and repainted its bottom, made a trifling alteration about the centre-board, overhauled the running gear, and sat up nearly all of Saturday night sewing on a new and much larger sail. So large did he make it, in fact, that additional ballast was imperative, and we stowed away nearly five hundred extra pounds of old railroad iron in the bottom of the boat.

Sunday came, and with it came Demetrios Contos, to break the law defiantly in open day. Again we had the afternoon sea-breeze, and again Demetrios cut loose some forty or more feet of his rotten net, and got up sail and under way under our very noses. But he had anticipated Charley's move, and his own sail peaked higher than ever, while a whole extra cloth had been added to the after leech.

It was nip and tuck across to the Contra Costa Hills, neither of us seeming to gain or to lose. But by the time we had made the return tack to the Sonoma Hills, we could see that, while we footed it at about equal speed, Demetrios had eaten into the wind the least bit more than we. Yet Charley was sailing our boat as finely and delicately as it was possible to sail it, and getting more out of it than he ever had before.

Of course, he could have drawn his revolver and fired at Demetrios; but we had long since found it contrary to our natures to

52

shoot at a fleeing man guilty of only a petty offence. Also a sort of tacit agreement seemed to have been reached between the patrolmen and the fishermen. If we did not shoot while they ran away, they, in turn, did not fight if we once laid hands on them. Thus Demetrios Contos ran away from us, and we did no more than try our best to overtake him; and, in turn, if our boat proved faster than his, or was sailed better, he would, we knew, make no resistance when we caught up with him.

With our large sails and the healthy breeze romping up the Carquinez Straits, we found that our sailing was what is called "ticklish." We had to be constantly on the alert to avoid a capsize, and while Charley steered I held the main-sheet in my hand with but a single turn round a pin, ready to let go at any moment. Demetrios, we could see, sailing his boat alone, had his hands full.

But it was a vain undertaking for us to attempt to catch him. Out of his inner consciousness he had evolved a boat that was better than ours. And though Charley sailed fully as well, if not the least bit better, the boat he sailed was not so good as the Greek's.

"Slack away the sheet," Charley commanded; and as our boat fell off before the wind, Demetrios's mocking laugh floated down to us.

Charley shook his head, saying, "It's no use. Demetrios has the better boat. If he tries his performance again, we must meet it with some new scheme."

This time it was my imagination that came to the rescue.

"What's the matter," I suggested, on the Wednesday following, "with my chasing Demetrios in the boat next Sunday, while you wait for him on the wharf at Vallejo when he arrives?"

Charley considered it a moment and slapped his knee.

"A good idea! You're beginning to use that head of yours. A credit to your teacher, I must say."

"But you mustn't chase him too far," he went on, the next moment, "or he'll head out into San Pablo Bay instead of running home to Vallejo, and there I'll be, standing lonely on the wharf and waiting in vain for him to arrive."

On Thursday Charley registered an objection to my plan.

"Everybody'll know I've gone to Vallejo, and you can depend upon it that Demetrios will know, too. I'm afraid we'll have to give up the idea."

This objection was only too valid, and for the rest of the day I struggled under my disappointment. But that night a new way seemed to open to me, and in my eagerness I awoke Charley from a sound sleep.

"Well," he grunted, "what's the matter? House afire?"

"No," I replied, "but my head is. Listen to this. On Sunday you and I will be around Benicia up to the very moment Demetrios's sail heaves into sight. This will lull everybody's suspicions. Then, when Demetrios's sail does heave in sight, do you stroll leisurely away and up-town. All the fishermen will think you're beaten and that you know you're beaten."

"So far, so good," Charley commented, while I paused to catch breath.

"And very good indeed," I continued proudly. "You stroll carelessly up-town, but when you're once out of sight you leg it for all you're worth for Dan Maloney's. Take the little mare of his, and strike out on the county road for Vallejo. The road's in fine condition, and you can make it in quicker time than Demetrios can beat all the way down against the wind."

"And I'll arrange right away for the mare, first thing in the morning," Charley said, accepting the modified plan without hesitation.

"But, I say," he said, a little later, this time waking me out of a sound sleep.

I could hear him chuckling in the dark.

"I say, lad, isn't it rather a novelty for the fish patrol to be taking to horseback?"

"Imagination," I answered. "It's what you're always preaching—'keep thinking one thought ahead of the other fellow, and you're bound to win out.'"

"He! he!" he chuckled. "And if one thought ahead, including a mare, doesn't take the other fellow's breath away this time, I'm not your humble servant, Charley Le Grant."

"But can you manage the boat alone?" he asked, on Friday. "Remember, we've a ripping big sail on her."

I argued my proficiency so well that he did not refer to the matter again till Saturday, when he suggested removing one whole cloth from the after leech. I guess it was the disappointment written on my face that made him desist; for I, also, had a pride in my boat-sailing abilities, and I was almost wild to get out alone with the big sail and go tearing down the Carquinez Straits in the wake of the flying Greek.

As usual, Sunday and Demetrios Contos arrived together. It had become the regular thing for the fishermen to assemble on Steamboat Wharf to greet his arrival and to laugh at our discomfiture. He lowered sail a couple of hundred yards out and set his customary fifty feet of rotten net.

"I suppose this nonsense will keep up as long as his old net holds out," Charley grumbled, with intention, in the hearing of several of the Greeks.

"Den I give-a heem my old-a net-a," one of them spoke up, promptly and maliciously.

"I don't care," Charley answered. "I've got some old net myself he can have—if he'll come around and ask for it."

They all laughed at this, for they could afford to be sweet-tempered with a man so badly outwitted as Charley was.

"Well, so long, lad," Charley called to me a moment later. "I think I'll go up-town to Maloney's."

"Let me take the boat out?" I asked.

"If you want to," was his answer, as he turned on his heel and walked slowly away.

Demetrios pulled two large salmon out of his net, and I jumped into the boat. The fishermen crowded around in a spirit of fun, and when I started to get up sail overwhelmed me with all sorts of jocular advice. They even offered extravagant bets to one another that I would surely catch Demetrios, and two of them, styling themselves the committee of judges, gravely asked permission to come along with me to see how I did it.

But I was in no hurry. I waited to give Charley all the time I could, and I pretended dissatisfaction with the stretch of the sail and slightly shifted the small tackle by which the huge sprit forces up the peak. It was not until I was sure that Charley had reached Dan Maloney's and was on the little mare's back, that I cast off from the wharf and gave the big sail to the wind. A stout puff filled it and suddenly pressed the lee gunwale down till a couple of buckets of water came inboard. A little thing like this will happen to the best small-boat sailors, and yet, though I instantly let go the sheet and righted, I was cheered sarcastically, as though I had been guilty of a very awkward blunder.

When Demetrios saw only one person in the fish patrol boat, and that one a boy, he proceeded to play with me. Making a short tack out, with me not thirty feet behind, he returned, with his sheet a little free, to Steamboat Wharf. And there he made short tacks, and turned and twisted and ducked around, to the great delight of his sympathetic audience. I was right behind him all the time, and I dared to do whatever he did, even when he squared away before the wind and jibed his big sail over—a most dangerous trick with such a sail in such a wind.

He depended upon the brisk sea breeze and the strong ebb tide, which together kicked up a nasty sea, to bring me to grief. But I was on my mettle, and never in all my life did I sail a boat better than on that day. I was keyed up to concert pitch, my brain was

55

working smoothly and quickly, my hands never fumbled once, and it seemed that I almost divined the thousand little things which a small-boat sailor must be taking into consideration every second.

It was Demetrios who came to grief instead. Something went wrong with his centre-board, so that it jammed in the case and would not go all the way down. In a moment's breathing space, which he had gained from me by a clever trick, I saw him working impatiently with the centre-board, trying to force it down. I gave him little time, and he was compelled quickly to return to the tiller and sheet.

The centre-board made him anxious. He gave over playing with me, and started on the long beat to Vallejo. To my joy, on the first long tack across, I found that I could eat into the wind just a little bit closer than he. Here was where another man in the boat would have been of value to him; for, with me but a few feet astern, he did not dare let go the tiller and run amidships to try to force down the centre-board.

Unable to hang on as close in the eye of the wind as formerly, he proceeded to slack his sheet a trifle and to ease off a bit, in order to outfoot me. This I permitted him to do till I had worked to windward, when I bore down upon him. As I drew close, he feinted at coming about. This led me to shoot into the wind to forestall him. But it was only a feint, cleverly executed, and he held back to his course while I hurried to make up lost ground.

He was undeniably smarter than I when it came to manœuvring. Time after time I all but had him, and each time he tricked me and escaped. Besides, the wind was freshening constantly, and each of us had his hands full to avoid capsizing. As for my boat, it could not have been kept afloat but for the extra ballast. I sat cocked over the weather gunwale, tiller in one hand and sheet in the other; and the sheet, with a single turn around a pin, I was very often forced to let go in the severer puffs. This allowed the sail to spill the wind, which was equivalent to taking off so much driving power, and of course I lost ground. My consolation was that Demetrios was as often compelled to do the same thing.

The strong ebb-tide, racing down the Straits in the teeth of the wind, caused an unusually heavy and spiteful sea, which dashed aboard continually. I was dripping wet, and even the sail was wet half-way up the after leech. Once I did succeed in outmanœuvring Demetrios, so that my bow bumped into him amidships. Here was where I should have had another man. Before I could run forward and leap aboard, he shoved the boats apart with an oar, laughing mockingly in my face as he did so.

We were now at the mouth of the Straits, in a bad stretch of water. Here the Vallejo Straits and the Carquinez Straits rushed directly at each other. Through the first flowed all the water of Napa River and the great tide-lands; through the second flowed all the water of Suisun Bay and the Sacramento and San Joaquin rivers. And where such immense bodies of water, flowing swiftly, clashed together, a terrible tide-rip was produced. To make it worse, the wind howled up San Pablo Bay for fifteen miles and drove in a tremendous sea upon the tide-rip.

Conflicting currents tore about in all directions, colliding, forming whirlpools, sucks, and boils, and shooting up spitefully into hollow waves which fell aboard as often from leeward as from windward. And through it all, confused, driven into a madness of motion, thundered the great smoking seas from San Pablo Bay.

I was as wildly excited as the water. The boat was behaving splendidly, leaping and lurching through the welter like a race-horse. I could hardly contain myself with the joy of it. The huge sail, the howling wind, the driving seas, the plunging boat—I, a pygmy, a mere speck in the midst of it, was mastering the elemental strife, flying through it and over it, triumphant and victorious.

And just then, as I roared along like a conquering hero, the boat received a frightful smash and came instantly to a dead stop. I was flung forward and into the bottom. As I sprang up I caught a fleeting glimpse of a greenish, barnacle-covered object, and knew it at once for what it was, that terror of navigation, a sunken pile. No man may guard against such a thing. Water-logged and floating just beneath the surface, it was impossible to sight it in the troubled water in time to escape.

The whole bow of the boat must have been crushed in, for in a few seconds the boat was half full. Then a couple of seas filled it, and it sank straight down, dragged to bottom by the heavy ballast. So quickly did it all happen that I was entangled in the sail and drawn under. When I fought my way to the surface, suffocating, my lungs almost bursting, I could see nothing of the oars. They must have been swept away by the chaotic currents. I saw Demetrios Contos looking back from his boat, and heard the vindictive and mocking tones of his voice as he shouted exultantly. He held steadily on his course, leaving me to perish.

There was nothing to do but to swim for it, which, in that wild confusion, was at the best a matter of but a few moments. Holding my breath and working with my hands, I managed to get off my heavy sea-boots and my jacket. Yet there was very little breath I could catch to hold, and I swiftly discovered that it was not so much a matter of swimming as of breathing.

I was beaten and buffeted, smashed under by the great San

Pablo whitecaps, and strangled by the hollow tide-rip waves which flung themselves into my eyes, nose, and mouth. Then the strange sucks would grip my legs and drag me under, to spout me up in some fierce boiling, where, even as I tried to catch my breath, a great whitecap would crash down upon my head.

It was impossible to survive any length of time. I was breathing more water than air, and drowning all the time. My senses began to leave me, my head to whirl around. I struggled on, spasmodically, instinctively, and was barely half conscious when I felt myself caught by the shoulders and hauled over the gunwale of a boat.

For some time I lay across a seat where I had been flung, face downward, and with the water running out of my mouth. After a while, still weak and faint, I turned around to see who was my rescuer. And there, in the stern, sheet in one hand and tiller in the other, grinning and nodding good-naturedly, sat Demetrios Contos. He had intended to leave me to drown,—he said so afterward,—but his better self had fought the battle, conquered, and sent him back to me.

"You all-a right?" he asked.

I managed to shape a "yes" on my lips, though I could not yet speak.

"You sail-a de boat verr-a good-a," he said. "So good-a as a man."

A compliment from Demetrios Contos was a compliment indeed, and I keenly appreciated it, though I could only nod my head in acknowledgment.

We held no more conversation, for I was busy recovering and he was busy with the boat. He ran in to the wharf at Vallejo, made the boat fast, and helped me out. Then it was, as we both stood on the wharf, that Charley stepped out from behind a net-rack and put his hand on Demetrios Contos's arm.

"He saved my life, Charley," I protested; "and I don't think he ought to be arrested."

A puzzled expression came into Charley's face, which cleared immediately after, in a way it had when he made up his mind.

"I can't help it, lad," he said kindly. "I can't go back on my duty, and it's plain duty to arrest him. To-day is Sunday; there are two salmon in his boat which he caught to-day. What else can I do?"

"But he saved my life," I persisted, unable to make any other argument.

Demetrios Contos's face went black with rage when he learned Charley's judgment. He had a sense of being unfairly treated. The better part of his nature had triumphed, he had performed a

58

generous act and saved a helpless enemy, and in return the enemy was taking him to jail.

Charley and I were out of sorts with each other when we went back to Benicia. I stood for the spirit of the law and not the letter; but by the letter Charley made his stand. As far as he could see, there was nothing else for him to do. The law said distinctly that no salmon should be caught on Sunday. He was a patrolman, and it was his duty to enforce that law. That was all there was to it. He had done his duty, and his conscience was clear. Nevertheless, the whole thing seemed unjust to me, and I felt very sorry for Demetrios Contos.

Two days later we went down to Vallejo to the trial. I had to go along as a witness, and it was the most hateful task that I ever performed in my life when I testified on the witness stand to seeing Demetrios catch the two salmon Charley had captured him with.

Demetrios had engaged a lawyer, but his case was hopeless. The jury was out only fifteen minutes, and returned a verdict of guilty. The judge sentenced Demetrios to pay a fine of one hundred dollars or go to jail for fifty days.

Charley stepped up to the clerk of the court. "I want to pay that fine," he said, at the same time placing five twenty-dollar gold pieces on the desk. "It—it was the only way out of it, lad," he stammered, turning to me.

The moisture rushed into my eyes as I seized his hand. "I want to pay—" I began.

"To pay your half?" he interrupted. "I certainly shall expect you to pay it."

In the meantime Demetrios had been informed by his lawyer that his fee likewise had been paid by Charley.

Demetrios came over to shake Charley's hand, and all his warm Southern blood flamed in his face. Then, not to be outdone in generosity, he insisted on paying his fine and lawyer's fee himself, and flew half-way into a passion because Charley refused to let him.

More than anything else we ever did, I think, this action of Charley's impressed upon the fishermen the deeper significance of the law. Also Charley was raised high in their esteem, while I came in for a little share of praise as a boy who knew how to sail a boat. Demetrios Contos not only never broke the law again, but he became a very good friend of ours, and on more than one occasion he ran up to Benicia to have a gossip with us.

VII

YELLOW HANDKERCHIEF

"I'm not wanting to dictate to you, lad," Charley said; "but I'm very much against your making a last raid. You've gone safely through rough times with rough men, and it would be a shame to have something happen to you at the very end."

"But how can I get out of making a last raid?" I demanded, with the cocksureness of youth. "There always has to be a last, you know, to anything."

Charley crossed his legs, leaned back, and considered the problem. "Very true. But why not call the capture of Demetrios Contos the last? You're back from it safe and sound and hearty, for all your good wetting, and—and—" His voice broke and he could not speak for a moment. "And I could never forgive myself if anything happened to you now."

I laughed at Charley's fears while I gave in to the claims of his affection, and agreed to consider the last raid already performed. We had been together for two years, and now I was leaving the fish patrol in order to go back and finish my education. I had earned and saved money to put me through three years at the high school, and though the beginning of the term was several months away, I intended doing a lot of studying for the entrance examinations.

My belongings were packed snugly in a sea-chest, and I was all ready to buy my ticket and ride down on the train to Oakland, when Neil Partington arrived in Benicia. The Reindeer was needed immediately for work far down on the Lower Bay, and Neil said he intended to run straight for Oakland. As that was his home and as I was to live with his family while going to school, he saw no reason, he said, why I should not put my chest aboard and come along.

So the chest went aboard, and in the middle of the afternoon we hoisted the Reindeer's big mainsail and cast off. It was tantalizing fall weather. The sea-breeze, which had blown steadily all summer, was gone, and in its place were capricious winds and murky skies which made the time of arriving anywhere extremely problematical. We started on the first of the ebb, and as we slipped down the Carquinez Straits, I looked my last for some time upon Benicia and the bight at Turner's Shipyard, where we had besieged the Lancashire Queen, and had captured Big Alec, the King of the Greeks. And at the mouth of the Straits I looked with not a little interest upon the spot where a few days before I should have drowned but for the good that was in the nature of Demetrios Contos.

A great wall of fog advanced across San Pablo Bay to meet us, and in a few minutes the Reindeer was running blindly through the damp obscurity. Charley, who was steering, seemed to have an instinct for that kind of work. How he did it, he himself confessed that he did not know; but he had a way of calculating winds, currents, distance, time, drift, and sailing speed that was truly marvellous.

"It looks as though it were lifting," Neil Partington said, a couple of hours after we had entered the fog. "Where do you say we are, Charley?"

Charley looked at his watch. "Six o'clock, and three hours more of ebb," he remarked casually.

"But where do you say we are?" Neil insisted.

Charley pondered a moment, and then answered, "The tide has edged us over a bit out of our course, but if the fog lifts right now, as it is going to lift, you'll find we're not more than a thousand miles off McNear's Landing."

"You might be a little more definite by a few miles, anyway," Neil grumbled, showing by his tone that he disagreed.

"All right, then," Charley said, conclusively, "not less than a quarter of a mile, not more than a half."

The wind freshened with a couple of little puffs, and the fog thinned perceptibly.

"McNear's is right off there," Charley said, pointing directly into the fog on our weather beam.

The three of us were peering intently in that direction, when the Reindeer struck with a dull crash and came to a standstill. We ran forward, and found her bowsprit entangled in the tanned rigging of a short, chunky mast. She had collided, head on, with a Chinese junk lying at anchor.

At the moment we arrived forward, five Chinese, like so many bees, came swarming out of the little 'tween-decks cabin, the sleep still in their eyes.

Leading them came a big, muscular man, conspicuous for his pock-marked face and the yellow silk handkerchief swathed about his head. It was Yellow Handkerchief, the Chinaman whom we had arrested for illegal shrimp-fishing the year before, and who, at that time, had nearly sunk the Reindeer, as he had nearly sunk it now by violating the rules of navigation.

"What d'ye mean, you yellow-faced heathen, lying here in a fairway without a horn a-going?" Charley cried hotly.

61

"Mean?" Neil calmly answered. "Just take a look—that's what he means."

Our eyes followed the direction indicated by Neil's finger, and we saw the open amid-ships of the junk, half filled, as we found on closer examination, with fresh-caught shrimps. Mingled with the shrimps were myriads of small fish, from a quarter of an inch upwards in size. Yellow Handkerchief had lifted the trap-net at high-water slack, and, taking advantage of the concealment offered by the fog, had boldly been lying by, waiting to lift the net again at low-water slack.

"Well," Neil hummed and hawed, "in all my varied and extensive experience as a fish patrolman, I must say this is the easiest capture I ever made. What'll we do with them, Charley?"

"Tow the junk into San Rafael, of course," came the answer. Charley turned to me. "You stand by the junk, lad, and I'll pass you a towing line. If the wind doesn't fail us, we'll make the creek before the tide gets too low, sleep at San Rafael, and arrive in Oakland to-morrow by midday."

So saying, Charley and Neil returned to the Reindeer and got under way, the junk towing astern. I went aft and took charge of the prize, steering by means of an antiquated tiller and a rudder with large, diamond-shaped holes, through which the water rushed back and forth.

By now the last of the fog had vanished, and Charley's estimate of our position was confirmed by the sight of McNear's Landing a short half-mile away. Following along the west shore, we rounded Point Pedro in plain view of the Chinese shrimp villages, and a great to-do was raised when they saw one of their junks towing behind the familiar fish patrol sloop.

The wind, coming off the land, was rather puffy and uncertain, and it would have been more to our advantage had it been stronger. San Rafael Creek, up which we had to go to reach the town, and turn over our prisoners to the authorities, ran through wide-stretching marshes, and was difficult to navigate on a falling tide, while at low tide it was impossible to navigate at all. So, with the tide already half-ebbed, it was necessary for us to make time. This the heavy junk prevented lumbering along behind and holding the Reindeer back by just so much dead weight.

"Tell those coolies to get up that sail" Charley finally called to me. "We don't want to hang up on the mud flats for the rest of the night."

I repeated the order to Yellow Handkerchief, who mumbled it huskily to his men. He was suffering from a bad cold, which doubled him up in convulsive coughing spells and made his eyes heavy and bloodshot. This made him more evil-looking than ever, and when he glared viciously at me, I remembered with a shiver the close shave I had had with him at the time of his previous arrest.

His crew sullenly tailed on to the halyards, and the strange, outlandish sail, lateen in rig and dyed a warm brown, rose in the air. We were sailing on the wind, and when Yellow Handkerchief flattened down the sheet the junk forged ahead and the tow-line went slack. Fast as the Reindeer could sail, the junk outsailed her; and to avoid running her down I hauled a little closer on the wind. But the junk likewise outpointed, and in a couple of minutes I was abreast of the Reindeer and to windward. The tow-line had now tautened, at right angles to the two boats and the predicament was laughable.

"Cast off!" I shouted.

Charley hesitated.

"It's all right," I added. "Nothing can happen. We'll make the creek on this tack, and you'll be right behind me all the way up to San Rafael."

At this Charley cast off, and Yellow Handkerchief sent one of his men forward to haul in the line. In the gathering darkness I could just make out the mouth of San Rafael Creek, and by the time we entered it I could barely see its banks. The Reindeer was fully five minutes astern, and we continued to leave her astern as we beat up the narrow, winding channel. With Charley behind us, it seemed I had little to fear from my five prisoners; but the darkness prevented my keeping a sharp eye on them, so I transferred my revolver from my trousers pocket to the side pocket of my coat, where I could more quickly put my hand on it.

Yellow Handkerchief was the one I feared, and that he knew it and made use of it, subsequent events will show. He was sitting a few feet away from me, on what then happened to be the weather side of the junk. I could scarcely see the outlines of his form, but I soon became convinced that he was slowly, very slowly, edging closer to me. I watched him carefully. Steering with my left hand, I slipped my right into my pocket and got hold of the revolver.

I saw him shift along for a couple of inches, and I was just about to order him back—the words were trembling on the tip of my tongue—when I was struck with great force by a heavy figure that had leaped through the air upon me from the lee side. It was one of the crew. He pinioned my right arm so that I could not withdraw my hand from my pocket, and at the same time clapped his other hand over my mouth. Of course, I could have struggled away from him and freed my hand or gotten my mouth clear so that I might cry an alarm, but in a trice Yellow Handkerchief was on top of me.

I struggled around to no purpose in the bottom of the junk, while my legs and arms were tied and my mouth securely bound in what I afterward found out to be a cotton shirt. Then I was left lying in the bottom. Yellow Handkerchief took the tiller, issuing his orders in whispers; and from our position at the time, and from the alteration of the sail, which I could dimly make out above me as a blot against the stars, I knew the junk was being headed into the mouth of a small slough which emptied at that point into San Rafael Creek.

In a couple of minutes we ran softly alongside the bank, and the sail was silently lowered. The Chinese kept very quiet. Yellow Handkerchief sat down in the bottom alongside of me, and I could feel him straining to repress his raspy, hacking cough. Possibly seven or eight minutes later I heard Charley's voice as the Reindeer went past the mouth of the slough.

"I can't tell you how relieved I am," I could plainly hear him saying to Neil, "that the lad has finished with the fish patrol without accident."

Here Neil said something which I could not catch, and then Charley's voice went on:

"The youngster takes naturally to the water, and if, when he finishes high school, he takes a course in navigation and goes deep sea, I see no reason why he shouldn't rise to be master of the finest and biggest ship afloat."

It was all very flattering to me, but lying there, bound and gagged by my own prisoners, with the voices growing faint and fainter as the Reindeer slipped on through the darkness toward San Rafael, I must say I was not in quite the proper situation to enjoy my smiling future. With the Reindeer went my last hope. What was to happen next I could not imagine, for the Chinese were a different race from mine, and from what I knew I was confident that fair play was no part of their make-up.

After waiting a few minutes longer, the crew hoisted the lateen sail, and Yellow Handkerchief steered down toward the mouth of San Rafael Creek. The tide was getting lower, and he had difficulty in escaping the mud-banks. I was hoping he would run aground, but he succeeded in making the Bay without accident.

As we passed out of the creek a noisy discussion arose, which I knew related to me. Yellow Handkerchief was vehement, but the other four as vehemently opposed him. It was very evident that he advocated doing away with me and they were afraid of the consequences. I was familiar enough with the Chinese character to know that fear alone restrained them. But what plan they offered in place of Yellow Handkerchief's murderous one, I could not make out.

My feelings, as my fate hung in the balance, may be guessed. The discussion developed into a quarrel, in the midst of which Yellow Handkerchief unshipped the heavy tiller and sprang toward me. But his four companions threw themselves between, and a clumsy struggle took place for possession of the tiller. In the end Yellow Handkerchief was over-come, and sullenly returned to the steering, while they soundly berated him for his rashness.

Not long after, the sail was run down and the junk slowly urged forward by means of the sweeps. I felt it ground gently on the soft mud. Three of the Chinese—they all wore long sea-boots—got over the side, and the other two passed me across the rail. With Yellow Handkerchief at my legs and his two companions at my shoulders, they began to flounder along through the mud. After some time their feet struck firmer footing, and I knew they were carrying me up some beach. The location of this beach was not doubtful in my mind. It could be none other than one of the Marin Islands, a group of rocky islets which lay off the Marin County shore.

When they reached the firm sand that marked high tide, I was dropped, and none too gently. Yellow Handkerchief kicked me spitefully in the ribs, and then the trio floundered back through the mud to the junk. A moment later I heard the sail go up and slat in the wind as they drew in the sheet. Then silence fell, and I was left to my own devices for getting free.

I remembered having seen tricksters writhe and squirm out of ropes with which they were bound, but though I writhed and squirmed like a good fellow, the knots remained as hard as ever, and there was no appreciable slack. In the course of my squirming, however, I rolled over upon a heap of clam-shells—the remains, evidently, of some yachting party's clam-bake. This gave me an idea. My hands were tied behind my back; and, clutching a shell in them, I rolled over and over, up the beach, till I came to the rocks I knew to be there.

Rolling about and searching, I finally discovered a narrow crevice, into which I shoved the shell. The edge of it was sharp, and across the sharp edge I proceeded to saw the rope that bound my wrists. The edge of the shell was also brittle, and I broke it by bearing too heavily upon it. Then I rolled back to the heap and returned with as many shells as I could carry in both hands. I broke many shells, cut my hands a number of times, and got cramps in my legs from my strained position and my exertions.

While I was suffering from the cramps, and resting, I heard

the familiar halloo drift across the water. It was Charley, searching for me. The gag in my mouth prevented me from replying, and I could only lie there, helplessly fuming, while he rowed past the island and his voice slowly lost itself in the distance.

I returned to the sawing process, and at the end of half an hour succeeded in severing the rope. The rest was easy. My hands once free, it was a matter of minutes to loosen my legs and to take the gag out of my mouth. I ran around the island to make sure it was an island and not by chance a portion of the mainland. An island it certainly was, one of the Marin group, fringed with a sandy beach and surrounded by a sea of mud. Nothing remained but to wait till daylight and to keep warm; for it was a cold, raw night for California, with just enough wind to pierce the skin and cause one to shiver.

To keep up the circulation, I ran around the island a dozen times or so, and clambered across its rocky backbone as many times more—all of which was of greater service to me, as I afterward discovered, than merely to warm me up. In the midst of this exercise I wondered if I had lost anything out of my pockets while rolling over and over in the sand. A search showed the absence of my revolver and pocket-knife. The first Yellow Handkerchief had taken; but the knife had been lost in the sand.

I was hunting for it when the sound of rowlocks came to my ears. At first, of course, I thought of Charley; but on second thought I knew Charley would be calling out as he rowed along. A sudden premonition of danger seized me. The Marin Islands are lonely places; chance visitors in the dead of night are hardly to be expected. What if it were Yellow Handkerchief? The sound made by the rowlocks grew more distinct. I crouched in the sand and listened intently. The boat, which I judged a small skiff from the quick stroke of the oars, was landing in the mud about fifty yards up the beach. I heard a raspy, hacking cough, and my heart stood still. It was Yellow Handkerchief. Not to be robbed of his revenge by his more cautious companions, he had stolen away from the village and come back alone.

I did some swift thinking. I was unarmed and helpless on a tiny islet, and a yellow barbarian, whom I had reason to fear, was coming after me. Any place was safer than the island, and I turned immediately to the water, or rather to the mud. As he began to flounder ashore through the mud. I started to flounder out into it, going over the same course which the Chinese had taken in landing me and in returning to the junk.

Yellow Handkerchief, believing me to be lying tightly bound, exercised no care, but came ashore noisily. This helped me, for, under the shield of his noise and making no more myself than necessary, I managed to cover fifty feet by the time he had made the beach. Here I lay down in the mud. It was cold and clammy, and made me shiver, but I did not care to stand up and run the risk of being discovered by his sharp eyes.

He walked down the beach straight to where he had left me lying, and I had a fleeting feeling of regret at not being able to see his surprise when he did not find me. But it was a very fleeting regret, for my teeth were chattering with the cold.

What his movements were after that I had largely to deduce from the facts of the situation, for I could scarcely see him in the dim starlight. But I was sure that the first thing he did was to make the circuit of the beach to learn if landings had been made by other boats. This he would have known at once by the tracks through the mud.

Convinced that no boat had removed me from the island, he next started to find out what had become of me. Beginning at the pile of clam-shells, he lighted matches to trace my tracks in the sand. At such times I could see his villanous face plainly, and, when the sulphur from the matches irritated his lungs, between the raspy cough that followed and the clammy mud in which I was lying, I confess I shivered harder than ever.

The multiplicity of my footprints puzzled him. Then the idea that I might be out in the mud must have struck him, for he waded out a few yards in my direction, and, stooping, with his eyes searched the dim surface long and carefully. He could not have been more than fifteen feet from me, and had he lighted a match he would surely have discovered me.

He returned to the beach and clambered about over the rocky backbone, again hunting for me with lighted matches. The closeness of the shore impelled me to further flight. Not daring to wade upright, on account of the noise made by floundering and by the suck of the mud, I remained lying down in the mud and propelled myself over its surface by means of my hands. Still keeping the trail made by the Chinese in going from and to the junk, I held on until I had reached the water. Into this I waded to a depth of three feet, and then I turned off to the side on a line parallel with the beach.

The thought came to me of going toward Yellow Handkerchief's skiff and escaping in it, but at that very moment he returned to the beach, and, as though fearing the very thing I had in mind, he slushed out through the mud to assure himself that the skiff was safe. This turned me in the opposite direction. Half swimming, half wading, with my head just out of water and avoiding splashing. I succeeded in putting about a hundred feet between myself and the spot ashore where the Chinese had begun to wade ashore from the junk. I drew myself out on the mud and remained lying flat.

Again Yellow Handkerchief returned to the beach and made a search of the island, and again he returned to the heap of clamshells. I knew what was running in his mind as well as he did himself. No one could leave or land without making tracks in the mud. The only tracks to be seen were those leading from his skiff and from where the junk had been. I was not on the island. I must have left it by one or other of those two tracks. He had just been over the one to his skiff, and was certain I had not left that way. Therefore I could have left the island only by going over the tracks of the junk landing. This he proceeded to verify by wading out over them himself, lighting matches as he came along.

When he arrived at the point where I had first lain, I knew, by the matches he burned and the time he took, that he had discovered the marks left by my body. These he followed straight to the water and into it, but in three feet of water he could no longer see them. On the other hand, as the tide was still falling, he could easily make out the impression made by the junk's bow, and could have likewise made out the impression of any other boat if it had landed at that particular spot. But there was no such mark; and I knew that he was absolutely convinced that I was hiding somewhere in the mud.

But to hunt on a dark night for a boy in a sea of mud would be like hunting for a needle in a haystack, and he did not attempt it. Instead he went back to the beach and prowled around for some time. I was hoping he would give up and go, for by this time I was suffering severely from the cold. At last he waded out to his skiff and rowed away. What if this departure of Yellow Handkerchief's were a sham? What if he had done it merely to entice me ashore?

The more I thought of it the more certain I became that he had made a little too much noise with his oars as he rowed away. So I remained, lying in the mud and shivering. I shivered till the muscles of the small of my back ached and pained me as badly as the cold, and I had need of all my self-control to force myself to remain in my miserable situation.

It was well that I did, however, for, possibly an hour later, I thought I could make out something moving on the beach. I watched intently, but my ears were rewarded first, by a raspy cough I knew only too well. Yellow Handkerchief had sneaked back, landed on the other side of the island, and crept around to surprise me if I had returned.

After that, though hours passed without sign of him, I was afraid to return to the island at all. On the other hand, I was equally

68

afraid that I should die of the exposure I was undergoing. I had never dreamed one could suffer so. I grew so cold and numb, finally, that I ceased to shiver. But my muscles and bones began to ache in a way that was agony. The tide had long since begun to rise, and, foot by foot, it drove me in toward the beach. High water came at three o'clock, and at three o'clock I drew myself up on the beach, more dead than alive, and too helpless to have offered any resistance had Yellow Handkerchief swooped down upon me.

But no Yellow Handkerchief appeared. He had given up and gone back to Point Pedro. Nevertheless, I was in a deplorable, not to say a dangerous, condition. I could not stand upon my feet, much less walk. My clammy, muddy, garments clung to me like sheets of ice. I thought I should never get them off. So numb and lifeless were my fingers, and so weak was I, that it seemed to take an hour to get off my shoes. I had not the strength to break the porpoise-hide laces, and the knots defied me. I repeatedly beat my hands upon the rocks to get some sort of life into them. Sometimes I felt sure I was going to die.

But in the end,—after several centuries, it seemed to me,—I got off the last of my clothes. The water was now close at hand, and I crawled painfully into it and washed the mud from my naked body. Still, I could not get on my feet and walk and I was afraid to lie still. Nothing remained but to crawl weakly, like a snail, and at the cost of constant pain, up and down the island. I kept this up as along as possible, but as the east paled with the coming of dawn I began to succumb. The sky grew rosy-red, and the golden rim of the sun, showing above the horizon, found me lying helpless and motionless among the clam-shells.

As in a dream, I saw the familiar mainsail of the Reindeer as she slipped out of San Rafael Creek on a light puff of morning air. This dream was very much broken. There are intervals I can never recollect on looking back over it. Three things, however, I distinctly remember: the first sight of the Reindeer's mainsail; her lying at anchor a few hundred feet away and a small boat leaving her side; and the cabin stove roaring red-hot, myself swathed all over with blankets, except on the chest and shoulders, which Charley was pounding and mauling unmercifully, and my mouth and throat burning with the coffee which Neil Partington was pouring down a trifle too hot.

But burn or no burn, I tell you it felt good. By the time we arrived in Oakland I was as limber and strong as ever,—though Charley and Neil Partington were afraid I was going to have pneumonia, and Mrs. Partington, for my first six months of school, kept an anxious eye upon me to discover the first symptoms of consumption.

Time flies. It seems but yesterday that I was a lad of sixteen on the fish patrol. Yet I know that I arrived this very morning from China, with a quick passage to my credit, and master of the barkentine Harvester. And I know that to-morrow morning I shall run over to Oakland to see Neil Partington and his wife and family, and later on up to Benicia to see Charley Le Grant and talk over old times. No; I shall not go to Benicia, now that I think about it. I expect to be a highly interested party to a wedding, shortly to take place. Her name is Alice Partington, and, since Charley has promised to be best man, he will have to come down to Oakland instead.

THE RED ONE

THE RED ONE

There it was! The abrupt liberation of sound! As he timed it with his watch, Bassett likened it to the trump of an archangel. Walls of cities, he meditated, might well fall down before so vast and compelling a summons. For the thousandth time vainly he tried to analyse the tone-quality of that enormous peal that dominated the land far into the strong-holds of the surrounding tribes. The mountain gorge which was its source rang to the rising tide of it until it brimmed over and flooded earth and sky and air. With the wantonness of a sick man's fancy, he likened it to the mighty cry of some Titan of the Elder World vexed with misery or wrath. Higher and higher it arose, challenging and demanding in such profounds of volume that it seemed intended for ears beyond the narrow confines of the solar system. There was in it, too, the clamour of protest in that there were no ears to hear and comprehend its utterance.

—Such the sick man's fancy. Still he strove to analyse the sound. Sonorous as thunder was it, mellow as a golden bell, thin and sweet as a thrummed taut cord of silver—no; it was none of these, nor a blend of these. There were no words nor semblances in his vocabulary and experience with which to describe the totality of that sound.

Time passed. Minutes merged into quarters of hours, and quarters of hours into half-hours, and still the sound persisted, ever changing from its initial vocal impulse yet never receiving fresh impulse—fading, dimming, dying as enormously as it had sprung into being. It became a confusion of troubled mutterings and babblings and colossal whisperings. Slowly it withdrew, sob by sob, into whatever great bosom had birthed it, until it whimpered deadly whispers of wrath and as equally seductive whispers of delight, striving still to be heard, to convey some cosmic secret, some understanding of infinite import and value. It dwindled to a ghost of sound that had lost its menace and promise, and became a thing that pulsed on in the sick man's consciousness for minutes after it had ceased. When he could hear it no longer, Bassett glanced at his watch. An hour had elapsed ere that archangel's trump had subsided into tonal nothingness.

Was this, then, his dark tower?—Bassett pondered, remembering his Browning and gazing at his skeleton-like and fever-wasted hands. And the fancy made him smile—of Childe Roland bearing a slug-horn to his lips with an arm as feeble as his was. Was it months, or years, he asked himself, since he first heard that mysterious call on the beach at Ringmanu? To save himself he could not tell. The long sickness had been most long. In conscious count of time he knew of months, many of them; but he had no way of estimating the long intervals of delirium and stupor. And how fared Captain Bateman of the blackbirder Nari? he wondered; and had Captain Bateman's drunken mate died of delirium tremens yet?

From which vain speculations, Bassett turned idly to review all that had occurred since that day on the beach of Ringmanu when he first heard the sound and plunged into the jungle after it. Sagawa had protested. He could see him yet, his queer little monkeyish face eloquent with fear, his back burdened with specimen cases, in his hands Bassett's butterfly net and naturalist's shot-gun, as he quavered, in Bêche-de-mer English: "Me fella too much fright along bush. Bad fella boy, too much stop'm along bush."

Bassett smiled sadly at the recollection. The little New Hanover boy had been frightened, but had proved faithful, following him without hesitancy into the bush in the quest after the source of the wonderful sound. No fire-hollowed tree-trunk, that, throbbing war through the jungle depths, had been Bassett's conclusion. Erroneous had been his next conclusion, namely, that the source or cause could not be more distant than an hour's walk, and that he would easily be back by mid-afternoon to be picked up by the Nari's whale-boat.

"That big fella noise no good, all the same devil-devil," Sagawa had adjudged. And Sagawa had been right. Had he not had his head hacked off within the day? Bassett shuddered. Without doubt Sagawa had been eaten as well by the "bad fella boys too much" that stopped along the bush. He could see him, as he had last seen him, stripped of the shot-gun and all the naturalist's gear of his master, lying on the narrow trail where he had been decapitated barely the moment before. Yes, within a minute the thing had happened. Within a minute, looking back, Bassett had seen him trudging patiently along under his burdens. Then Bassett's own trouble had come upon him. He looked at the cruelly healed stumps of the first

72

and second fingers of his left hand, then rubbed them softly into the indentation in the back of his skull. Quick as had been the flash of the long handled tomahawk, he had been quick enough to duck away his head and partially to deflect the stroke with his up-flung hand. Two fingers and a hasty scalp-wound had been the price he paid for his life. With one barrel of his ten-gauge shot-gun he had blown the life out of the bushman who had so nearly got him; with the other barrel he had peppered the bushmen bending over Sagawa, and had the pleasure of knowing that the major portion of the charge had gone into the one who leaped away with Sagawa's head. Everything had occurred in a flash. Only himself, the slain bushman, and what remained of Sagawa, were in the narrow, wild-pig run of a path. From the dark jungle on either side came no rustle of movement or sound of life. And he had suffered distinct and dreadful shock. For the first time in his life he had killed a human being, and he knew nausea as he contemplated the mess of his handiwork.

Then had begun the chase. He retreated up the pig-run before his hunters, who were between him and the beach. How many there were, he could not guess. There might have been one, or a hundred, for aught he saw of them. That some of them took to the trees and travelled along through the jungle roof he was certain; but at the most he never glimpsed more than an occasional flitting of shadows. No bow-strings twanged that he could hear; but every little while, whence discharged he knew not, tiny arrows whispered past him or struck tree-boles and fluttered to the ground beside him. They were bone-tipped and feather shafted, and the feathers, torn from the breasts of humming-birds, iridesced like jewels.

Once—and now, after the long lapse of time, he chuckled gleefully at the recollection—he had detected a shadow above him that came to instant rest as he turned his gaze upward. He could make out nothing, but, deciding to chance it, had fired at it a heavy charge of number five shot. Squalling like an infuriated cat, the shadow crashed down through tree-ferns and orchids and thudded upon the earth at his feet, and, still squalling its rage and pain, had sunk its human teeth into the ankle of his stout tramping boot. He, on the other hand, was not idle, and with his free foot had done what reduced the squalling to silence. So inured to savagery has Bassett since become, that he chuckled again with the glee of the recollection.

What a night had followed! Small wonder that he had accumulated such a virulence and variety of fevers, he thought, as he recalled that sleepless night of torment, when the throb of his wounds was as nothing compared with the myriad stings of the mosquitoes. There had been no escaping them, and he had not dared to light a fire. They had literally pumped his body full of poison, so that, with the coming of day, eyes swollen almost shut, he had stumbled blindly on, not caring much when his head should be hacked off and his carcass started on the way of Sagawa's to the cooking fire. Twenty-four hours had made a wreck of him—of mind as well as body. He had scarcely retained his wits at all, so maddened was he by the tremendous inoculation of poison he had received. Several times he fired his shot-gun with effect into the shadows that dogged him. Stinging day insects and gnats added to his torment, while his bloody wounds attracted hosts of loathsome flies that clung sluggishly to his flesh and had to be brushed off and crushed off.

Once, in that day, he heard again the wonderful sound, seemingly more distant, but rising imperiously above the nearer war-drums in the bush. Right there was where he had made his mistake. Thinking that he had passed beyond it and that, therefore, it was between him and the beach of Ringmanu, he had worked back toward it when in reality he was penetrating deeper and deeper into the mysterious heart of the unexplored island. That night, crawling in among the twisted roots of a banyan tree, he had slept from exhaustion while the mosquitoes had had their will of him.

Followed days and nights that were vague as nightmares in his memory. One clear vision he remembered was of suddenly finding himself in the midst of a bush village and watching the old men and children fleeing into the jungle. All had fled but one. From close at hand and above him, a whimpering as of some animal in pain and terror had startled him. And looking up he had seen her—a girl, or young woman rather, suspended by one arm in the cooking sun. Perhaps for days she had so hung. Her swollen, protruding tongue spoke as much. Still alive, she gazed at him with eyes of terror. Past help, he decided, as he noted the swellings of her legs which advertised that the joints had been crushed and the great bones broken. He resolved to shoot her, and there the vision terminated. He could not remember whether he had or not, any more than could he remember how he chanced to be in that village, or how he succeeded in getting away from it.

Many pictures, unrelated, came and went in Bassett's mind as he reviewed that period of his terrible wanderings. He remembered invading another village of a dozen houses and driving all before him with his shot-gun save, for one old man, too feeble to flee, who spat at him and whined and snarled as he dug open a ground-oven and from amid the hot stones dragged forth a roasted pig that steamed its essence deliciously through its green-leaf wrappings. It was at this place that a wantonness of savagery had seized upon him. Having feasted, ready to depart with a hind-quarter of the pig in his hand, he deliberately fired the grass thatch of a house with his burning glass.

But seared deepest of all in Bassett's brain, was the dank and noisome jungle. It actually stank with evil, and it was always twilight. Rarely did a shaft of sunlight penetrate its matted roof a hundred feet overhead. And beneath that roof was an aerial ooze of vegetation, a monstrous, parasitic dripping of decadent life-forms that rooted in death and lived on death. And through all this he drifted, ever pursued by the flitting shadows of the anthropophagi, themselves ghosts of evil that dared not face him in battle but that knew that, soon or late, they would feed on him. Bassett remembered that at the time, in lucid moments, he had likened himself to a wounded bull pursued by plains' coyotes too cowardly to battle with him for the meat of him, yet certain of the inevitable end of him when they would be full gorged. As the bull's horns and stamping hoofs kept off the coyotes, so his shot-gun kept off these Solomon Islanders, these twilight shades of bushmen of the island of Guadalcanal.

Came the day of the grass lands. Abruptly, as if cloven by the sword of God in the hand of God, the jungle terminated. The edge of it, perpendicular and as black as the infamy of it, was a hundred feet up and down. And, beginning at the edge of it, grew the grass— sweet, soft, tender, pasture grass that would have delighted the eyes and beasts of any husbandman and that extended, on and on, for leagues and leagues of velvet verdure, to the backbone of the great island, the towering mountain range flung up by some ancient earth-cataclysm, serrated and gullied but not yet erased by the erosive tropic rains. But the grass! He had crawled into it a dozen yards, buried his face in it, smelled it, and broken down in a fit of involuntary weeping.

And, while he wept, the wonderful sound had pealed forth—if by peal, he had often thought since, an adequate description could be given of the enunciation of so vast a sound melting sweet. Sweet it was, as no sound ever heard. Vast it was, of so mighty a resonance that it might have proceeded from some brazen-throated monster. And yet it called to him across that leagues-wide savannah, and was like a benediction to his long-suffering, pain racked spirit.

He remembered how he lay there in the grass, wet-cheeked

but no longer sobbing, listening to the sound and wondering that he had been able to hear it on the beach of Ringmanu. Some freak of air pressures and air currents, he reflected, had made it possible for the sound to carry so far. Such conditions might not happen again in a thousand days or ten thousand days, but the one day it had happened had been the day he landed from the Nari for several hours' collecting. Especially had he been in quest of the famed jungle butterfly, a foot across from wing-tip to wing-tip, as velvet-dusky of lack of colour as was the gloom of the roof, of such lofty arboreal habits that it resorted only to the jungle roof and could be brought down only by a dose of shot. It was for this purpose that Sagawa had carried the ten-gauge shot-gun.

Two days and nights he had spent crawling across that belt of grass land. He had suffered much, but pursuit had ceased at the jungle-edge. And he would have died of thirst had not a heavy thunderstorm revived him on the second day.

And then had come Balatta. In the first shade, where the savannah yielded to the dense mountain jungle, he had collapsed to die. At first she had squealed with delight at sight of his helplessness, and was for beating his brain out with a stout forest branch. Perhaps it was his very utter helplessness that had appealed to her, and perhaps it was her human curiosity that made her refrain. At any rate, she had refrained, for he opened his eyes again under the impending blow, and saw her studying him intently. What especially struck her about him were his blue eyes and white skin. Coolly she had squatted on her hams, spat on his arm, and with her finger-tips scrubbed away the dirt of days and nights of muck and jungle that sullied the pristine whiteness of his skin.

And everything about her had struck him especially, although there was nothing conventional about her at all. He laughed weakly at the recollection, for she had been as innocent of garb as Eve before the fig-leaf adventure. Squat and lean at the same time, asymmetrically limbed, string-muscled as if with lengths of cordage, dirt-caked from infancy save for casual showers, she was as unbeautiful a prototype of woman as he, with a scientist's eye, had ever gazed upon. Her breasts advertised at the one time her maturity and youth; and, if by nothing else, her sex was advertised by the one article of finery with which she was adorned, namely a pig's tail, thrust though a hole in her left ear-lobe. So lately had the tail been severed, that its raw end still oozed blood that dried upon her shoulder like so much candle-droppings. And her face! A twisted and wizened complex of apish features, perforated by upturned, sky-open, Mongolian nostrils, by a mouth that sagged from a huge upper-lip and faded precipitately into a retreating chin, by peering querulous eyes that blinked as blink the eyes of denizens of monkey-cages.

Not even the water she brought him in a forest-leaf, and the ancient and half-putrid chunk of roast pig, could redeem in the slightest the grotesque hideousness of her. When he had eaten weakly for a space, he closed his eyes in order not to see her, although again and again she poked them open to peer at the blue of them. Then had come the sound. Nearer, much nearer, he knew it to be; and he knew equally well, despite the weary way he had come, that it was still many hours distant. The effect of it on her had been startling. She cringed under it, with averted face, moaning and chattering with fear. But after it had lived its full life of an hour, he closed his eyes and fell asleep with Balatta brushing the flies from him.

When he awoke it was night, and she was gone. But he was aware of renewed strength, and, by then too thoroughly inoculated by the mosquito poison to suffer further inflammation, he closed his eyes and slept an unbroken stretch till sun-up. A little later Balatta had returned, bringing with her a half-dozen women who, unbeautiful as they were, were patently not so unbeautiful as she. She evidenced by her conduct that she considered him her find, her property, and the pride she took in showing him off would have been ludicrous had his situation not been so desperate.

Later, after what had been to him a terrible journey of miles, when he collapsed in front of the devil-devil house in the shadow of the breadfruit tree, she had shown very lively ideas on the matter of retaining possession of him. Ngurn, whom Bassett was to know afterward as the devil-devil doctor, priest, or medicine man of the village, had wanted his head. Others of the grinning and chattering monkey-men, all as stark of clothes and bestial of appearance as Balatta, had wanted his body for the roasting oven. At that time he had not understood their language, if by language might be dignified the uncouth sounds they made to represent ideas. But Bassett had thoroughly understood the matter of debate, especially when the men pressed and prodded and felt of the flesh of him as if he were so much commodity in a butcher's stall.

Balatta had been losing the debate rapidly, when the accident happened. One of the men, curiously examining Bassett's shot-gun, managed to cock and pull a trigger. The recoil of the butt into the pit of the man's stomach had not been the most sanguinary result, for the charge of shot, at a distance of a yard, had blown the head of one of the debaters into nothingness.

Even Balatta joined the others in flight, and, ere they returned, his senses already reeling from the oncoming fever-attack, Bassett had regained possession of the gun. Whereupon, although his teeth chattered with the ague and his swimming eyes could scarcely see, he held on to his fading consciousness until he could intimidate the bushmen with the simple magics of compass, watch, burning glass, and matches. At the last, with due emphasis, of solemnity and awfulness, he had killed a young pig with his shot-gun and promptly fainted.

Bassett flexed his arm-muscles in quest of what possible strength might reside in such weakness, and dragged himself slowly and totteringly to his feet. He was shockingly emaciated; yet, during the various convalescences of the many months of his long sickness, he had never regained quite the same degree of strength as this time. What he feared was another relapse such as he had already frequently experienced. Without drugs, without even quinine, he had managed so far to live through a combination of the most pernicious and most malignant of malarial and black-water fevers. But could he continue to endure? Such was his everlasting query. For, like the genuine scientist he was, he would not be content to die until he had solved the secret of the sound.

Supported by a staff, he staggered the few steps to the devil-devil house where death and Ngurn reigned in gloom. Almost as infamously dark and evil-stinking as the jungle was the devil-devil house—in Bassett's opinion. Yet therein was usually to be found his favourite crony and gossip, Ngurn, always willing for a yarn or a discussion, the while he sat in the ashes of death and in a slow smoke shrewdly revolved curing human heads suspended from the rafters. For, through the months' interval of consciousness of his long sickness, Bassett had mastered the psychological simplicities and lingual difficulties of the language of the tribe of Ngurn and Balatta and Vngngn—the latter the addle-headed young chief who was ruled by Ngurn, and who, whispered intrigue had it, was the son of Ngurn.

"Will the Red One speak to-day?" Bassett asked, by this time so accustomed to the old man's gruesome occupation as to take even an interest in the progress of the smoke-curing.

With the eye of an expert Ngurn examined the particular head he was at work upon.

78

"It will be ten days before I can say 'finish,'" he said. "Never has any man fixed heads like these."

Bassett smiled inwardly at the old fellow's reluctance to talk with him of the Red One. It had always been so. Never, by any chance, had Ngurn or any other member of the weird tribe divulged the slightest hint of any physical characteristic of the Red One. Physical the Red One must be, to emit the wonderful sound, and though it was called the Red One, Bassett could not be sure that red represented the colour of it. Red enough were the deeds and powers of it, from what abstract clues he had gleaned. Not alone, had Ngurn informed him, was the Red One more bestial powerful than the neighbour tribal gods, ever athirst for the red blood of living human sacrifices, but the neighbour gods themselves were sacrificed and tormented before him. He was the god of a dozen allied villages similar to this one, which was the central and commanding village of the federation. By virtue of the Red One many alien villages had been devastated and even wiped out, the prisoners sacrificed to the Red One. This was true to-day, and it extended back into old history carried down by word of mouth through the generations. When he, Ngurn, had been a young man, the tribes beyond the grass lands had made a war raid. In the counter raid, Ngurn and his fighting folk had made many prisoners. Of children alone over five score living had been bled white before the Red One, and many, many more men and women.

The Thunderer was another of Ngurn's names for the mysterious deity. Also at times was he called The Loud Shouter, The God-Voiced, The Bird-Throated, The One with the Throat Sweet as the Throat of the Honey-Bird, The Sun Singer, and The Star-Born.

Why The Star-Born? In vain Bassett interrogated Ngurn. According to that old devil-devil doctor, the Red One had always been, just where he was at present, for ever singing and thundering his will over men. But Ngurn's father, wrapped in decaying grass-matting and hanging even then over their heads among the smoky rafters of the devil-devil house, had held otherwise. That departed wise one had believed that the Red One came from out of the starry night, else why—so his argument had run—had the old and forgotten ones passed his name down as the Star-Born? Bassett could not but recognize something cogent in such argument. But Ngurn affirmed the long years of his long life, wherein he had gazed upon many starry nights, yet never had he found a star on grass land or in jungle depth—and he had looked for them. True, he had beheld shooting stars (this in reply to Bassett's contention); but likewise had he beheld the phosphorescence of fungoid growths and rotten meat and fireflies on dark nights, and the flames of wood-fires and of blazing candle-nuts; yet what were flame and blaze and glow when they had flamed and blazed and glowed? Answer: memories, memories only, of things which had ceased to be, like memories of matings accomplished, of feasts forgotten, of desires that were the ghosts of desires, flaring, flaming, burning, yet unrealized in achievement of easement and satisfaction. Where was the appetite of yesterday? the roasted flesh of the wild pig the hunter's arrow failed to slay? the maid, unwed and dead ere the young man knew her?

A memory was not a star, was Ngurn's contention. How could a memory be a star? Further, after all his long life he still observed the starry night-sky unaltered. Never had he noted the absence of a single star from its accustomed place. Besides, stars were fire, and the Red One was not fire—which last involuntary betrayal told Bassett nothing.

"Will the Red One speak to-morrow?" he queried.

Ngurn shrugged his shoulders as who should say.

"And the day after?—and the day after that?" Bassett persisted.

"I would like to have the curing of your head," Ngurn changed the subject. "It is different from any other head. No devil-devil has a head like it. Besides, I would cure it well. I would take months and months. The moons would come and the moons would go, and the smoke would be very slow, and I should myself gather the materials for the curing smoke. The skin would not wrinkle. It would be as smooth as your skin now."

He stood up, and from the dim rafters, grimed with the smoking of countless heads, where day was no more than a gloom, took down a matting-wrapped parcel and began to open it.

"It is a head like yours," he said, "but it is poorly cured."

Bassett had pricked up his ears at the suggestion that it was a white man's head; for he had long since come to accept that these jungle-dwellers, in the midmost centre of the great island, had never had intercourse with white men. Certainly he had found them without the almost universal bêche-de-mer English of the west South Pacific. Nor had they knowledge of tobacco, nor of gunpowder. Their few precious knives, made from lengths of hoop-iron, and their few and more precious tomahawks from cheap trade hatchets, he had surmised they had captured in war from the bushmen of the jungle beyond the grass lands, and that they, in turn, had similarly gained them from the salt-water men who fringed the coral beaches of the shore and had contact with the occasional white men.

"The folk in the out beyond do not know how to cure heads," old Ngurn explained, as he drew forth from the filthy matting and placed in Bassett's hands an indubitable white man's head.

Ancient it was beyond question; white it was as the blond hair attested. He could have sworn it once belonged to an Englishman, and to an Englishman of long before by token of the heavy gold circlets still threaded in the withered ear-lobes.

"Now your head..." the devil-devil doctor began on his favourite topic.

"I'll tell you what," Bassett interrupted, struck by a new idea. "When I die I'll let you have my head to cure, if, first, you take me to look upon the Red One."

"I will have your head anyway when you are dead," Ngurn rejected the proposition. He added, with the brutal frankness of the savage: "Besides, you have not long to live. You are almost a dead man now. You will grow less strong. In not many months I shall have you here turning and turning in the smoke. It is pleasant, through the long afternoons, to turn the head of one you have known as well as I know you. And I shall talk to you and tell you the many secrets you want to know. Which will not matter, for you will be dead."

"Ngurn," Bassett threatened in sudden anger. "You know the Baby Thunder in the Iron that is mine." (This was in reference to his all-potent and all-awful shotgun.) "I can kill you any time, and then you will not get my head."

"Just the same, will Vngngn, or some one else of my folk get it," Ngurn complacently assured him. "And just the same will in the end turn devil-devil house in the smoke. The quicker you slay me with your Baby Thunder, the quicker will your head turn in the smoke."

And Bassett knew he was beaten in the discussion.

What was the Red One?—Bassett asked himself a thousand times in the succeeding week, while he seemed to grow stronger. What was the source of the wonderful sound? What was this Sun Singer, this Star-Born One, this mysterious deity, as bestial-conducted as the black and kinky-headed and monkey-like human beasts who worshipped it, and whose silver-sweet, bull-mouthed singing and commanding he had heard at the taboo distance for so long?

Ngurn had he failed to bribe with the inevitable curing of his head when he was dead. Vngngn, imbecile and chief that he was,

was too imbecilic, too much under the sway of Ngurn, to be considered. Remained Balatta, who, from the time she found him and poked his blue eyes open to recrudescence of her grotesque female hideousness, had continued his adorer. Woman she was, and he had long known that the only way to win from her treason of her tribe was through the woman's heart of her.

Bassett was a fastidious man. He had never recovered from the initial horror caused by Balatta's female awfulness. Back in England, even at best the charm of woman, to him, had never been robust. Yet now, resolutely, as only a man can do who is capable of martyring himself for the cause of science, he proceeded to violate all the fineness and delicacy of his nature by making love to the unthinkably disgusting bushwoman.

He shuddered, but with averted face hid his grimaces and swallowed his gorge as he put his arm around her dirt-crusted shoulders and felt the contact of her rancid oily and kinky hair with his neck and chin. But he nearly screamed when she succumbed to that caress so at the very first of the courtship and mowed and gibbered and squealed little, queer, pig-like gurgly noises of delight. It was too much. And the next he did in the singular courtship was to take her down to the stream and give her a vigorous scrubbing.

From then on he devoted himself to her like a true swain as frequently and for as long at a time as his will could override his repugnance. But marriage, which she ardently suggested, with due observance of tribal custom, he balked at. Fortunately, taboo rule was strong in the tribe. Thus, Ngurn could never touch bone, or flesh, or hide of crocodile. This had been ordained at his birth. Vngngn was denied ever the touch of woman. Such pollution, did it chance to occur, could be purged only by the death of the offending female. It had happened once, since Bassett's arrival, when a girl of nine, running in play, stumbled and fell against the sacred chief. And the girl-child was seen no more. In whispers, Balatta told Bassett that she had been three days and nights in dying before the Red One. As for Balatta, the breadfruit was taboo to her. For which Bassett was thankful. The taboo might have been water.

For himself, he fabricated a special taboo. Only could he marry, he explained, when the Southern Cross rode highest in the sky. Knowing his astronomy, he thus gained a reprieve of nearly nine months; and he was confident that within that time he would either be dead or escaped to the coast with full knowledge of the Red One and of the source of the Red One's wonderful voice. At first he had fancied the Red One to be some colossal statue, like Memnon, rendered vocal under certain temperature conditions of sunlight. But when, after a war raid, a batch of prisoners was brought in and the sacrifice made at night, in the midst of rain, when the sun could play no part, the Red One had been more vocal than usual, Bassett discarded that hypothesis.

In company with Balatta, sometimes with men and parties of women, the freedom of the jungle was his for three quadrants of the compass. But the fourth quadrant, which contained the Red One's abiding place, was taboo. He made more thorough love to Balatta—also saw to it that she scrubbed herself more frequently. Eternal female she was, capable of any treason for the sake of love. And, though the sight of her was provocative of nausea and the contact of her provocative of despair, although he could not escape her awfulness in his dream-haunted nightmares of her, he nevertheless was aware of the cosmic verity of sex that animated her and that made her own life of less value than the happiness of her lover with whom she hoped to mate. Juliet or Balatta? Where was the intrinsic difference? The soft and tender product of ultra-civilization, or her bestial prototype of a hundred thousand years before her?—there was no difference.

Bassett was a scientist first, a humanist afterward. In the jungle-heart of Guadalcanal he put the affair to the test, as in the laboratory he would have put to the test any chemical reaction. He increased his feigned ardour for the bushwoman, at the same time increasing the imperiousness of his will of desire over her to be led to look upon the Red One face to face. It was the old story, he recognized, that the woman must pay, and it occurred when the two of them, one day, were catching the unclassified and unnamed little black fish, an inch long, half-eel and half-scaled, rotund with salmon-golden roe, that frequented the fresh water, and that were esteemed, raw and whole, fresh or putrid, a perfect delicacy. Prone in the muck of the decaying jungle-floor, Balatta threw herself, clutching his ankles with her hands kissing his feet and making slubbery noises that chilled his backbone up and down again. She begged him to kill her rather than exact this ultimate love-payment. She told him of the penalty of breaking the taboo of the Red One—a week of torture, living, the details of which she yammered out from her face in the mire until he realized that he was yet a tyro in knowledge of the frightfulness the human was capable of wreaking on the human.

Yet did Bassett insist on having his man's will satisfied, at the woman's risk, that he might solve the mystery of the Red One's singing, though she should die long and horribly and screaming. And Balatta, being mere woman, yielded. She led him into the forbidden quadrant. An abrupt mountain, shouldering in from the north to meet a similar intrusion from the south, tormented the stream in which they had fished into a deep and gloomy gorge. After a mile along the gorge, the way plunged sharply upward until they crossed a saddle of raw limestone which attracted his geologist's eye. Still climbing, although he paused often from sheer physical weakness, they scaled forest-clad heights until they emerged on a naked mesa or tableland. Bassett recognized the stuff of its composition as black volcanic sand, and knew that a pocket magnet could have captured a full load of the sharply angular grains he trod upon.

And then holding Balatta by the hand and leading her onward, he came to it—a tremendous pit, obviously artificial, in the heart of the plateau. Old history, the South Seas Sailing Directions, scores of remembered data and connotations swift and furious, surged through his brain. It was Mendana who had discovered the islands and named them Solomon's, believing that he had found that monarch's fabled mines. They had laughed at the old navigator's child-like credulity; and yet here stood himself, Bassett, on the rim of an excavation for all the world like the diamond pits of South Africa.

But no diamond this that he gazed down upon. Rather was it a pearl, with the depth of iridescence of a pearl; but of a size all pearls of earth and time, welded into one, could not have totalled; and of a colour undreamed of in any pearl, or of anything else, for that matter, for it was the colour of the Red One. And the Red One himself Bassett knew it to be on the instant. A perfect sphere, full two hundred feet in diameter, the top of it was a hundred feet below the level of the rim. He likened the colour quality of it to lacquer. Indeed, he took it to be some sort of lacquer, applied by man, but a lacquer too marvellously clever to have been manufactured by the bush-folk. Brighter than bright cherry-red, its richness of colour was as if it were red builded upon red. It glowed and iridesced in the sunlight as if gleaming up from underlay under underlay of red.

In vain Balatta strove to dissuade him from descending. She threw herself in the dirt; but, when he continued down the trail that spiralled the pit-wall, she followed, cringing and whimpering her terror. That the red sphere had been dug out as a precious thing, was patent. Considering the paucity of members of the federated twelve villages and their primitive tools and methods, Bassett knew that the toil of a myriad generations could scarcely have made that enormous excavation.

He found the pit bottom carpeted with human bones, among

84

which, battered and defaced, lay village gods of wood and stone. Some, covered with obscene totemic figures and designs, were carved from solid tree trunks forty or fifty feet in length. He noted the absence of the shark and turtle gods, so common among the shore villages, and was amazed at the constant recurrence of the helmet motive. What did these jungle savages of the dark heart of Guadalcanal know of helmets? Had Mendana's men-at-arms worn helmets and penetrated here centuries before? And if not, then whence had the bush-folk caught the motive?

Advancing over the litter of gods and bones, Balatta whimpering at his heels, Bassett entered the shadow of the Red One and passed on under its gigantic overhang until he touched it with his finger-tips. No lacquer that. Nor was the surface smooth as it should have been in the case of lacquer. On the contrary, it was corrugated and pitted, with here and there patches that showed signs of heat and fusing. Also, the substance of it was metal, though unlike any metal, or combination of metals, he had ever known. As for the colour itself, he decided it to be no application. It was the intrinsic colour of the metal itself.

He moved his finger-tips, which up to that had merely rested, along the surface, and felt the whole gigantic sphere quicken and live and respond. It was incredible! So light a touch on so vast a mass! Yet did it quiver under the finger-tip caress in rhythmic vibrations that became whisperings and rustlings and mutterings of sound—but of sound so different; so elusively thin that it was shimmeringly sibilant; so mellow that it was maddening sweet, piping like an elfin horn, which last was just what Bassett decided would be like a peal from some bell of the gods reaching earthward from across space.

He looked at Balatta with swift questioning; but the voice of the Red One he had evoked had flung her face downward and moaning among the bones. He returned to contemplation of the prodigy. Hollow it was, and of no metal known on earth, was his conclusion. It was right-named by the ones of old-time as the Star-Born. Only from the stars could it have come, and no thing of chance was it. It was a creation of artifice and mind. Such perfection of form, such hollowness that it certainly possessed, could not be the result of mere fortuitousness. A child of intelligences, remote and unguessable, working corporally in metals, it indubitably was. He stared at it in amaze, his brain a racing wild-fire of hypotheses to account for this far-journeyer who had adventured the night of space, threaded the stars, and now rose before him and above him, exhumed by patient anthropophagi, pitted and lacquered by its fiery bath in two atmospheres.

But was the colour a lacquer of heat upon some familiar metal? Or was it an intrinsic quality of the metal itself? He thrust in the blue-point of his pocket-knife to test the constitution of the stuff. Instantly the entire sphere burst into a mighty whispering, sharp with protest, almost twanging goldenly, if a whisper could possibly be considered to twang, rising higher, sinking deeper, the two extremes of the registry of sound threatening to complete the circle and coalesce into the bull-mouthed thundering he had so often heard beyond the taboo distance.

Forgetful of safety, of his own life itself, entranced by the wonder of the unthinkable and unguessable thing, he raised his knife to strike heavily from a long stroke, but was prevented by Balatta. She upreared on her own knees in an agony of terror, clasping his knees and supplicating him to desist. In the intensity of her desire to impress him, she put her forearm between her teeth and sank them to the bone.

He scarcely observed her act, although he yielded automatically to his gentler instincts and withheld the knife-hack. To him, human life had dwarfed to microscopic proportions before this colossal portent of higher life from within the distances of the sidereal universe. As had she been a dog, he kicked the ugly little bushwoman to her feet and compelled her to start with him on an encirclement of the base. Part way around, he encountered horrors. Even, among the others, did he recognize the sun-shrivelled remnant of the nine-years girl who had accidentally broken Chief Vngngn's personality taboo. And, among what was left of these that had passed, he encountered what was left of one who had not yet passed. Truly had the bush-folk named themselves into the name of the Red One, seeing in him their own image which they strove to placate and please with such red offerings.

Farther around, always treading the bones and images of humans and gods that constituted the floor of this ancient charnel-house of sacrifice, he came upon the device by which the Red One was made to send his call singing thunderingly across the jungle-belts and grass-lands to the far beach of Ringmanu. Simple and primitive was it as was the Red One's consummate artifice. A great king-post, half a hundred feet in length, seasoned by centuries of superstitious care, carven into dynasties of gods, each superimposed, each helmeted, each seated in the open mouth of a crocodile, was slung by ropes, twisted of climbing vegetable parasites, from the apex of a tripod of three great forest trunks, themselves carved into grinning and grotesque adumbrations of man's modern concepts of art and god. From the striker king-post, were suspended ropes of climbers to which men could apply their strength and direction. Like a battering ram, this king-post could be driven end-onward against the mighty red-iridescent sphere.

Here was where Ngurn officiated and functioned religiously for himself and the twelve tribes under him. Bassett laughed aloud, almost with madness, at the thought of this wonderful messenger, winged with intelligence across space, to fall into a bushman stronghold and be worshipped by ape-like, man-eating and head-hunting savages. It was as if God's World had fallen into the muck mire of the abyss underlying the bottom of hell; as if Jehovah's Commandments had been presented on carved stone to the monkeys of the monkey cage at the Zoo; as if the Sermon on the Mount had been preached in a roaring bedlam of lunatics.

The slow weeks passed. The nights, by election, Bassett spent on the ashen floor of the devil-devil house, beneath the ever-swinging, slow-curing heads. His reason for this was that it was taboo to the lesser sex of woman, and therefore, a refuge for him from Balatta, who grew more persecutingly and perilously loverly as the Southern Cross rode higher in the sky and marked the imminence of her nuptials. His days Bassett spent in a hammock swung under the shade of the great breadfruit tree before the devil-devil house. There were breaks in this programme, when, in the comas of his devastating fever-attacks, he lay for days and nights in the house of heads. Ever he struggled to combat the fever, to live, to continue to live, to grow strong and stronger against the day when he would be strong enough to dare the grass-lands and the belted jungle beyond, and win to the beach, and to some labour-recruiting, black-birding ketch or schooner, and on to civilization and the men of civilization, to whom he could give news of the message from other worlds that lay, darkly worshipped by beastmen, in the black heart of Guadalcanal's midmost centre.

On the other nights, lying late under the breadfruit tree, Bassett spent long hours watching the slow setting of the western stars beyond the black wall of jungle where it had been thrust back by the clearing for the village. Possessed of more than a cursory knowledge of astronomy, he took a sick man's pleasure in speculating as to the dwellers on the unseen worlds of those incredibly remote suns, to haunt whose houses of light, life came forth, a shy visitant, from the rayless crypts of matter. He could no more apprehend limits to time than bounds to space. No subversive radium speculations had shaken his steady scientific faith in the conservation of energy and the indestructibility of matter. Always and forever must there have been stars. And surely, in that cosmic ferment, all must be comparatively alike, comparatively of the same substance, or substances, save for the freaks of the ferment. All must obey, or compose, the same laws that ran without infraction through the entire experience of man. Therefore, he argued and agreed, must worlds and life be appanages to all the suns as they were appanages to the particular of his own solar system.

Even as he lay here, under the breadfruit tree, an intelligence that stared across the starry gulfs, so must all the universe be exposed to the ceaseless scrutiny of innumerable eyes, like his, though grantedly different, with behind them, by the same token, intelligences that questioned and sought the meaning and the construction of the whole. So reasoning, he felt his soul go forth in kinship with that august company, that multitude whose gaze was forever upon the arras of infinity.

Who were they, what were they, those far distant and superior ones who had bridged the sky with their gigantic, red-iridescent, heaven-singing message? Surely, and long since, had they, too, trod the path on which man had so recently, by the calendar of the cosmos, set his feet. And to be able to send a message across the pit of space, surely they had reached those heights to which man, in tears and travail and bloody sweat, in darkness and confusion of many counsels, was so slowly struggling. And what were they on their heights? Had they won Brotherhood? Or had they learned that the law of love imposed the penalty of weakness and decay? Was strife, life? Was the rule of all the universe the pitiless rule of natural selection? And, and most immediately and poignantly, were their far conclusions, their long-won wisdoms, shut even then in the huge, metallic heart of the Red One, waiting for the first earth-man to read? Of one thing he was certain: No drop of red dew shaken from the lion-mane of some sun in torment, was the sounding sphere. It was of design, not chance, and it contained the speech and wisdom of the stars.

What engines and elements and mastered forces, what lore and mysteries and destiny-controls, might be there! Undoubtedly, since so much could be enclosed in so little a thing as the foundation stone of a public building, this enormous sphere should contain vast histories, profounds of research achieved beyond man's wildest guesses, laws and formulæ that, easily mastered, would make man's life on earth, individual and collective, spring up from its present mire to inconceivable heights of purity and power. It was Time's greatest gift to blindfold, insatiable, and sky-aspiring man. And to him, Bassett, had been vouchsafed the lordly fortune to be the first to receive this message from man's interstellar kin!

No white man, much less no outland man of the other bush-tribes, had gazed upon the Red One and lived. Such the law expounded by Ngurn to Bassett. There was such a thing as blood brotherhood. Bassett, in return, had often argued in the past. But Ngurn had stated solemnly no. Even the blood brotherhood was outside the favour of the Red One. Only a man born within the tribe could look upon the Red One and live. But now, his guilty secret known only to Balatta, whose fear of immolation before the Red One fast-sealed her lips, the situation was different. What he had to do was to recover from the abominable fevers that weakened him, and gain to civilization. Then would he lead an expedition back, and, although the entire population of Guadalcanal he destroyed, extract from the heart of the Red One the message of the world from other worlds.

But Bassett's relapses grew more frequent, his brief convalescences less and less vigorous, his periods of coma longer, until he came to know, beyond the last promptings of the optimism inherent in so tremendous a constitution as his own, that he would never live to cross the grass lands, perforate the perilous coast jungle, and reach the sea. He faded as the Southern Cross rose higher in the sky, till even Balatta knew that he would be dead ere the nuptial date determined by his taboo. Ngurn made pilgrimage personally and gathered the smoke materials for the curing of Bassett's head, and to him made proud announcement and exhibition of the artistic perfectness of his intention when Bassett should be dead. As for himself, Bassett was not shocked. Too long and too deeply had life ebbed down in him to bite him with fear of its impending extinction. He continued to persist, alternating periods of unconsciousness with periods of semi-consciousness, dreamy and unreal, in which he idly wondered whether he had ever truly beheld the Red One or whether it was a nightmare fancy of delirium.

Came the day when all mists and cob-webs dissolved, when he found his brain clear as a bell, and took just appraisement of his body's weakness. Neither hand nor foot could he lift. So little control of his body did he have, that he was scarcely aware of possessing one. Lightly indeed his flesh sat upon his soul, and his soul, in its briefness of clarity, knew by its very clarity that the black of cessation was near. He knew the end was close; knew that in all truth he had with his eyes beheld the Red One, the messenger between the worlds; knew that he would never live to carry that message to the world—that message, for aught to the contrary, which might already have waited man's hearing in the heart of Guadalcanal for ten thousand years. And Bassett stirred with resolve, calling Ngurn to him, out under the shade of the breadfruit tree, and with the old devil-devil doctor discussing the terms and arrangements of his last life effort, his final adventure in the quick of the flesh.

"I know the law, O Ngurn," he concluded the matter. "Whoso is not of the folk may not look upon the Red One and live. I shall not live anyway. Your young men shall carry me before the face of the Red One, and I shall look upon him, and hear his voice, and thereupon die, under your hand, O Ngurn. Thus will the three things be satisfied: the law, my desire, and your quicker possession of my head for which all your preparations wait."

To which Ngurn consented, adding:

"It is better so. A sick man who cannot get well is foolish to live on for so little a while. Also is it better for the living that he should go. You have been much in the way of late. Not but what it was good for me to talk to such a wise one. But for moons of days we have held little talk. Instead, you have taken up room in the house of heads, making noises like a dying pig, or talking much and loudly in your own language which I do not understand. This has been a confusion to me, for I like to think on the great things of the light and dark as I turn the heads in the smoke. Your much noise has thus been a disturbance to the long-learning and hatching of the final wisdom that will be mine before I die. As for you, upon whom the dark has already brooded, it is well that you die now. And I promise you, in the long days to come when I turn your head in the smoke, no man of the tribe shall come in to disturb us. And I will tell you many secrets, for I am an old man and very wise, and I shall be adding wisdom to wisdom as I turn your head in the smoke."

So a litter was made, and, borne on the shoulders of half a dozen of the men, Bassett departed on the last little adventure that was to cap the total adventure, for him, of living. With a body of which he was scarcely aware, for even the pain had been exhausted out of it, and with a bright clear brain that accommodated him to a quiet ecstasy of sheer lucidness of thought, he lay back on the lurching litter and watched the fading of the passing world, beholding for the last time the breadfruit tree before the devil-devil house, the dim day beneath the matted jungle roof, the gloomy gorge between the shouldering mountains, the saddle of raw limestone, and the mesa of black volcanic sand.

Down the spiral path of the pit they bore him, encircling the sheening, glowing Red One that seemed ever imminent to iridesce from colour and light into sweet singing and thunder. And over bones and logs of immolated men and gods they bore him, past the horrors of other immolated ones that yet lived, to the three-king-post tripod and the huge king-post striker.

Here Bassett, helped by Ngurn and Balatta, weakly sat up, swaying weakly from the hips, and with clear, unfaltering, all-seeing eyes gazed upon the Red One.

"Once, O Ngurn," he said, not taking his eyes from the sheening, vibrating surface whereon and wherein all the shades of cherry-red played unceasingly, ever a-quiver to change into sound, to become silken rustlings, silvery whisperings, golden thrummings of cords, velvet pipings of elfland, mellow distances of thunderings.

"I wait," Ngurn prompted after a long pause, the long-handled tomahawk unassumingly ready in his hand.

"Once, O Ngurn," Bassett repeated, "let the Red One speak so that I may see it speak as well as hear it. Then strike, thus, when I raise my hand; for, when I raise my hand, I shall drop my head forward and make place for the stroke at the base of my neck. But, O Ngurn, I, who am about to pass out of the light of day for ever, would like to pass with the wonder-voice of the Red One singing greatly in my ears."

"And I promise you that never will a head be so well cured as yours," Ngurn assured him, at the same time signalling the tribesmen to man the propelling ropes suspended from the king-post striker. "Your head shall be my greatest piece of work in the curing of heads."

Bassett smiled quietly to the old one's conceit, as the great carved log, drawn back through two-score feet of space, was released. The next moment he was lost in ecstasy at the abrupt and thunderous liberation of sound. But such thunder! Mellow it was with preciousness of all sounding metals. Archangels spoke in it; it was magnificently beautiful before all other sounds; it was invested with the intelligence of supermen of planets of other suns; it was the voice of God, seducing and commanding to be heard. And—the everlasting miracle of that interstellar metal! Bassett, with his own eyes, saw colour and colours transform into sound till the whole visible surface of the vast sphere was a-crawl and titillant and vaporous with what he could not tell was colour or was sound. In that moment the interstices of matter were his, and the interfusings and intermating transfusings of matter and force.

Time passed. At the last Bassett was brought back from his ecstasy by an impatient movement of Ngurn. He had quite forgotten the old devil-devil one. A quick flash of fancy brought a husky chuckle into Bassett's throat. His shot-gun lay beside him in the litter. All he had to do, muzzle to head, was to press the trigger and blow his head into nothingness.

But why cheat him? was Bassett's next thought. Head-hunting, cannibal beast of a human that was as much ape as human, nevertheless Old Ngurn had, according to his lights, played squarer than square. Ngurn was in himself a forerunner of ethics and contract, of consideration, and gentleness in man. No, Bassett decided; it would be a ghastly pity and an act of dishonour to cheat the old fellow at the last. His head was Ngurn's, and Ngurn's head to cure it would be.

And Bassett, raising his hand in signal, bending forward his head as agreed so as to expose cleanly the articulation to his taut spinal cord, forgot Balatta, who was merely a woman, a woman merely and only and undesired. He knew, without seeing, when the razor-edged hatchet rose in the air behind him. And for that instant, ere the end, there fell upon Bassett the shadows of the Unknown, a sense of impending marvel of the rending of walls before the imaginable. Almost, when he knew the blow had started and just ere the edge of steel bit the flesh and nerves it seemed that he gazed upon the serene face of the Medusa, Truth—And, simultaneous with the bite of the steel on the onrush of the dark, in a flashing instant of fancy, he saw the vision of his head turning slowly, always turning, in the devil-devil house beside the breadfruit tree.

THE END

Waikiki, Honolulu
May 22, 1916

THE HUSSY

There are some stories that have to be true—the sort that cannot be fabricated by a ready fiction-reckoner. And by the same token there are some men with stories to tell who cannot be doubted. Such a man was Julian Jones. Although I doubt if the average reader of this will believe the story Julian Jones told me. Nevertheless I believe it. So thoroughly am I convinced of its verity that I am willing, nay, eager, to invest capital in the enterprise and embark personally on the adventure to a far land.

It was in the Australian Building at the Panama Pacific Exposition that I met him. I was standing before an exhibit of facsimiles of the record nuggets which had been discovered in the goldfields of the Antipodes. Knobbed, misshapen and massive, it was as difficult to believe that they were not real gold as it was to believe the accompanying statistics of their weights and values.

"That's what those kangaroo-hunters call a nugget," boomed over my shoulder directly at the largest of the specimens.

I turned and looked up into the dim blue eyes of Julian Jones. I looked up, for he stood something like six feet four inches in height. His hair, a wispy, sandy yellow, seemed as dimmed and faded as his eyes. It may have been the sun which had washed out his colouring; at least his face bore the evidence of a prodigious and ardent sun-burn which had long since faded to yellow. As his eyes turned from the exhibit and focussed on mine I noted a queer look in them as of one who vainly tries to recall some fact of supreme importance.

"What's the matter with it as a nugget?" I demanded.

The remote, indwelling expression went out of his eyes as he boomed

"Why, its size."

"It does seem large," I admitted. "But there's no doubt it's authentic. The Australian Government would scarcely dare—"

"Large!" he interrupted, with a sniff and a sneer.

"Largest ever discovered—" I started on.

"Ever discovered!" His dim eyes smouldered hotly as he proceeded. "Do you think that every lump of gold ever discovered has got into the newspapers and encyclopedias?"

"Well," I replied judicially, "if there's one that hasn't, I don't see how we're to know about it. If a really big nugget, or nugget-finder, elects to blush unseen—"

"But it didn't," he broke in quickly. "I saw it with my own eyes, and, besides, I'm too tanned to blush anyway. I'm a railroad man and I've been in the tropics a lot. Why, I used to be the colour of mahogany—real old mahogany, and have been taken for a blue-eyed Spaniard more than once—"

It was my turn to interrupt, and I did.

"Was that nugget bigger than those in there, Mr.—er—?"

"Jones, Julian Jones is my name."

He dug into an inner pocket and produced an envelope addressed to such a person, care of General Delivery, San Francisco; and I, in turn, presented him with my card.

"Pleased to know you, sir," he said, extending his hand, his voice booming as if accustomed to loud noises or wide spaces. "Of course I've heard of you, seen your picture in the papers, and all that, and, though I say it that shouldn't, I want to say that I didn't care a rap about those articles you wrote on Mexico. You're wrong, all wrong. You make the mistake of all Gringos in thinking a Mexican is a white man. He ain't. None of them ain't—Greasers, Spiggoties, Latin-Americans and all the rest of the cattle. Why, sir, they don't think like we think, or reason, or act. Even their multiplication table is different. You think seven times seven is forty-nine; but not them. They work it out different. And white isn't white to them, either. Let me give you an example. Buying coffee retail for house-keeping in one-pound or ten-pound lots—"

"How big was that nugget you referred to?" I queried firmly. "As big as the biggest of those?"

"Bigger," he said quietly. "Bigger than the whole blamed exhibit of them put together, and then some." He paused and regarded me with a steadfast gaze. "I don't see no reason why I shouldn't go into the matter with you. You've got a reputation a man ought to be able to trust, and I've read you've done some tall skylarking yourself in out-of-the-way places. I've been browsing around with an eye open for some one to go in with me on the proposition."

"You can trust me," I said.

And here I am, blazing out into print with the whole story just as he told it to me as we sat on a bench by the lagoon before the Palace of Fine Arts with the cries of the sea gulls in our ears. Well, he should have kept his appointment with me. But I anticipate.

As we started to leave the building and hunt for a seat, a small woman, possibly thirty years of age, with a washed-out complexion of the farmer's wife sort, darted up to him in a bird-like way, for all the world like the darting veering gulls over our heads and fastened herself to his arm with the accuracy and dispatch and inevitableness of a piece of machinery.

"There you go!" she shrilled. "A-trottin' right off and never givin' me a thought."

I was formally introduced to her. It was patent that she had never heard of me, and she surveyed me bleakly with shrewd black eyes, set close together and as beady and restless as a bird's.

"You ain't goin' to tell him about that hussy?" she complained.

"Well, now, Sarah, this is business, you see," he argued plaintively. "I've been lookin' for a likely man this long while, and now that he's shown up it seems to me I got a right to give him the hang of what happened."

The small woman made no reply, but set her thin lips in a needle-like line. She gazed straight before her at the Tower of Jewels with so austere an expression that no glint of refracted sunlight could soften it. We proceeded slowly to the lagoon, managed to obtain an unoccupied seat, and sat down with mutual sighs of relief as we released our weights from our tortured sightseeing feet.

"One does get so mortal weary," asserted the small woman, almost defiantly.

Two swans waddled up from the mirroring water and investigated us. When their suspicions of our niggardliness or lack of peanuts had been confirmed, Jones half-turned his back on his life-partner and gave me his story.

"Ever been in Ecuador? Then take my advice—and don't. Though I take that back, for you and me might be hitting it for there together if you can rustle up the faith in me and the backbone in yourself for the trip. Well, anyway, it ain't so many years ago that I came ambling in there on a rusty, foul-bottomed, tramp collier from Australia, forty-three days from land to land. Seven knots was her speed when everything favoured, and we'd had a two weeks' gale to the north'ard of New Zealand, and broke our engines down for two days off Pitcairn Island.

"I was no sailor on her. I'm a locomotive engineer. But I'd made friends with the skipper at Newcastle an' come along as his guest for as far as Guayaquil. You see, I'd heard wages was 'way up on the American railroad runnin' from that place over the Andes to Quito. Now Guayaquil—"

"Is a fever-hole," I interpolated.

Julian Jones nodded.

"Thomas Nast died there of it within a month after he landed.—He was our great American cartoonist," I added.

"Don't know him," Julian Jones said shortly. "But I do know

95

he wasn't the first to pass out by a long shot. Why, look you the way I found it. The pilot grounds is sixty miles down the river. 'How's the fever?' said I to the pilot who came aboard in the early morning. 'See that Hamburg barque,' said he, pointing to a sizable ship at anchor. 'Captain and fourteen men dead of it already, and the cook and two men dying right now, and they're the last left of her.'

"And by jinks he told the truth. And right then they were dying forty a day in Guayaquil of Yellow Jack. But that was nothing, as I was to find out. Bubonic plague and small-pox were raging, while dysentery and pneumonia were reducing the population, and the railroad was raging worst of all. I mean that. For them that insisted in riding on it, it was more dangerous than all the other diseases put together.

"When we dropped anchor off Guayaquil half a dozen skippers from other steamers came on board to warn our skipper not to let any of his crew or officers go ashore except the ones he wanted to lose. A launch came off for me from Duran, which is on the other side of the river and is the terminal of the railroad. And it brought off a man that soared up the gangway three jumps at a time he was that eager to get aboard. When he hit the deck he hadn't time to speak to any of us. He just leaned out over the rail and shook his fist at Duran and shouted: 'I beat you to it! I beat you to it!'

"'Who'd you beat to it, friend?' I asked. 'The railroad,' he said, as he unbuckled the straps and took off a big '44 Colt's automatic from where he wore it handy on his left side under his coat, 'I staved as long as I agreed—three months—and it didn't get me. I was a conductor.'

"And that was the railroad I was to work for. All of which was nothing to what he told me in the next few minutes. The road ran from sea level at Duran up to twelve thousand feet on Chimborazo and down to ten thousand at Quito on the other side the range. And it was so dangerous that the trains didn't run nights. The through passengers had to get off and sleep in the towns at night while the train waited for daylight. And each train carried a guard of Ecuadoriano soldiers which was the most dangerous of all. They were supposed to protect the train crews, but whenever trouble started they unlimbered their rifles and joined the mob. You see, whenever a train wreck occurred, the first cry of the spiggoties was 'Kill the Gringos!' They always did that, and proceeded to kill the train crew and whatever chance Gringo passengers that'd escaped being killed in the accident. Which is their kind of arithmetic, which I told you a while back as being different from ours.

"Shucks! Before the day was out I was to find out for myself that that ex-conductor wasn't lying. It was over at Duran. I was to take my run on the first division out to Quito, for which place I was to start next morning—only one through train running every twenty-four hours. It was the afternoon of my first day, along about four o'clock, when the boilers of the Governor Hancock exploded and she sank in sixty feet of water alongside the dock. She was the big ferry boat that carried the railroad passengers across the river to Guayaquil. It was a bad accident, but it was the cause of worse that followed. By half-past four, big trainloads began to arrive. It was a feast day and they'd run an excursion up country but of Guayaquil, and this was the crowd coming back.

"And the crowd—there was five thousand of them—wanted to get ferried across, and the ferry was at the bottom of the river, which wasn't our fault. But by the Spiggoty arithmetic, it was. 'Kill the Gringos!' shouts one of them. And right there the beans were spilled. Most of us got away by the skin of our teeth. I raced on the heels of the Master Mechanic, carrying one of his babies for him, for the locomotives that was just pulling out. You see, way down there away from everywhere they just got to save their locomotives in times of trouble, because, without them, a railroad can't be run. Half a dozen American wives and as many children were crouching on the cab floors along with the rest of us when we pulled out; and the Ecuadoriano soldiers, who should have been protecting our lives and property, turned loose with their rifles and must have given us all of a thousand rounds before we got out of range.

"We camped up country and didn't come back to clean up until next day. It was some cleaning. Every flat-car, box-car, coach, asthmatic switch engine, and even hand-car that mob of Spiggoties had shoved off the dock into sixty feet of water on top of the Governor Hancock. They'd burnt the round house, set fire to the coal bunkers, and made a scandal of the repair shops. Oh, yes, and there were three of our fellows they'd got that we had to bury mighty quick. It's hot weather all the time down there."

Julian Jones came to a full pause and over his shoulder studied the straight-before-her gaze and forbidding expression of his wife's face.

"I ain't forgotten the nugget," he assured me.

"Nor the hussy," the little woman snapped, apparently at the mud-hens paddling on the surface of the lagoon.

"I've been travelling toward the nugget right along—"

"There was never no reason for you to stay in that dangerous country," his wife snapped in on him.

"Now, Sarah," he appealed. "I was working for you right along." And to me he explained: "The risk was big, but so was the

97

pay. Some months I earned as high as five hundred gold. And here was Sarah waiting for me back in Nebraska—"

"An' us engaged two years," she complained to the Tower of Jewels.

"—What of the strike, and me being blacklisted, and getting typhoid down in Australia, and everything," he went on. "And luck was with me on that railroad. Why, I saw fellows fresh from the States pass out, some of them not a week on their first run. If the diseases and the railroad didn't get them, then it was the Spiggoties got them. But it just wasn't my fate, even that time I rode my engine down to the bottom of a forty-foot washout. I lost my fireman; and the conductor and the Superintendent of Rolling Stock (who happened to be running down to Duran to meet his bride) had their heads knifed off by the Spiggoties and paraded around on poles. But I lay snug as a bug under a couple of feet of tender coal, and they thought I'd headed for tall timber—lay there a day and a night till the excitement cooled down. Yes, I was lucky. The worst that happened to me was I caught a cold once, and another time had a carbuncle. But the other fellows! They died like flies, what of Yellow Jack, pneumonia, the Spiggoties, and the railroad. The trouble was I didn't have much chance to pal with them. No sooner'd I get some intimate with one of them he'd up and die—all but a fireman named Andrews, and he went loco for keeps.

"I made good on my job from the first, and lived in Quito in a 'dobe house with whacking big Spanish tiles on the roof that I'd rented. And I never had much trouble with the Spiggoties, what of letting them sneak free rides in the tender or on the cowcatcher. Me throw them off? Never! I took notice, when Jack Harris put off a bunch of them, that I attended his funeral muy pronto—"

"Speak English," the little woman beside him snapped.

"Sarah just can't bear to tolerate me speaking Spanish," he apologized. "It gets so on her nerves that I promised not to. Well, as I was saying, the goose hung high and everything was going hunky-dory, and I was piling up my wages to come north to Nebraska and marry Sarah, when I run on to Vahna—"

"The hussy!" Sarah hissed.

"Now, Sarah," her towering giant of a husband begged, "I just got to mention her or I can't tell about the nugget.—It was one night when I was taking a locomotive—no train—down to Amato, about thirty miles from Quito. Seth Manners was my fireman. I was breaking him in to engineer for himself, and I was letting him run the locomotive while I sat up in his seat meditating about Sarah here. I'd just got a letter from her, begging as usual for me to come home and hinting as usual about the dangers of an unmarried man like me running around loose in a country full of senoritas and fandangos. Lord! If she could only a-seen them. Positive frights, that's what they are, their faces painted white as corpses and their lips red as—as some of the train wrecks I've helped clean up.

"It was a lovely April night, not a breath of wind, and a tremendous big moon shining right over the top of Chimborazo.— Some mountain that. The railroad skirted it twelve thousand feet above sea level, and the top of it ten thousand feet higher than that.

"Mebbe I was drowsing, with Seth running the engine; but he slammed on the brakes so sudden hard that I darn near went through the cab window.

"'What the—' I started to yell, and 'Holy hell,' Seth says, as both of us looked at what was on the track. And I agreed with Seth entirely in his remark. It was an Indian girl—and take it from me, Indians ain't Spiggoties by any manner of means. Seth had managed to fetch a stop within twenty feet of her, and us bowling down hill at that! But the girl. She—"

I saw the form of Mrs. Julian Jones stiffen, although she kept her gaze fixed balefully upon two mud-hens that were prowling along the lagoon shallows below us. "The hussy!" she hissed, once and implacably. Jones had stopped at the sound, but went on immediately.

"She was a tall girl, slim and slender, you know the kind, with black hair, remarkably long hanging, down loose behind her, as she stood there no more afraid than nothing, her arms spread out to stop the engine. She was wearing a slimpsy sort of garment wrapped around her that wasn't cloth but ocelot skins, soft and dappled, and silky. It was all she had on—"

"The hussy!" breathed Mrs. Jones.

But Mr. Jones went on, making believe that he was unaware of the interruption.

"'Hell of a way to stop a locomotive,' I complained at Seth, as I climbed down on to the right of way. I walked past our engine and up to the girl, and what do you think? Her eyes were shut tight. She was trembling that violent that you would see it by the moonlight. And she was barefoot, too.

"'What's the row?' I said, none too gentle. She gave a start, seemed to come out of her trance, and opened her eyes. Say! They were big and black and beautiful. Believe me, she was some looker—"

"The hussy!" At which hiss the two mud-hens veered away a few feet. But Jones was getting himself in hand, and didn't even blink.

"'What are you stopping this locomotive for?' I demanded in

Spanish. Nary an answer. She stared at me, then at the snorting engine and then burst into tears, which you'll admit is uncommon behaviour for an Indian woman.

"'If you try to get rides that way,' I slung at her in Spiggoty Spanish (which they tell me is some different from regular Spanish), 'you'll be taking one smeared all over our cowcatcher and headlight, and it'll be up to my fireman to scrape you off.'

"My Spiggoty Spanish wasn't much to brag on, but I could see she understood, though she only shook her head and wouldn't speak. But great Moses, she was some looker—"

I glanced apprehensively at Mrs. Jones, who must have caught me out of the tail of her eye, for she muttered: "If she hadn't been do you think he'd a-taken her into his house to live?"

"Now hold on, Sarah," he protested. "That ain't fair. Besides, I'm telling this.—Next thing, Seth yells at me, 'Goin' to stay here all night?'

"'Come on,' I said to the girl, 'and climb on board. But next time you want a ride don't flag a locomotive between stations.' She followed along; but when I got to the step and turned to give her a lift-up, she wasn't there. I went forward again. Not a sign of her. Above and below was sheer cliff, and the track stretched ahead a hundred yards clear and empty. And then I spotted her, crouched down right against the cowcatcher, that close I'd almost stepped on her. If we'd started up, we'd have run over her in a second. It was all so nonsensical, I never could make out her actions. Maybe she was trying to suicide. I grabbed her by the wrist and jerked her none too gentle to her feet. And she came along all right. Women do know when a man means business."

I glanced from this Goliath to his little, bird-eyed spouse, and wondered if he had ever tried to mean business with her.

"Seth kicked at first, but I boosted her into the cab and made her sit up beside me—"

"And I suppose Seth was busy running the engine," Mrs. Jones observed.

"I was breaking him in, wasn't I?" Mr. Jones protested. "So we made the run into Amato. She'd never opened her mouth once, and no sooner'd the engine stopped than she'd jumped to the ground and was gone. Just like that. Not a thank you kindly. Nothing.

"But next morning when we came to pull out for Quito with a dozen flat cars loaded with rails, there she was in the cab waiting for us; and in the daylight I could see how much better a looker she was than the night before.

"'Huh! she's adopted you,' Seth grins. And it looked like it.

100

She just stood there and looked at me—at us—like a loving hound dog that you love, that you've caught with a string of sausages inside of him, and that just knows you ain't going to lift a hand to him. 'Go chase yourself!' I told her pronto." (Mrs. Jones her proximity noticeable with a wince at the Spanish word.) "You see, Sarah, I'd no use for her, even at the start."

Mrs. Jones stiffened. Her lips moved soundlessly, but I knew to what syllables.

"And what made it hardest was Seth jeering at me. 'You can't shake her that way,' he said. 'You saved her life—' 'I didn't,' I said sharply; 'it was you.' 'But she thinks you did, which is the same thing,' he came back at me. 'And now she belongs to you. Custom of the country, as you ought to know.'"

"Heathenish," said Mrs. Jones, and though her steady gaze was set upon the Tower of Jewels I knew she was making no reference to its architecture.

"'She's come to do light housekeeping for you,' Seth grinned. I let him rave, though afterwards I kept him throwing in the coal too fast to work his mouth very much. Why, say, when I got to the spot where I picked her up, and stopped the train for her to get off, she just flopped down on her knees, got a hammerlock with her arms around my knees, and cried all over my shoes. What was I to do?"

With no perceptible movement that I was aware of, Mrs. Jones advertised her certitude of knowledge of what she would have done.

"And the moment we pulled into Quito, she did what she'd done before—vanished. Sarah never believes me when I say how relieved I felt to be quit of her. But it was not to be. I got to my 'dobe house and managed a cracking fine dinner my cook had ready for me. She was mostly Spiggoty and half Indian, and her name was Paloma.—Now, Sarah, haven't I told you she was older'n a grandmother, and looked more like a buzzard than a dove? Why, I couldn't bear to eat with her around where I could look at her. But she did make things comfortable, and she was some economical when it came to marketing.

"That afternoon, after a big long siesta, what'd I find in the kitchen, just as much at home as if she belonged there, but that blamed Indian girl. And old Paloma was squatting at the girl's feet and rubbing the girl's knees and legs like for rheumatism, which I knew the girl didn't have from the way I'd sized up the walk of her, and keeping time to the rubbing with a funny sort of gibberish chant. And I let loose right there and then. As Sarah knows, I never could a-bear women around the house—young, unmarried women, I mean. But it was no go! Old Paloma sided with the girl, and said if the girl went she went, too. Also, she called me more kinds of a fool than the English language has accommodation for. You'd like the Spanish lingo, Sarah, for expressing yourself in such ways, and you'd have liked old Paloma, too. She was a good woman, though she didn't have any teeth and her face could kill a strong man's appetite in the cradle.

"I gave in. I had to. Except for the excuse that she needed Vahna's help around the house (which she didn't at all), old Paloma never said why she stuck up for the girl. Anyway, Vahna was a quiet thing, never in the way. And she never gadded. Just sat in-doors jabbering with Paloma and helping with the chores. But I wasn't long in getting on to that she was afraid of something. She would look up, that anxious it hurt, whenever anybody called, like some of the boys to have a gas or a game of pedro. I tried to worm it out of Paloma what was worrying the girl, but all the old woman did was to look solemn and shake her head like all the devils in hell was liable to precipitate a visit on us.

"And then one day Vahna had a visitor. I'd just come in from a run and was passing the time of day with her—I had to be polite, even if she had butted in on me and come to live in my house for keeps—when I saw a queer expression come into her eyes. In the doorway stood an Indian boy. He looked like her, but was younger and slimmer. She took him into the kitchen and they must have had a great palaver, for he didn't leave until after dark. Inside the week he came back, but I missed him. When I got home, Paloma put a fat nugget of gold into my hand, which Vahna had sent him for. The blamed thing weighed all of two pounds and was worth more than five hundred dollars. She explained that Vahna wanted me to take it to pay for her keep. And I had to take it to keep peace in the house.

"Then, after a long time, came another visitor. We were sitting before the fire—"

"Him and the hussy," quoth Mrs. Jones.

"And Paloma," he added quickly.

"Him and his cook and his light housekeeper sitting by the fire," she amended.

"Oh, I admit Vahna did like me a whole heap," he asserted recklessly, then modified with a pang of caution: "A heap more than was good for her, seeing that I had no inclination her way.

"Well, as I was saying, she had another visitor. He was a lean, tall, white-headed old Indian, with a beak on him like an eagle. He walked right in without knocking. Vahna gave a little cry that was half like a yelp and half like a gasp, and flumped down on her knees before me, pleading to me with deer's eyes and to him with the eyes of a deer about to be killed that don't want to be killed. Then, for a minute that seemed as long as a life-time, she and the old fellow glared at each other. Paloma was the first to talk, in his own lingo, for he talked back to her. But great Moses, if he wasn't the high and mighty one! Paloma's old knees were shaking, and she cringed to him like a hound dog. And all this in my own house! I'd have thrown him out on his neck, only he was so old.

"If the things he said to Vahna were as terrible as the way he looked! Say! He just spit words at her! But Paloma kept whimpering and butting in, till something she said got across, because his face relaxed. He condescended to give me the once over and fired some question at Vahna. She hung her head, and looked foolish, and blushed, and then replied with a single word and a shake of the head. And with that he just naturally turned on his heel and beat it. I guess she'd said 'No.'

"For some time after that Vahna used to fluster up whenever she saw me. Then she took to the kitchen for a spell. But after a long time she began hanging around the big room again. She was still mighty shy, but she'd keep on following me about with those big eyes of hers—"

"The hussy!" I heard plainly. But Julian Jones and I were pretty well used to it by this time.

"I don't mind saying that I was getting some interested myself—oh, not in the way Sarah never lets up letting me know she thinks. That two-pound nugget was what had me going. If Vahna'd put me wise to where it came from, I could say good-bye to railroading and hit the high places for Nebraska and Sarah.

"And then the beans were spilled . . . by accident. Come a letter from Wisconsin. My Aunt Eliza 'd died and up and left me her big farm. I let out a whoop when I read it; but I could have canned my joy, for I was jobbed out of it by the courts and lawyers afterward—not a cent to me, and I'm still paying 'm in instalments.

"But I didn't know, then; and I prepared to pull back to God's country. Paloma got sore, and Vahna got the weeps. 'Don't go! Don't go!' That was her song. But I gave notice on my job, and wrote a letter to Sarah here—didn't I, Sarah?

"That night, sitting by the fire like at a funeral, Vahna really loosened up for the first time.

"'Don't go,' she says to me, with old Paloma nodding agreement with her. 'I'll show you where my brother got the nugget, if you don't go.' 'Too late,' said I. And I told her why.

"And told her about me waiting for you back in Nebraska," Mrs. Jones observed in cold, passionless tones.

"Now, Sarah, why should I hurt a poor Indian girl's feelings? Of course I didn't.

"Well, she and Paloma talked Indian some more, and then Vahna says: 'If you stay, I'll show you the biggest nugget that is the father of all other nuggets.' 'How big?' I asked. 'As big as me?' She laughed. 'Bigger than you,' she says, 'much, much bigger.' 'They don't grow that way,' I said. But she said she'd seen it and Paloma backed her up. Why, to listen to them you'd have thought there was millions in that one nugget. Paloma 'd never seen it herself, but she'd heard about it. A secret of the tribe which she couldn't share, being only half Indian herself."

Julian Jones paused and heaved a sigh.

"And they kept on insisting until I fell for—"

"The hussy," said Mrs. Jones, pert as a bird, at the ready instant.

"'No; for the nugget. What of Aunt Eliza's farm I was rich enough to quit railroading, but not rich enough to turn my back on big money—and I just couldn't help believing them two women. Gee! I could be another Vanderbilt, or J. P. Morgan. That's the way I thought; and I started in to pump Vahna. But she wouldn't give down. 'You come along with me,' she says. 'We can be back here in a couple of weeks with all the gold the both of us can carry.' 'We'll take a burro, or a pack-train of burros,' was my suggestion. But nothing doing. And Paloma agreed with her. It was too dangerous. The Indians would catch us.

"The two of us pulled out when the nights were moonlight. We travelled only at night, and laid up in the days. Vahna wouldn't let me light a fire, and I missed my coffee something fierce. We got up in the real high mountains of the main Andes, where the snow on one pass gave us some trouble; but the girl knew the trails, and, though we didn't waste any time, we were a full week getting there. I know the general trend of our travel, because I carried a pocket compass; and the general trend is all I need to get there again, because of that peak. There's no mistaking it. There ain't another peak like it in the world. Now, I'm not telling you its particular shape, but when you and I head out for it from Quito I'll take you straight to it.

"It's no easy thing to climb, and the person doesn't live that can climb it at night. We had to take the daylight to it, and didn't reach the top till after sunset. Why, I could take hours and hours telling you about that last climb, which I won't. The top was flat as a billiard table, about a quarter of an acre in size, and was almost clean of snow. Vahna told me that the great winds that usually blew, kept the snow off of it.

104

"We were winded, and I got mountain sickness so bad that I had to stretch out for a spell. Then, when the moon come up, I took a prowl around. It didn't take long, and I didn't catch a sight or a smell of anything that looked like gold. And when I asked Vahna, she only laughed and clapped her hands. Meantime my mountain sickness tuned up something fierce, and I sat down on a big rock to wait for it to ease down.

"'Come on, now,' I said, when I felt better. 'Stop your fooling and tell me where that nugget is.' 'It's nearer to you right now than I'll ever get,' she answered, her big eyes going sudden wistful. 'All you Gringos are alike. Gold is the love of your heart, and women don't count much.'

"I didn't say anything. That was no time to tell her about Sarah here. But Vahna seemed to shake off her depressed feelings, and began to laugh and tease again. 'How do you like it?' she asked. 'Like what?' 'The nugget you're sitting on.'

"I jumped up as though it was a red-hot stove. And all it was was a rock. I felt nay heart sink. Either she had gone clean loco or this was her idea of a joke. Wrong on both counts. She gave me the hatchet and told me to take a hack at the boulder, which I did, again and again, for yellow spots sprang up from under every blow. By the great Moses! it was gold! The whole blamed boulder!"

Jones rose suddenly to his full height and flung out his long arms, his face turned to the southern skies. The movement shot panic into the heart of a swan that had drawn nearer with amiably predatory designs. Its consequent abrupt retreat collided it with a stout old lady, who squealed and dropped her bag of peanuts. Jones sat down and resumed.

"Gold, I tell you, solid gold and that pure and soft that I chopped chips out of it. It had been coated with some sort of rain-proof paint or lacquer made out of asphalt or something. No wonder I'd taken it for a rock. It was ten feet long, all of five feet through, and tapering to both ends like an egg. Here. Take a look at this."

From his pocket he drew and opened a leather case, from which he took an object wrapped in tissue-paper. Unwrapping it, he dropped into my hand a chip of pure soft gold, the size of a ten-dollar gold-piece. I could make out the greyish substance on one side with which it had been painted.

"I chopped that from one end of the thing," Jones went on, replacing the chip in its paper and leather case. "And lucky I put it in my pocket. For right at my back came one loud word—more like a croak than a word, in my way of thinking. And there was that lean old fellow with the eagle beak that had dropped in on us one night.

And there was about thirty Indians with him—all slim young fellows.

"Vahna'd flopped down and begun whimpering, but I told her, 'Get up and make friends with them for me.' 'No, no,' she cried. 'This is death. Good-bye, amigo—'"

Here Mrs. Jones winced, and her husband abruptly checked the particular flow of his narrative.

"'Then get up and fight along with me,' I said to her. And she did. She was some hellion, there on the top of the world, clawing and scratching tooth and nail—a regular she cat. And I wasn't idle, though all I had was that hatchet and my long arms. But they were too many for me, and there was no place for me to put my back against a wall. When I come to, minutes after they'd cracked me on the head—here, feel this."

Removing his hat, Julian Jones guided my finger tips through his thatch of sandy hair until they sank into an indentation. It was fully three inches long, and went into the bone itself of the skull.

"When I come to, there was Vahna spread-eagled on top of the nugget, and the old fellow with a beak jabbering away solemnly as if going through some sort of religious exercises. In his hand he had a stone knife—you know, a thin, sharp sliver of some obsidian-like stuff same as they make arrow-heads out of. I couldn't lift a hand, being held down, and being too weak besides. And—well, anyway, that stone knife did for her, and me they didn't even do the honour of killing there on top their sacred peak. They chucked me off of it like so much carrion.

"And the buzzards didn't get me either. I can see the moonlight yet, shining on all those peaks of snow, as I went down. Why, sir, it was a five-hundred-foot fall, only I didn't make it. I went into a big snow-drift in a crevice. And when I come to (hours after I know, for it was full day when I next saw the sun), I found myself in a regular snow-cave or tunnel caused by the water from the melting snow running along the ledge. In fact, the stone above actually overhung just beyond where I first landed. A few feet more to the side, either way, and I'd almost be going yet. It was a straight miracle, that's what it was.

"But I paid for it. It was two years and over before I knew what happened. All I knew was that I was Julian Jones and that I'd been blacklisted in the big strike, and that I was married to Sarah here. I mean that. I didn't know anything in between, and when Sarah tried to talk about it, it gave me pains in the head. I mean my head was queer, and I knew it was queer.

"And then, sitting on the porch of her father's farmhouse back in Nebraska one moonlight evening, Sarah came out and put that

106

gold chip into my hand. Seems she'd just found it in the torn lining of the trunk I'd brought back from Ecuador—I who for two years didn't even know I'd been to Ecuador, or Australia, or anything! Well, I just sat there looking at the chip in the moonlight, and turning it over and over and figuring what it was and where it'd come from, when all of a sudden there was a snap inside my head as if something had broken, and then I could see Vahna spread-eagled on that big nugget and the old fellow with the beak waving the stone knife, and . . . and everything. That is, everything that had happened from the time I first left Nebraska to when I crawled to the daylight out of the snow after they had chucked me off the mountain-top. But everything that'd happened after that I'd clean forgotten. When Sarah said I was her husband, I wouldn't listen to her. Took all her family and the preacher that'd married us to convince me.

"Later on I wrote to Seth Manners. The railroad hadn't killed him yet, and he pieced out a lot for me. I'll show you his letters. I've got them at the hotel. One day, he said, making his regular run, I crawled out on to the track. I didn't stand upright, I just crawled. He took me for a calf, or a big dog, at first. I wasn't anything human, he said, and I didn't know him or anything. As near as I can make out, it was ten days after the mountain-top to the time Seth picked me up. What I ate I don't know. Maybe I didn't eat. Then it was doctors at Quito, and Paloma nursing me (she must have packed that gold chip in my trunk), until they found out I was a man without a mind, and the railroad sent me back to Nebraska. At any rate, that's what Seth writes me. Of myself, I don't know. But Sarah here knows. She corresponded with the railroad before they shipped me and all that."

Mrs. Jones nodded affirmation of his words, sighed and evidenced unmistakable signs of eagerness to go.

"I ain't been able to work since," her husband continued. "And I ain't been able to figure out how to get back that big nugget. Sarah's got money of her own, and she won't let go a penny—"

"He won't get down to that country no more!" she broke forth.

"But, Sarah, Vahna's dead—you know that," Julian Jones protested.

"I don't know anything about anything," she answered decisively, "except that that country is no place for a married man."

Her lips snapped together, and she fixed an unseeing stare across to where the afternoon sun was beginning to glow into sunset. I gazed for a moment at her face, white, plump, tiny, and implacable, and gave her up.

"How do you account for such a mass of gold being there?" I

queried of Julian Jones. "A solid-gold meteor that fell out of the sky?"

"Not for a moment." He shook his head. " It was carried there by the Indians."

"Up a mountain like that—and such enormous weight and size!" I objected.

"Just as easy," he smiled. "I used to be stumped by that proposition myself, after I got my memory back. Now how in Sam Hill—' I used to begin, and then spend hours figuring at it. And then when I got the answer I felt downright idiotic, it was that easy." He paused, then announced: "They didn't."

"But you just—said they did."

"They did and they didn't," was his enigmatic reply. "Of course they never carried that monster nugget up there. What they did was to carry up its contents."

He waited until he saw enlightenment dawn in my face.

"And then of course melted all the gold, or welded it, or smelted it, all into one piece. You know the first Spaniards down there, under a leader named Pizarro, were a gang of robbers and cut-throats. They went through the country like the hoof-and-mouth disease, and killed the Indians off like cattle. You see, the Indians had lots of gold. Well, what the Spaniards didn't get, the surviving Indians hid away in that one big chunk on top the mountain, and it's been waiting there ever since for me—and for you, if you want to go in on it."

And here, by the Lagoon of the Palace of Fine Arts, ended my acquaintance with Julian Jones. On my agreeing to finance the adventure, he promised to call on me at my hotel next morning with the letters of Seth Manners and the railroad, and conclude arrangements. But he did not call. That evening I telephoned his hotel and was informed by the clerk that Mr. Julian Jones and wife had departed in the early afternoon, with their baggage.

Can Mrs. Jones have rushed him back and hidden him away in Nebraska? I remember that as we said good-bye, there was that in her smile that recalled the vulpine complacency of Mona Lisa, the Wise.

THE END

Kohala, Hawaii
May 5, 1916

LIKE ARGUS OF THE ANCIENT TIMES

It was the summer of 1897, and there was trouble in the Tarwater family. Grandfather Tarwater, after remaining properly subdued and crushed for a quiet decade, had broken out again. This time it was the Klondike fever. His first and one unvarying symptom of such attacks was song. One chant only he raised, though he remembered no more than the first stanza and but three lines of that. And the family knew his feet were itching and his brain was tingling with the old madness, when he lifted his hoarse-cracked voice, now falsetto-cracked, in:

Like Argus of the ancient times,
  We leave this modern Greece,
Tum-tum, tum-tum, tum, tum, tum-tum,
  To shear the Golden Fleece.

Ten years earlier he had lifted the chant, sung to the air of the "Doxology," when afflicted with the fever to go gold-mining in Patagonia. The multitudinous family had sat upon him, but had had a hard time doing it. When all else had failed to shake his resolution, they had applied lawyers to him, with the threat of getting out guardianship papers and of confining him in the state asylum for the insane—which was reasonable for a man who had, a quarter of a century before, speculated away all but ten meagre acres of a California principality, and who had displayed no better business acumen ever since.

The application of lawyers to John Tarwater was like the application of a mustard plaster. For, in his judgment, they were the gentry, more than any other, who had skinned him out of the broad Tarwater acres. So, at the time of his Patagonian fever, the very thought of so drastic a remedy was sufficient to cure him. He quickly demonstrated he was not crazy by shaking the fever from him and agreeing not to go to Patagonia.

Next, he demonstrated how crazy he really was, by deeding over to his family, unsolicited, the ten acres on Tarwater Flat, the house, barn, outbuildings, and water-rights. Also did he turn over the eight hundred dollars in bank that was the long-saved salvage of his wrecked fortune. But for this the family found no cause for committal to the asylum, since such committal would necessarily invalidate what he had done.

"Grandfather is sure peeved," said Mary, his oldest daughter, herself a grandmother, when her father quit smoking.

All he had retained for himself was a span of old horses, a mountain buckboard, and his one room in the crowded house. Further, having affirmed that he would be beholden to none of them, he got the contract to carry the United States mail, twice a week, from Kelterville up over Tarwater Mountain to Old Almaden—which was a sporadically worked quick-silver mine in the upland cattle country. With his old horses it took all his time to make the two weekly round trips. And for ten years, rain or shine, he had never missed a trip. Nor had he failed once to pay his week's board into Mary's hand. This board he had insisted on, in the convalescence from his Patagonian fever, and he had paid it strictly, though he had given up tobacco in order to be able to do it.

"Huh!" he confided to the ruined water wheel of the old Tarwater Mill, which he had built from the standing timber and which had ground wheat for the first settlers. "Huh! They'll never put me in the poor farm so long as I support myself. And without a penny to my name it ain't likely any lawyer fellows'll come snoopin' around after me."

And yet, precisely because of these highly rational acts, it was held that John Tarwater was mildly crazy!

The first time he had lifted the chant of "Like Argus of the Ancient Times," had been in 1849, when, twenty-two years' of age, violently attacked by the Californian fever, he had sold two hundred and forty Michigan acres, forty of it cleared, for the price of four yoke of oxen, and a wagon, and had started across the Plains.

"And we turned off at Fort Hall, where the Oregon emigration went north'ard, and swung south for Californy," was his way of concluding the narrative of that arduous journey. "And Bill Ping and me used to rope grizzlies out of the underbrush of Cache Slough in the Sacramento Valley."

Years of freighting and mining had followed, and, with a stake gleaned from the Merced placers, he satisfied the land-hunger of his race and time by settling in Sonoma County.

During the ten years of carrying the mail across Tarwater Township, up Tarwater Valley, and over Tarwater Mountain, most all of which land had once been his, he had spent his time dreaming of winning back that land before he died. And now, his huge gaunt form more erect than it had been for years, with a glinting of blue fires in his small and close-set eyes, he was lifting his ancient chant again.

"There he goes now—listen to him," said William Tarwater.

110

"Nobody at home," laughed Harris Topping, day labourer, husband of Annie Tarwater, and father of her nine children.

The kitchen door opened to admit the old man, returning from feeding his horses. The song had ceased from his lips; but Mary was irritable from a burnt hand and a grandchild whose stomach refused to digest properly diluted cows' milk.

"Now there ain't no use you carryin' on that way, father," she tackled him. "The time's past for you to cut and run for a place like the Klondike, and singing won't buy you nothing."

"Just the same," he answered quietly. "I bet I could go to that Klondike place and pick up enough gold to buy back the Tarwater lands."

"Old fool!" Annie contributed.

"You couldn't buy them back for less'n three hundred thousand and then some," was William's effort at squelching him.

"Then I could pick up three hundred thousand, and then some, if I was only there," the old man retorted placidly.

"Thank God you can't walk there, or you'd be startin', I know," Mary cried. "Ocean travel costs money."

"I used to have money," her father said humbly.

"Well, you ain't got any now—so forget it," William advised. "Them times is past, like roping bear with Bill Ping. There ain't no more bear."

"Just the same—"

But Mary cut him off. Seizing the day's paper from the kitchen table, she flourished it savagely under her aged progenitor's nose.

"What do those Klondikers say? There it is in cold print. Only the young and robust can stand the Klondike. It's worse than the north pole. And they've left their dead a-plenty there themselves. Look at their pictures. You're forty years older 'n the oldest of them."

John Tarwater did look, but his eyes strayed to other photographs on the highly sensational front page.

"And look at the photys of them nuggets they brought down," he said. "I know gold. Didn't I gopher twenty thousand outa the Merced? And wouldn't it a-ben a hundred thousand if that cloudburst hadn't busted my wing-dam? Now if I was only in the Klondike—"

"Crazy as a loon," William sneered in open aside to the rest.

"A nice way to talk to your father," Old Man Tarwater censured mildly. "My father'd have walloped the tar out of me with a single-tree if I'd spoke to him that way."

"But you are crazy, father—" William began.

111

"Reckon you're right, son. And that's where my father wasn't crazy. He'd a-done it."

"The old man's been reading some of them magazine articles about men who succeeded after forty," Annie jibed.

"And why not, daughter?" he asked. "And why can't a man succeed after he's seventy? I was only seventy this year. And mebbe I could succeed if only I could get to the Klondike—"

"Which you ain't going to get to," Mary shut him off.

"Oh, well, then," he sighed, "seein's I ain't, I might just as well go to bed."

He stood up, tall, gaunt, great-boned and gnarled, a splendid ruin of a man. His ragged hair and whiskers were not grey but snowy white, as were the tufts of hair that stood out on the backs of his huge bony fingers. He moved toward the door, opened it, sighed, and paused with a backward look.

"Just the same," he murmured plaintively, "the bottoms of my feet is itching something terrible."

Long before the family stirred next morning, his horses fed and harnessed by lantern light, breakfast cooked and eaten by lamp light, Old Man Tarwater was off and away down Tarwater Valley on the road to Kelterville. Two things were unusual about this usual trip which he had made a thousand and forty times since taking the mail contract. He did not drive to Kelterville, but turned off on the main road south to Santa Rosa. Even more remarkable than this was the paper-wrapped parcel between his feet. It contained his one decent black suit, which Mary had been long reluctant to see him wear any more, not because it was shabby, but because, as he guessed what was at the back of her mind, it was decent enough to bury him in.

And at Santa Rosa, in a second-hand clothes shop, he sold the suit outright for two dollars and a half. From the same obliging shopman he received four dollars for the wedding ring of his long-dead wife. The span of horses and the wagon he disposed of for seventy-five dollars, although twenty-five was all he received down in cash. Chancing to meet Alton Granger on the street, to whom never before had he mentioned the ten dollars loaned him in '74, he reminded Alton Granger of the little affair, and was promptly paid. Also, of all unbelievable men to be in funds, he so found the town drunkard for whom he had bought many a drink in the old and palmy days. And from him John Tarwater borrowed a dollar. Finally, he took the afternoon train to San Francisco.

A dozen days later, carrying a half-empty canvas sack of blankets and old clothes, he landed on the beach of Dyea in the thick of the great Klondike Rush. The beach was screaming bedlam.

Ten thousand tons of outfit lay heaped and scattered, and twice ten thousand men struggled with it and clamoured about it. Freight, by Indian-back, over Chilcoot to Lake Linderman, had jumped from sixteen to thirty cents a pound, which latter was a rate of six hundred dollars a ton. And the sub-arctic winter gloomed near at hand. All knew it, and all knew that of the twenty thousand of them very few would get across the passes, leaving the rest to winter and wait for the late spring thaw.

Such the beach old John Tarwater stepped upon; and straight across the beach and up the trail toward Chilcoot he headed, cackling his ancient chant, a very Grandfather Argus himself, with no outfit worry in the world, for he did not possess any outfit. That night he slept on the flats, five miles above Dyea, at the head of canoe navigation. Here the Dyea River became a rushing mountain torrent, plunging out of a dark canyon from the glaciers that fed it far above.

And here, early next morning, he beheld a little man weighing no more than a hundred, staggering along a foot-log under all of a hundred pounds of flour strapped on his back. Also, he beheld the little man stumble off the log and fall face-downward in a quiet eddy where the water was two feet deep and proceed quietly to drown. It was no desire of his to take death so easily, but the flour on his back weighed as much as he and would not let him up.

"Thank you, old man," he said to Tarwater, when the latter had dragged him up into the air and ashore.

While he unlaced his shoes and ran the water out, they had further talk. Next, he fished out a ten-dollar gold-piece and offered it to his rescuer.

Old Tarwater shook his head and shivered, for the ice-water had wet him to his knees.

"But I reckon I wouldn't object to settin' down to a friendly meal with you."

"Ain't had breakfast?" the little man, who was past forty and who had said his name was Anson, queried with a glance frankly curious.

"Nary bite," John Tarwater answered.

"Where's your outfit? Ahead?"

"Nary outfit."

"Expect to buy your grub on the Inside?"

"Nary a dollar to buy it with, friend. Which ain't so important as a warm bite of breakfast right now."

In Anson's camp, a quarter of a mile on, Tarwater found a slender, red-whiskered young man of thirty cursing over a fire of wet willow wood. Introduced as Charles, he transferred his scowl and wrath to Tarwater, who, genially oblivious, devoted himself to the fire, took advantage of the chill morning breeze to create a draught which the other had left stupidly blocked by stones, and soon developed less smoke and more flame. The third member of the party, Bill Wilson, or Big Bill as they called him, came in with a hundred-and-forty-pound pack; and what Tarwater esteemed to be a very rotten breakfast was dished out by Charles. The mush was half cooked and mostly burnt, the bacon was charred carbon, and the coffee was unspeakable.

Immediately the meal was wolfed down the three partners took their empty pack-straps and headed down trail to where the remainder of their outfit lay at the last camp a mile away. And old Tarwater became busy. He washed the dishes, foraged dry wood, mended a broken pack-strap, put an edge on the butcher-knife and camp-axe, and repacked the picks and shovels into a more carryable parcel.

What had impressed him during the brief breakfast was the sort of awe in which Anson and Big Bill stood of Charles. Once, during the morning, while Anson took a breathing spell after bringing in another hundred-pound pack, Tarwater delicately hinted his impression.

"You see, it's this way," Anson said. "We've divided our leadership. We've got specialities. Now I'm a carpenter. When we get to Lake Linderman, and the trees are chopped and whipsawed into planks, I'll boss the building of the boat. Big Bill is a logger and miner. So he'll boss getting out the logs and all mining operations. Most of our outfit's ahead. We went broke paying the Indians to pack that much of it to the top of Chilcoot. Our last partner is up there with it, moving it along by himself down the other side. His name's Liverpool, and he's a sailor. So, when the boat's built, he's the boss of the outfit to navigate the lakes and rapids to Klondike.

"And Charles—this Mr. Crayton—what might his speciality be?" Tarwater asked.

"He's the business man. When it comes to business and organization he's boss."

"Hum," Tarwater pondered. "Very lucky to get such a bunch of specialities into one outfit."

"More than luck," Anson agreed. "It was all accident, too. Each of us started alone. We met on the steamer coming up from San Francisco, and formed the party.—Well, I got to be goin'. Charles is liable to get kicking because I ain't packin' my share' just the same, you can't expect a hundred-pound man to pack as much as a hundred-and-sixty-pounder."

"Stick around and cook us something for dinner," Charles, on

114

his next load in and noting the effects of the old man's handiness, told Tarwater.

And Tarwater cooked a dinner that was a dinner, washed the dishes, had real pork and beans for supper, and bread baked in a frying-pan that was so delectable that the three partners nearly foundered themselves on it. Supper dishes washed, he cut shavings and kindling for a quick and certain breakfast fire, showed Anson a trick with foot-gear that was invaluable to any hiker, sang his "Like Argus of the Ancient Times," and told them of the great emigration across the Plains in Forty-nine.

"My goodness, the first cheerful and hearty-like camp since we hit the beach," Big Bill remarked as he knocked out his pipe and began pulling off his shoes for bed.

"Kind of made things easy, boys, eh?" Tarwater queried genially.

All nodded. "Well, then, I got a proposition, boys. You can take it or leave it, but just listen kindly to it. You're in a hurry to get in before the freeze-up. Half the time is wasted over the cooking by one of you that he might be puttin' in packin' outfit. If I do the cookin' for you, you all'll get on that much faster. Also, the cookin' 'll be better, and that'll make you pack better. And I can pack quite a bit myself in between times, quite a bit, yes, sir, quite a bit."

Big Bill and Anson were just beginning to nod their heads in agreement, when Charles stopped them.

"What do you expect of us in return?" he demanded of the old man.

"Oh, I leave it up to the boys."

"That ain't business," Charles reprimanded sharply. "You made the proposition. Now finish it."

"Well, it's this way—"

"You expect us to feed you all winter, eh?" Charles interrupted.

"No, siree, I don't. All I reckon is a passage to Klondike in your boat would be mighty square of you."

"You haven't an ounce of grub, old man. You'll starve to death when you get there."

"I've been feedin' some long time pretty successful," Old Tarwater replied, a whimsical light in his eyes. "I'm seventy, and ain't starved to death never yet."

"Will you sign a paper to the effect that you shift for yourself as soon as you get to Dawson?" the business one demanded.

"Oh, sure," was the response.

Again Charles checked his two partners' expressions of satisfaction with the arrangement.

"One other thing, old man. We're a party of four, and we all have a vote on questions like this. Young Liverpool is ahead with the main outfit. He's got a say so, and he isn't here to say it."

"What kind of a party might he be?" Tarwater inquired.

"He's a rough-neck sailor, and he's got a quick, bad temper."

"Some turbulent," Anson contributed.

"And the way he can cuss is simply God-awful," Big Bill testified.

"But he's square," Big Bill added.

Anson nodded heartily to this appraisal.

"Well, boys," Tarwater summed up, "I set out for Californy and I got there. And I'm going to get to Klondike. Ain't a thing can stop me, ain't a thing. I'm going to get three hundred thousand outa the ground, too. Ain't a thing can stop me, ain't a thing, because I just naturally need the money. I don't mind a bad temper so long's the boy is square. I'll take my chance, an' I'll work along with you till we catch up with him. Then, if he says no to the proposition, I reckon I'll lose. But somehow I just can't see 'm sayin' no, because that'd mean too close up to freeze-up and too late for me to find another chance like this. And, as I'm sure going to get to Klondike, it's just plumb impossible for him to say no."

Old John Tarwater became a striking figure on a trail unusually replete with striking figures. With thousands of men, each back-tripping half a ton of outfit, retracing every mile of the trail twenty times, all came to know him and to hail him as "Father Christmas." And, as he worked, ever he raised his chant with his age-falsetto voice. None of the three men he had joined could complain about his work. True, his joints were stiff—he admitted to a trifle of rheumatism. He moved slowly, and seemed to creak and crackle when he moved; but he kept on moving. Last into the blankets at night, he was first out in the morning, so that the other three had hot coffee before their one before-breakfast pack. And, between breakfast and dinner and between dinner and supper, he always managed to back-trip for several packs himself. Sixty pounds was the limit of his burden, however. He could manage seventy-five, but he could not keep it up. Once, he tried ninety, but collapsed on the trail and was seriously shaky for a couple of days afterward.

Work! On a trail where hard-working men learned for the first time what work was, no man worked harder in proportion to his strength than Old Tarwater. Driven desperately on by the near-thrust of winter, and lured madly on by the dream of gold, they worked to their last ounce of strength and fell by the way. Others, when failure made certain, blew out their brains. Some went mad, and still others, under the irk of the man-destroying strain, broke partnerships and dissolved life-time friendships with fellows just as good as themselves and just as strained and mad.

Work! Old Tarwater could shame them all, despite his creaking and crackling and the nasty hacking cough he had developed. Early and late, on trail or in camp beside the trail he was ever in evidence, ever busy at something, ever responsive to the hail of "Father Christmas." Weary back-trippers would rest their packs on a log or rock alongside of where he rested his, and would say: "Sing us that song of yourn, dad, about Forty-Nine." And, when he had wheezingly complied, they would arise under their loads, remark that it was real heartening, and hit the forward trail again.

"If ever a man worked his passage and earned it," Big Bill confided to his two partners, "that man's our old Skeezicks."

"You bet," Anson confirmed. "He's a valuable addition to the party, and I, for one, ain't at all disagreeable to the notion of making him a regular partner—"

"None of that!" Charles Crayton cut in. "When we get to Dawson we're quit of him—that's the agreement. We'd only have to bury him if we let him stay on with us. Besides, there's going to be a famine, and every ounce of grub'll count. Remember, we're feeding him out of our own supply all the way in. And if we run short in the pinch next year, you'll know the reason. Steamboats can't get up grub to Dawson till the middle of June, and that's nine months away."

"Well, you put as much money and outfit in as the rest of us," Big Bill conceded, "and you've a say according."

"And I'm going to have my say," Charles asserted with increasing irritability. "And it's lucky for you with your fool sentiments that you've got somebody to think ahead for you, else you'd all starve to death. I tell you that famine's coming. I've been studying the situation. Flour will be two dollars a pound, or ten, and no sellers. You mark my words."

Across the rubble-covered flats, up the dark canyon to Sheep Camp, past the over-hanging and ever-threatening glaciers to the Scales, and from the Scales up the steep pitches of ice-scoured rock where packers climbed with hands and feet, Old Tarwater camp-cooked and packed and sang. He blew across Chilcoot Pass, above timberline, in the first swirl of autumn snow. Those below, without firewood, on the bitter rim of Crater Lake, heard from the driving obscurity above them a weird voice chanting:

> *"Like Argus of the ancient times,*
> *We leave this modern Greece,*

Tum-tum, tum-tum, tum, tum, tum-tum,
To shear the Golden Fleece."

And out of the snow flurries they saw appear a tall, gaunt form, with whiskers of flying white that blended with the storm, bending under a sixty-pound pack of camp dunnage.

"Father Christmas!" was the hail. And then: "Three rousing cheers for Father Christmas!"

Two miles beyond Crater Lake lay Happy Camp—so named because here was found the uppermost fringe of the timber line, where men might warm themselves by fire again. Scarcely could it be called timber, for it was a dwarf rock-spruce that never raised its loftiest branches higher than a foot above the moss, and that twisted and grovelled like a pig-vegetable under the moss. Here, on the trail leading into Happy Camp, in the first sunshine of half a dozen days, Old Tarwater rested his pack against a huge boulder and caught his breath. Around this boulder the trail passed, laden men toiling slowly forward and men with empty pack-straps limping rapidly back for fresh loads. Twice Old Tarwater essayed to rise and go on, and each time, warned by his shakiness, sank back to recover more strength. From around the boulder he heard voices in greeting, recognized Charles Crayton's voice, and realized that at last they had met up with Young Liverpool. Quickly, Charles plunged into business, and Tarwater heard with great distinctness every word of Charles' unflattering description of him and the proposition to give him passage to Dawson.

"A dam fool proposition," was Liverpool's judgment, when Charles had concluded. "An old granddad of seventy! If he's on his last legs, why in hell did you hook up with him? If there's going to be a famine, and it looks like it, we need every ounce of grub for ourselves. We only out-fitted for four, not five."

"It's all right," Tarwater heard Charles assuring the other. "Don't get excited. The old codger agreed to leave the final decision to you when we caught up with you. All you've got to do is put your foot down and say no."

"You mean it's up to me to turn the old one down, after your encouraging him and taking advantage of his work clear from Dyea here?"

"It's a hard trail, Liverpool, and only the men that are hard will get through," Charles strove to palliate.

"And I'm to do the dirty work?" Liverpool complained, while Tarwater's heart sank.

"That's just about the size of it," Charles said. "You've got the deciding."

Then old Tarwater's heart uprose again as the air was rent by a cyclone of profanity, from the midst of which crackled sentences like:—"Dirty skunks! . . . See you in hell first! . . . My mind's made up! . . . Hell's fire and corruption! . . . The old codger goes down the Yukon with us, stack on that, my hearty! . . . Hard? You don't know what hard is unless I show you! . . . I'll bust the whole outfit to hell and gone if any of you try to side-track him! . . . Just try to side-track him, that is all, and you'll think the Day of Judgment and all God's blastingness has hit the camp in one chunk!"

Such was the invigoratingness of Liverpool's flow of speech that, quite without consciousness of effort, the old man arose easily under his load and strode on toward Happy Camp.

From Happy Camp to Long Lake, from Long Lake to Deep Lake, and from Deep Lake up over the enormous hog-back and down to Linderman, the man-killing race against winter kept on. Men broke their hearts and backs and wept beside the trail in sheer exhaustion. But winter never faltered. The fall gales blew, and amid bitter soaking rains and ever-increasing snow flurries, Tarwater and the party to which he was attached piled the last of their outfit on the beach.

There was no rest. Across the lake, a mile above a roaring torrent, they located a patch of spruce and built their saw-pit. Here, by hand, with an inadequate whipsaw, they sawed the spruce-trunks into lumber. They worked night and day. Thrice, on the night-shift, underneath in the saw-pit, Old Tarwater fainted. By day he cooked as well, and, in the betweenwhiles, helped Anson in the building of the boat beside the torrent as the green planks came down.

The days grew shorter. The wind shifted into the north and blew unending gales. In the mornings the weary men crawled from their blankets and in their socks thawed out their frozen shoes by the fire Tarwater always had burning for them. Ever arose the increasing tale of famine on the Inside. The last grub steamboats up from Bering Sea were stalled by low water at the beginning of the Yukon Flats hundreds of miles north of Dawson. In fact, they lay at the old Hudson Bay Company's post at Fort Yukon inside the Arctic Circle. Flour in Dawson was up to two dollars a pound, but no one would sell. Bonanza and Eldorado Kings, with money to burn, were leaving for the Outside because they could buy no grub. Miners' Committees were confiscating all grub and putting the population on strict rations. A man who held out an ounce of grub was shot like a dog. A score had been so executed already.

And, under a strain which had broken so many younger men, Old Tarwater began to break. His cough had become terrible, and had not his exhausted comrades slept like the dead, he would have

119

kept them awake nights. Also, he began to take chills, so that he dressed up to go to bed. When he had finished so dressing, not a rag of garment remained in his clothes bag. All he possessed was on his back and swathed around his gaunt old form.

"Gee!" said Big Bill. "If he puts all he's got on now, when it ain't lower than twenty above, what'll he do later on when it goes down to fifty and sixty below?"

They lined the rough-made boat down the mountain torrent, nearly losing it a dozen times, and rowed across the south end of Lake Linderman in the thick of a fall blizzard. Next morning they planned to load and start, squarely into the teeth of the north, on their perilous traverse of half a thousand miles of lakes and rapids and box canyons. But before he went to bed that night, Young Liverpool was out over the camp. He returned to find his whole party asleep. Rousing Tarwater, he talked with him in low tones.

"Listen, dad," he said.—"You've got a passage in our boat, and if ever a man earned a passage you have. But you know yourself you're pretty well along in years, and your health right now ain't exciting. If you go on with us you'll croak surer'n hell.—Now wait till I finish, dad. The price for a passage has jumped to five hundred dollars. I've been throwing my feet and I've hustled a passenger. He's an official of the Alaska Commercial and just has to get in. He's bid up to six hundred to go with me in our boat. Now the passage is yours. You sell it to him, poke the six hundred into your jeans, and pull South for California while the goin's good. You can be in Dyea in two days, and in California in a week more. What d'ye say?"

Tarwater coughed and shivered for a space, ere he could get freedom of breath for speech.

"Son," he said, "I just want to tell you one thing. I drove my four yoke of oxen across the Plains in Forty-nine and lost nary a one. I drove them plumb to Californy, and I freighted with them afterward out of Sutter's Fort to American Bar. Now I'm going to Klondike. Ain't nothing can stop me, ain't nothing at all. I'm going to ride that boat, with you at the steering sweep, clean to Klondike, and I'm going to shake three hundred thousand out of the moss-roots. That being so, it's contrary to reason and common sense for me to sell out my passage. But I thank you kindly, son, I thank you kindly."

The young sailor shot out his hand impulsively and gripped the old man's.

"By God, dad!" he cried. "You're sure going to go then. You're the real stuff." He looked with undisguised contempt across the

120

sleepers to where Charles Crayton snored in his red beard. "They don't seem to make your kind any more, dad."

Into the north they fought their way, although old-timers, coming out, shook their heads and prophesied they would be frozen in on the lakes. That the freeze-up might come any day was patent, and delays of safety were no longer considered. For this reason, Liverpool decided to shoot the rapid stream connecting Linderman to Lake Bennett with the fully loaded boat. It was the custom to line the empty boats down and to portage the cargoes across. Even then many empty boats had been wrecked. But the time was past for such precaution.

"Climb out, dad," Liverpool commanded as he prepared to swing from the bank and enter the rapids.

Old Tarwater shook his white head.

"I'm sticking to the outfit," he declared. "It's the only way to get through. You see, son, I'm going to Klondike. If I stick by the boat, then the boat just naturally goes to Klondike, too. If I get out, then most likely you'll lose the boat."

"Well, there's no use in overloading," Charles announced, springing abruptly out on the bank as the boat cast off.

"Next time you wait for my orders!" Liverpool shouted ashore as the current gripped the boat. "And there won't be any more walking around rapids and losing time waiting to pick you up!"

What took them ten minutes by river, took Charles half an hour by land, and while they waited for him at the head of Lake Bennett they passed the time of day with several dilapidated old-timers on their way out. The famine news was graver than ever. The North-west Mounted Police, stationed at the foot of Lake Marsh where the gold-rushers entered Canadian territory, were refusing to let a man past who did not carry with him seven hundred pounds of grub. In Dawson City a thousand men, with dog-teams, were waiting the freeze-up to come out over the ice. The trading companies could not fill their grub-contracts, and partners were cutting the cards to see which should go and which should stay and work the claims.

"That settles it," Charles announced, when he learned of the action of the mounted police on the boundary. "Old Man, you might as well start back now."

"Climb aboard!" Liverpool commanded. "We're going to Klondike, and old dad is going along."

A shift of gale to the south gave them a fair wind down Lake Bennett, before which they ran under a huge sail made by Liverpool. The heavy weight of outfit gave such ballast that he cracked on as a daring sailor should when moments counted. A shift of four points into the south-west, coming just at the right time as they entered upon Caribou Crossing, drove them down that connecting link to lakes Tagish and Marsh. In stormy sunset and twilight—they made the dangerous crossing of Great Windy Arm, wherein they beheld two other boat-loads of gold-rushers capsize and drown.

Charles was for beaching for the night, but Liverpool held on, steering down Tagish by the sound of the surf on the shoals and by the occasional shore-fires that advertised wrecked or timid argonauts. At four in the morning, he aroused Charles. Old Tarwater, shiveringly awake, heard Liverpool order Crayton aft beside him at the steering-sweep, and also heard the one-sided conversation.

"Just listen, friend Charles, and keep your own mouth shut," Liverpool began. "I want you to get one thing into your head and keep it there: old dad's going by the police. Understand? He's going by. When they examine our outfit, old dad's got a fifth share in it, savvee? That'll put us all 'way under what we ought to have, but we can bluff it through. Now get this, and get it hard: there ain't going to be any fall-down on this bluff—"

"If you think I'd give away on the old codger—" Charles began indignantly.

"You thought that," Liverpool checked him, "because I never mentioned any such thing. Now—get me and get me hard: I don't care what you've been thinking. It's what you're going to think. We'll make the police post some time this afternoon, and we've got to get ready to pull the bluff without a hitch, and a word to the wise is plenty."

"If you think I've got it in my mind—" Charles began again.

"Look here," Liverpool shut him off. "I don't know what's in your mind. I don't want to know. I want you to know what's in my mind. If there's any slip-up, if old dad gets turned back by the police, I'm going to pick out the first quiet bit of landscape and take you ashore on it. And then I'm going to beat you up to the Queen's taste. Get me, and get me hard. It ain't going to be any half-way beating, but a real, two-legged, two-fisted, he-man beating. I don't expect I'll kill you, but I'll come damn near to half-killing you."

"But what can I do?" Charles almost whimpered.

"Just one thing," was Liverpool's final word. "You just pray. You pray so hard that old dad gets by the police that he does get by. That's all. Go back to your blankets."

Before they gained Lake Le Barge, the land was sheeted with snow that would not melt for half a year. Nor could they lay their boat at will against the bank, for the rim-ice was already forming. Inside the mouth of the river, just ere it entered Lake Le Barge, they

122

found a hundred storm-bound boats of the argonauts. Out of the north, across the full sweep of the great lake, blew an unending snow gale. Three mornings they put out and fought it and the cresting seas it drove that turned to ice as they fell in-board. While the others broke their hearts at the oars, Old Tarwater managed to keep up just sufficient circulation to survive by chopping ice and throwing it overboard.

Each day for three days, beaten to helplessness, they turned tail on the battle and ran back into the sheltering river. By the fourth day, the hundred boats had increased to three hundred, and the two thousand argonauts on board knew that the great gale heralded the freeze-up of Le Barge. Beyond, the rapid rivers would continue to run for days, but unless they got beyond, and immediately, they were doomed to be frozen in for six months to come.

"This day we go through," Liverpool announced. "We turn back for nothing. And those of us that dies at the oars will live again and go on pulling."

And they went through, winning half the length of the lake by nightfall and pulling on through all the night hours as the wind went down, falling asleep at the oars and being rapped awake by Liverpool, toiling on through an age-long nightmare while the stars came out and the surface of the lake turned to the unruffledness of a sheet of paper and froze skin-ice that tinkled like broken glass as their oar-blades shattered it.

As day broke clear and cold, they entered the river, with behind them a sea of ice. Liverpool examined his aged passenger and found him helpless and almost gone. When he rounded the boat to against the rim-ice to build a fire and warm up Tarwater inside and out, Charles protested against such loss of time.

"This ain't business, so don't you come horning in," Liverpool informed him. "I'm running the boat trip. So you just climb out and chop firewood, and plenty of it. I'll take care of dad. You, Anson, make a fire on the bank. And you, Bill, set up the Yukon stove in the boat. Old dad ain't as young as the rest of us, and for the rest of this voyage he's going to have a fire on board to sit by."

All of which came to pass; and the boat, in the grip of the current, like a river steamer with smoke rising from the two joints of stove-pipe, grounded on shoals, hung up on split currents, and charged rapids and canyons, as it drove deeper into the Northland winter. The Big and Little Salmon rivers were throwing mush-ice into the main river as they passed, and, below the riffles, anchor-ice arose from the river bottom and coated the surface with crystal scum. Night and day the rim-ice grew, till, in quiet places, it extended out a hundred yards from shore. And Old Tarwater, with all his clothes on, sat by the stove and kept the fire going. Night and day, not daring to stop for fear of the imminent freeze-up, they dared to run, an increasing mushiness of ice running with them.

"What ho, old hearty?" Liverpool would call out at times.

"Cheer O," Old Tarwater had learned to respond.

"What can I ever do for you, son, in payment?" Tarwater, stoking the fire, would sometimes ask Liverpool, beating now one released hand and now the other as he fought for circulation where he steered in the freezing stern-sheets.

"Just break out that regular song of yours, old Forty-Niner," was the invariable reply.

And Tarwater would lift his voice in the cackling chant, as he lifted it at the end, when the boat swung in through driving cake-ice and moored to the Dawson City bank, and all waterfront Dawson pricked its ears to hear the triumphant pæan:

> *Like Argus of the ancient times,*
> *We leave this modern Greece,*
> *Tum-tum, tum-tum, tum, tum, tum-tum,*
> *To shear the Golden Fleece,*

Charles did it, but he did it so discreetly that none of his party, least of all the sailor, ever learned of it. He saw two great open barges being filled up with men, and, on inquiry, learned that these were grubless ones being rounded up and sent down the Yukon by the Committee of Safety. The barges were to be towed by the last little steamboat in Dawson, and the hope was that Fort Yukon, where lay the stranded steamboats, would be gained before the river froze. At any rate, no matter what happened to them, Dawson would be relieved of their grub-consuming presence. So to the Committee of Safety Charles went, privily to drop a flea in its ear concerning Tarwater's grubless, moneyless, and aged condition. Tarwater was one of the last gathered in, and when Young Liverpool returned to the boat, from the bank he saw the barges in a run of cake-ice, disappearing around the bend below Moose-hide Mountain.

Running in cake-ice all the way, and several times escaping jams in the Yukon Flats, the barges made their hundreds of miles of progress farther into the north and froze up cheek by jowl with the grub-fleet. Here, inside the Arctic Circle, Old Tarwater settled down to pass the long winter. Several hours' work a day, chopping firewood for the steamboat companies, sufficed to keep him in food.

124

For the rest of the time there was nothing to do but hibernate in his log cabin.

Warmth, rest, and plenty to eat, cured his hacking cough and put him in as good physical condition as was possible for his advanced years. But, even before Christmas, the lack of fresh vegetables caused scurvy to break out, and disappointed adventurer after disappointed adventurer took to his bunk in abject surrender to this culminating misfortune. Not so Tarwater. Even before the first symptoms appeared on him, he was putting into practice his one prescription, namely, exercise. From the junk of the old trading post he resurrected a number of rusty traps, and from one of the steamboat captains he borrowed a rifle.

Thus equipped, he ceased from wood-chopping, and began to make more than a mere living. Nor was he downhearted when the scurvy broke out on his own body. Ever he ran his trap-lines and sang his ancient chant. Nor could the pessimist shake his surety of the three hundred thousand of Alaskan gold he as going to shake out of the moss-roots.

"But this ain't gold-country," they told him.

"Gold is where you find it, son, as I should know who was mining before you was born, 'way back in Forty-Nine," was his reply. "What was Bonanza Creek but a moose-pasture? No miner'd look at it; yet they washed five-hundred-dollar pans and took out fifty million dollars. Eldorado was just as bad. For all you know, right under this here cabin, or right over the next hill, is millions just waiting for a lucky one like me to come and shake it out."

At the end of January came his disaster. Some powerful animal that he decided was a bob-cat, managing to get caught in one of his smaller traps, dragged it away. A heavy snow-fall put a stop midway to his pursuit, losing the trail for him and losing himself. There were but several hours of daylight each day between the twenty hours of intervening darkness, and his efforts in the grey light and continually falling snow succeeded only in losing him more thoroughly. Fortunately, when winter snow falls in the Northland the thermometer invariably rises; so, instead of the customary forty and fifty and even sixty degrees below zero, the temperature remained fifteen below. Also, he was warmly clad and had a full matchbox. Further to mitigate his predicament, on the fifth day he killed a wounded moose that weighed over half a ton. Making his camp beside it on a spruce-bottom, he was prepared to last out the winter, unless a searching party found him or his scurvy grew worse.

But at the end of two weeks there had been no sign of search, while his scurvy had undeniably grown worse. Against his fire, banked from outer cold by a shelter-wall of spruce-boughs, he crouched long hours in sleep and long hours in waking. But the waking hours grew less, becoming semi-waking or half-dreaming hours as the process of hibernation worked their way with him. Slowly the sparkle point of consciousness and identity that was John Tarwater sank, deeper and deeper, into the profounds of his being that had been compounded ere man was man, and while he was becoming man, when he, first of all animals, regarded himself with an introspective eye and laid the beginnings of morality in foundations of nightmare peopled by the monsters of his own ethic-thwarted desires.

Like a man in fever, waking to intervals of consciousness, so Old Tarwater awoke, cooked his moose-meat, and fed the fire; but more and more time he spent in his torpor, unaware of what was day-dream and what was sleep-dream in the content of his unconsciousness. And here, in the unforgetable crypts of man's unwritten history, unthinkable and unrealizable, like passages of nightmare or impossible adventures of lunacy, he encountered the monsters created of man's first morality that ever since have vexed him into the spinning of fantasies to elude them or do battle with them.

In short, weighted by his seventy years, in the vast and silent loneliness of the North, Old Tarwater, as in the delirium of drug or anæsthetic, recovered within himself, the infantile mind of the child-man of the early world. It was in the dusk of Death's fluttery wings that Tarwater thus crouched, and, like his remote forebear, the child-man, went to myth-making, and sun-heroizing, himself hero-maker and the hero in quest of the immemorial treasure difficult of attainment.

Either must he attain the treasure—for so ran the inexorable logic of the shadow-land of the unconscious—or else sink into the all-devouring sea, the blackness eater of the light that swallowed to extinction the sun each night . . . the sun that arose ever in rebirth next morning in the east, and that had become to man man's first symbol of immortality through rebirth. All this, in the deeps of his unconsciousness (the shadowy western land of descending light), was the near dusk of Death down into which he slowly ebbed.

But how to escape this monster of the dark that from within him slowly swallowed him? Too deep-sunk was he to dream of escape or feel the prod of desire to escape. For him reality had ceased. Nor from within the darkened chamber of himself could reality recrudesce. His years were too heavy upon him, the debility of disease and the lethargy and torpor of the silence and the cold were too profound. Only from without could reality impact upon him and reawake within him an awareness of reality. Otherwise he would ooze down through the shadow-realm of the unconscious into the all-darkness of extinction.

But it came, the smash of reality from without, crashing upon his ear drums in a loud, explosive snort. For twenty days, in a temperature that had never risen above fifty below, no breath of wind had blown movement, no slightest sound had broken the silence. Like the smoker on the opium couch refocusing his eyes from the spacious walls of dream to the narrow confines of the mean little room, so Old Tarwater stared vague-eyed before him across his dying fire, at a huge moose that stared at him in startlement, dragging a wounded leg, manifesting all signs of extreme exhaustion; it, too, had been straying blindly in the shadow-land, and had wakened to reality only just ere it stepped into Tarwater's fire.

He feebly slipped the large fur mitten lined with thickness of wool from his right hand. Upon trial he found the trigger finger too numb for movement. Carefully, slowly, through long minutes, he worked the bare hand inside his blankets, up under his fur parka, through the chest openings of his shirts, and into the slightly warm hollow of his left arm-pit. Long minutes passed ere the finger could move, when, with equal slowness of caution, he gathered his rifle to his shoulder and drew bead upon the great animal across the fire.

At the shot, of the two shadow-wanderers, the one reeled downward to the dark and the other reeled upward to the light, swaying drunkenly on his scurvy-ravaged legs, shivering with nervousness and cold, rubbing swimming eyes with shaking fingers, and staring at the real world all about him that had returned to him with such sickening suddenness. He shook himself together, and realized that for long, how long he did not know, he had bedded in the arms of Death. He spat, with definite intention, heard the spittle crackle in the frost, and judged it must be below and far below sixty below. In truth, that day at Fort Yukon, the spirit thermometer registered seventy-five degrees below zero, which, since freezing-point is thirty-two above, was equivalent to one hundred and seven degrees of frost.

Slowly Tarwater's brain reasoned to action. Here, in the vast alone, dwelt Death. Here had come two wounded moose. With the clearing of the sky after the great cold came on, he had located his bearings, and he knew that both wounded moose had trailed to him from the east. Therefore, in the east, were men—whites or Indians he could not tell, but at any rate men who might stand by him in his need and help moor him to reality above the sea of dark.

He moved slowly, but he moved in reality, girding himself

127

with rifle, ammunition, matches, and a pack of twenty pounds of moose-meat. Then, an Argus rejuvenated, albeit lame of both legs and tottery, he turned his back on the perilous west and limped into the sun-arising, re-birthing east. . . .

Days later—how many days later he was never to know—dreaming dreams and seeing visions, cackling his old gold-chant of Forty-Nine, like one drowning and swimming feebly to keep his consciousness above the engulfing dark, he came out upon the snow-slope to a canyon and saw below smoke rising and men who ceased from work to gaze at him. He tottered down the hill to them, still singing; and when he ceased from lack of breath they called him variously: Santa Claus, Old Christmas, Whiskers, the Last of the Mohicans, and Father Christmas. And when he stood among them he stood very still, without speech, while great tears welled out of his eyes. He cried silently, a long time, till, as if suddenly bethinking himself, he sat down in the snow with much creaking and crackling of his joints, and from this low vantage point toppled sidewise and fainted calmly and easily away.

In less than a week Old Tarwater was up and limping about the housework of the cabin, cooking and dish-washing for the five men of the creek. Genuine sourdoughs (pioneers) they were, tough and hard-bitten, who had been buried so deeply inside the Circle that they did not know there was a Klondike Strike. The news he brought them was their first word of it. They lived on an almost straight-meat diet of moose, caribou, and smoked salmon, eked out with wild berries and somewhat succulent wild roots they had stocked up with in the summer. They had forgotten the taste of coffee, made fire with a burning glass, carried live fire-sticks with them wherever they travelled, and in their pipes smoked dry leaves that bit the tongue and were pungent to the nostrils.

Three years before, they had prospected from the head-reaches of the Koyokuk northward and clear across to the mouth of the Mackenzie on the Arctic Ocean. Here, on the whaleships, they had beheld their last white men and equipped themselves with the last white man's grub, consisting principally of salt and smoking tobacco. Striking south and west on the long traverse to the junction of the Yukon and Porcupine at Fort Yukon, they had found gold on this creek and remained over to work the ground.

They hailed the advent of Tarwater with joy, never tired of listening to his tales of Forty-Nine, and rechristened him Old Hero. Also, with tea made from spruce needles, with concoctions brewed from the inner willow bark, and with sour and bitter roots and bulbs from the ground, they dosed his scurvy out of him, so that he ceased limping and began to lay on flesh over his bony framework.

Further, they saw no reason at all why he should not gather a rich treasure of gold from the ground.

"Don't know about all of three hundred thousand," they told him one morning, at breakfast, ere they departed to their work, "but how'd a hundred thousand do, Old Hero? That's what we figure a claim is worth, the ground being badly spotted, and we've already staked your location notices."

"Well, boys," Old Tarwater answered, "and thanking you kindly, all I can say is that a hundred thousand will do nicely, and very nicely, for a starter. Of course, I ain't goin' to stop till I get the full three hundred thousand. That's what I come into the country for."

They laughed and applauded his ambition and reckoned they'd have to hunt a richer creek for him. And Old Hero reckoned that as the spring came on and he grew spryer, he'd have to get out and do a little snooping around himself.

"For all anybody knows," he said, pointing to a hillside across the creek bottom, "the moss under the snow there may be plumb rooted in nugget gold."

He said no more, but as the sun rose higher and the days grew longer and warmer, he gazed often across the creek at the definite bench-formation half way up the hill. And, one day, when the thaw was in full swing, he crossed the stream and climbed to the bench. Exposed patches of ground had already thawed an inch deep. On one such patch he stopped, gathered a bunch of moss in his big gnarled hands, and ripped it out by the roots. The sun smouldered on dully glistening yellow. He shook the handful of moss, and coarse nuggets, like gravel, fell to the ground. It was the Golden Fleece ready for the shearing.

Not entirely unremembered in Alaskan annals is the summer stampede of 1898 from Fort Yukon to the bench diggings of Tarwater Hill. And when Tarwater sold his holdings to the Bowdie interests for a sheer half-million and faced for California, he rode a mule over a new-cut trail, with convenient road houses along the way, clear to the steamboat landing at Fort Yukon.

At the first meal on the ocean-going steamship out of St. Michaels, a waiter, greyish-haired, pain-ravaged of face, scurvy-twisted of body, served him. Old Tarwater was compelled to look him over twice in order to make certain he was Charles Crayton.

"Got it bad, eh, son?" Tarwater queried.

"Just my luck," the other complained, after recognition and greeting. "Only one of the party that the scurvy attacked. I've been through hell. The other three are all at work and healthy, getting grub-stake to prospect up White River this winter. Anson's earning twenty-five a day at carpentering, Liverpool getting twenty logging for the saw-mill, and Big Bill's getting forty a day as chief sawyer. I tried my best, and if it hadn't been for scurvy . . ."

"Sure, son, you done your best, which ain't much, you being naturally irritable and hard from too much business. Now I'll tell you what. You ain't fit to work crippled up this way. I'll pay your passage with the captain in kind remembrance of the voyage you gave me, and you can lay up and take it easy the rest of the trip. And what are your circumstances when you land at San Francisco?"

Charles Crayton shrugged his shoulders.

"Tell you what," Tarwater continued. "There's work on the ranch for you till you can start business again."

"I could manage your business for you—" Charles began eagerly.

"No, siree," Tarwater declared emphatically. "But there's always post-holes to dig, and cordwood to chop, and the climate's fine ... "

Tarwater arrived home a true prodigal grandfather for whom the fatted calf was killed and ready. But first, ere he sat down at table, he must stroll out and around. And sons and daughters of his flesh and of the law needs must go with him fulsomely eating out of the gnarled old hand that had half a million to disburse. He led the way, and no opinion he slyly uttered was preposterous or impossible enough to draw dissent from his following. Pausing by the ruined water wheel which he had built from the standing timber, his face beamed as he gazed across the stretches of Tarwater Valley, and on and up the far heights to the summit of Tarwater Mountain—now all his again.

A thought came to him that made him avert his face and blow his nose in order to hide the twinkle in his eyes. Still attended by the entire family, he strolled on to the dilapidated barn. He picked up an age-weathered single-tree from the ground.

"William," he said. "Remember that little conversation we had just before I started to Klondike? Sure, William, you remember. You told me I was crazy. And I said my father'd have walloped the tar out of me with a single-tree if I'd spoke to him that way."

"Aw, but that was only foolin'," William temporized.

William was a grizzled man of forty-five, and his wife and grown sons stood in the group, curiously watching Grandfather Tarwater take off his coat and hand it to Mary to hold.

"William—come here," he commanded imperatively.

No matter how reluctantly, William came.

"Just a taste, William, son, of what my father give me often

130

enough," Old Tarwater crooned, as he laid on his son's back and shoulders with the single-tree. "Observe, I ain't hitting you on the head. My father had a gosh-wollickin' temper and never drew the line at heads when he went after tar.—Don't jerk your elbows back that way! You're likely to get a crack on one by accident. And just tell me one thing, William, son: is there nary notion in your head that I'm crazy?"

"No!" William yelped out in pain, as he danced about. "You ain't crazy, father of course you ain't crazy!"

"You said it," Old Tarwater remarked sententiously, tossing the single-tree aside and starting to struggle into his coat. "Now let's all go in and eat."

THE END

Glen Ellen, California
September 14, 1916

THE PRINCESS

A fire burned cheerfully in the jungle camp, and beside the fire lolled a cheerful-seeming though horrible-appearing man. This was a hobo jungle, pitched in a thin strip of woods that lay between a railroad embankment and the bank of a river. But no hobo was the man. So deep-sunk was he in the social abyss that a proper hobo would not sit by the same fire with him. A gay-cat, who is an ignorant new-comer on the "Road," might sit with such as he, but only long enough to learn better. Even low down bindle-stiffs and stew-bums, after a once-over, would have passed this man by. A genuine hobo, a couple of punks, or a bunch of tender-yeared road-kids might have gone through his rags for any stray pennies or nickels and kicked him out into the darkness. Even an alki-stiff would have reckoned himself immeasurably superior.

For this man was that hybrid of tramp-land, an alki-stiff that has degenerated into a stew-bum, with so little self-respect that he will never "boil-up," and with so little pride that he will eat out of a garbage can. He was truly horrible-appearing. He might have been sixty years of age; he might have been ninety. His garments might have been discarded by a rag-picker. Beside him, an unrolled bundle showed itself as consisting of a ragged overcoat and containing an empty and smoke-blackened tomato can, an empty and battered condensed milk can, some dog-meat partly wrapped in brown paper and evidently begged from some butcher-shop, a carrot that had been run over in the street by a wagon-wheel, three greenish-cankered and decayed potatoes, and a sugar-bun with a mouthful bitten from it and rescued from the gutter, as was made patent by the gutter-filth that still encrusted it.

A prodigious growth of whiskers, greyish-dirty and untrimmed for years, sprouted from his face. This hirsute growth should have been white, but the season was summer and it had not been exposed to a rain-shower for some time. What was visible of the face looked as if at some period it had stopped a hand-grenade. The nose was so variously malformed in its healed brokenness that there was no bridge, while one nostril, the size of a pea, opened downward, and the other, the size of a robin's egg, tilted upward to the sky. One eye, of normal size, dim-brown and misty, bulged to the verge of popping out, and as if from senility wept copiously and continuously. The other eye, scarcely larger than a squirrel's and as uncannily bright, twisted up obliquely into the hairy scar of a bone-crushed eyebrow. And he had but one arm.

Yet was he cheerful. On his face, in mild degree, was depicted sensuous pleasure as he lethargically scratched his ribs with his one hand. He pawed over his food-scraps, debated, then drew a twelve-ounce druggist bottle from his inside coat-pocket. The bottle was full of a colourless liquid, the contemplation of which made his little eye burn brighter and quickened his movements. Picking up the tomato can, he arose, went down the short path to the river, and returned with the can filled with not-nice river water. In the condensed milk can he mixed one part of water with two parts of fluid from the bottle. This colourless fluid was druggist's alcohol, and as such is known in tramp-land as "alki."

Slow footsteps, coming down the side of the railroad embankment, alarmed him ere he could drink. Placing the can carefully upon the ground between his legs, he covered it with his hat and waited anxiously whatever impended.

Out of the darkness emerged a man as filthy ragged as he. The new-comer, who might have been fifty, and might have been sixty, was grotesquely fat. He bulged everywhere. He was composed of bulges. His bulbous nose was the size and shape of a turnip. His eyelids bulged and his blue eyes bulged in competition with them. In many places the seams of his garments had parted across the bulges of body. His calves grew into his feet, for the broken elastic sides of his Congress gaiters were swelled full with the fat of him. One arm only he sported, from the shoulder of which was suspended a small and tattered bundle with the mud caked dry on the outer covering from the last place he had pitched his doss. He advanced with tentative caution, made sure of the harmlessness of the man beside the fire, and joined him.

"Hello, grandpa," the new-comer greeted, then paused to stare at the other's flaring, sky-open nostril. "Say, Whiskers, how'd ye keep the night dew out of that nose o' yourn?"

Whiskers growled an incoherence deep in his throat and spat into the fire in token that he was not pleased by the question.

"For the love of Mike," the fat man chuckled, "if you got caught out in a rainstorm without an umbrella you'd sure drown, wouldn't you?"

"Can it, Fatty, can it," Whiskers muttered wearily. "They ain't nothin' new in that line of chatter. Even the bulls hand it out to me."

"But you can still drink, I hope"; Fatty at the same time mollified and invited, with his one hand deftly pulling the slip-knots that fastened his bundle.

From within the bundle he brought to light a twelve-ounce bottle of alki. Footsteps coming down the embankment alarmed

133

him, and he hid the bottle under his hat on the ground between his legs.

But the next comer proved to be not merely one of their own ilk, but likewise to have only one arm. So forbidding of aspect was he that greetings consisted of no more than grunts. Huge-boned, tall, gaunt to cadaverousness, his face a dirty death's head, he was as repellent a nightmare of old age as ever Doré imagined. His toothless, thin-lipped mouth was a cruel and bitter slash under a great curved nose that almost met the chin and that was like a buzzard's beak. His one hand, lean and crooked, was a talon. The beady grey eyes, unblinking and unwavering, were bitter as death, as bleak as absolute zero and as merciless. His presence was a chill, and Whiskers and Fatty instinctively drew together for protection against the unguessed threat of him. Watching his chance, privily, Whiskers snuggled a chunk of rock several pounds in weigh close to his hand if need for action should arise. Fatty duplicated the performance.

Then both sat licking their lips, guiltily embarrassed, while the unblinking eyes of the terrible one bored into them, now into one, now into another, and then down at the rock-chunks of their preparedness.

"Huh!" sneered the terrible one, with such dreadfulness of menace as to cause Whiskers and Fatty involuntarily to close their hands down on their cave-man's weapons.

"Huh!" the other repeated, reaching his one talon into his side coat pocket with swift definiteness. "A hell of a chance you two cheap bums 'd have with me."

The talon emerged, clutching ready for action a six-pound iron quoit.

"We ain't lookin' for trouble, Slim," Fatty quavered.

"Who in hell are you to call me 'Slim'?" came the snarling answer.

"Me? I'm just Fatty, an' seein' 's I never seen you before—"

"An' I suppose that's Whiskers, there, with the gay an' festive lamp tan-going into his eyebrow an' the God-forgive-us nose joy-riding all over his mug?"

"It'll do, it'll do," Whiskers muttered uncomfortably. "One monica's as good as another, I find, at my time of life. And everybody hands it out to me anyway. And I need an umbrella when it rains to keep from getting drowned, an' all the rest of it."

"I ain't used to company—don't like it," Slim growled. "So if you guys want to stick around, mind your step, that's all, mind your step."

He fished from his pocket a cigar stump, self-evidently shot from the gutter, and prepared to put it in his mouth to chew. Then he changed his mind, glared at his companions savagely, and unrolled his bundle. Appeared in his hand a druggist's bottle of alki.

"Well," he snarled, "I suppose I gotta give you cheap skates a drink when I ain't got more'n enough for a good petrification for myself."

Almost a softening flicker of light was imminent in his withered face as he beheld the others proudly lift their hats and exhibit their own supplies.

"Here's some water for the mixin's," Whiskers said, proffering his tomato-can of river slush. "Stockyards just above," he added apologetically. "But they say—"

"Huh!" Slim snapped short, mixing the drink. "I've drunk worse'n stockyards in my time."

Yet when all was ready, cans of alki in their solitary hands, the three things that had once been men hesitated, as if of old habit, and next betrayed shame as if at self-exposure.

Whiskers was the first to brazen it.

"I've sat in at many a finer drinking," he bragged.

"With the pewter," Slim sneered.

"With the silver," Whiskers corrected.

Slim turned a scorching eye-interrogation on Fatty.

Fatty nodded.

"Beneath the salt," said Slim.

"Above it," came Fatty's correction. "I was born above it, and I've never travelled second class. First or steerage, but no intermediate in mine."

"Yourself?" Whiskers queried of Slim.

"In broken glass to the Queen, God bless her," Slim answered, solemnly, without snarl or sneer.

"In the pantry?" Fatty insinuated.

Simultaneously Slim reached for his quoit, and Whiskers and Fatty for their rocks.

"Now don't let's get feverish," Fatty said, dropping his own weapon. "We aren't scum. We're gentlemen. Let's drink like gentlemen."

"Let it be a real drinking," Whiskers approved.

"Let's get petrified," Slim agreed. "Many a distillery's flowed under the bridge since we were gentlemen; but let's forget the long road we've travelled since, and hit our doss in the good old fashion in which every gentleman went to bed when we were young."

"My father done it—did it," Fatty concurred and corrected, as old recollections exploded long-sealed brain-cells of connotation and correct usage.

The other two nodded a descent from similar fathers, and elevated their tin cans of alcohol.

By the time each had finished his own bottle and from his rags fished forth a second one, their brains were well-mellowed and a-glow, although they had not got around to telling their real names. But their English had improved. They spoke it correctly, while the argo of tramp-land ceased from their lips.

"It's my constitution," Whiskers was explaining. "Very few men could go through what I have and live to tell the tale. And I never took any care of myself. If what the moralists and the physiologists say were true, I'd have been dead long ago. And it's the same with you two. Look at us, at our advanced years, carousing as the young ones don't dare, sleeping out in the open on the ground, never sheltered from frost nor rain nor storm, never afraid of pneumonia or rheumatism that would put half the young ones on their backs in hospital."

He broke off to mix another drink, and Fatty took up the tale.

"And we've had our fun," he boasted, "and speaking of sweethearts and all," he cribbed from Kipling, "'We've rogued and we've ranged—'"

"'In our time,'" Slim completed the crib for him.

"I should say so, I should say so," Fatty confirmed. "And been loved by princesses—at least I have."

"Go on and tell us about it," Whiskers urged. "The night's young, and why shouldn't we remember back to the roofs of kings?"

Nothing loth, Fatty cleared his throat for the recital and cast about in his mind for the best way to begin.

"It must be known that I came of good family. Percival Delaney, let us say, yes, let us say Percival Delaney, was not unknown at Oxford once upon a time—not for scholarship, I am frank to admit; but the gay young dogs of that day, if any be yet alive, would remember him—"

"My people came over with the Conqueror," Whiskers interrupted, extending his hand to Fatty's in acknowledgment of the introduction.

"What name?" Fatty queried. "I did not seem quite to catch it."

"Delarouse, Chauncey Delarouse. The name will serve as well as any."

Both completed the handshake and glanced to Slim.

"Oh, well, while we're about it . . . " Fatty urged.

136

"Bruce Cadogan Cavendish," Slim growled morosely. "Go on, Percival, with your princesses and the roofs of kings."

"Oh, I was a rare young devil," Percival obliged, "after I played ducks and drakes at home and sported out over the world. And I was some figure of a man before I lost my shape—polo, steeple-chasing, boxing. I won medals at buckjumping in Australia, and I held more than several swimming records from the quarter of a mile up. Women turned their heads to look when I went by. The women! God bless them!"

And Fatty, alias Percival Delaney, a grotesque of manhood, put his bulgy hand to his puffed lips and kissed audibly into the starry vault of the sky.

"And the Princess!" he resumed, with another kiss to the stars. "She was as fine a figure of a woman as I was a man, as high-spirited and courageous, as reckless and dare-devilish. Lord, Lord, in the water she was a mermaid, a sea-goddess. And when it came to blood, beside her I was parvenu. Her royal line traced back into the mists of antiquity.

"She was not a daughter of a fair-skinned folk. Tawny golden was she, with golden-brown eyes, and her hair that fell to her knees was blue-black and straight, with just the curly tendrilly tendency that gives to woman's hair its charm. Oh, there were no kinks in it, any more than were there kinks in the hair of her entire genealogy. For she was Polynesian, glowing, golden, lovely and lovable, royal Polynesian."

Again he paused to kiss his hand to the memory of her, and Slim, alias Bruce Cadogan Cavendish, took advantage to interject:

"Huh! Maybe you didn't shine in scholarship, but at least you gleaned a vocabulary out of Oxford."

"And in the South Seas garnered a better vocabulary from the lexicon of Love," Percival was quick on the uptake.

"It was the island of Talofa," he went on, "meaning love, the Isle of Love, and it was her island. Her father, the king, an old man, sat on his mats with paralysed knees and drank squareface gin all day and most of the night, out of grief, sheer grief. She, my princess, was the only issue, her brother having been lost in their double canoe in a hurricane while coming up from a voyage to Samoa. And among the Polynesians the royal women have equal right with the men to rule. In fact, they trace their genealogies always by the female line."

To this both Chauncey Delarouse and Bruce Cadogan Cavendish nodded prompt affirmation.

"Ah," said Percival, "I perceive you both know the South Seas, wherefore, without undue expenditure of verbiage on my part, I am

137

assured that you will appreciate the charm of my princess, the Princess Tui-nui of Talofa, the Princess of the Isle of Love."

He kissed his hand to her, sipped from his condensed milk can a man-size drink of druggist's alcohol, and to her again kissed her hand.

"But she was coy, and ever she fluttered near to me but never near enough. When my arm went out to her to girdle her, presto, she was not there. I knew, as never before, nor since, the thousand dear and delightful anguishes of love frustrated but ever resilient and beckoned on by the very goddess of love."

"Some vocabulary," Bruce Cadogan Cavendish muttered in aside to Chauncey Delarouse. But Percival Delaney was not to be deterred. He kissed his pudgy hand aloft into the night and held warmly on.

"No fond agonies of rapture deferred that were not lavished upon me by my dear Princess, herself ever a luring delight of promise flitting just beyond my reach. Every sweet lover's inferno unguessed of by Dante she led me through. Ah! Those swooning tropic nights, under our palm trees, the distant surf a languourous murmur as from some vast sea shell of mystery, when she, my Princess, all but melted to my yearning, and with her laughter, that was as silver strings by buds and blossoms smitten, all but made lunacy of my lover's ardency.

"It was by my wrestling with the champions of Talofa that I first interested her. It was by my prowess at swimming that I awoke her. And it was by a certain swimming deed that I won from her more than coquettish smiles and shy timidities of feigned retreat.

"We were squidding that day, out on the reef—you know how, undoubtedly, diving down the face of the wall of the reef, five fathoms, ten fathoms, any depth within reason, and shoving our squid-sticks into the likely holes and crannies of the coral where squid might be lairing. With the squid-stick, bluntly sharp at both ends, perhaps a foot long, and held crosswise in the hand, the trick was to gouge any lazying squid until he closed his tentacles around fist, stick and arm.—Then you had him, and came to the surface with him, and hit him in the head which is in the centre of him, and peeled him off into the waiting canoe. . . . And to think I used to do that!"

Percival Delaney paused a moment, a glimmer of awe on his rotund face, as he contemplated the mighty picture of his youth.

"Why, I've pulled out a squid with tentacles eight feet long, and done it under fifty feet of water. I could stay down four minutes. I've gone down, with a coral-rock to sink me, in a hundred and ten feet to clear a fouled anchor. And I could back-dive with a once-over and go in feet-first from eighty feet above the surface—"

"Quit it, delete it, cease it," Chauncey Delarouse admonished testily. "Tell of the Princess. That's what makes old blood leap again. Almost can I see her. Was she wonderful?"

Percival Delaney kissed unutterable affirmation.

"I have said she was a mermaid. She was. I know she swam thirty-six hours before being rescued, after her schooner was capsized in a double-squall. I have seen her do ninety feet and bring up pearl shell in each hand. She was wonderful. As a woman she was ravishing, sublime. I have said she was a sea-goddess. She was. Oh, for a Phidias or a Praxiteles to have made the wonder of her body immortal!

"And that day, out for squid on the reef, I was almost sick for her. Mad—I know I was mad for her. We would step over the side from the big canoe, and swim down, side by side, into the delicious depths of cool and colour, and she would look at me, as we swam, and with her eyes tantalize me to further madness. And at last, down, far down, I lost myself and reached for her. She eluded me like the mermaid she was, and I saw the laughter on her face as she fled. She fled deeper, and I knew I had her for I was between her and the surface; but in the muck coral sand of the bottom she made a churning with her squid stick. It was the old trick to escape a shark. And she worked it on me, rolling the water so that I could not see her. And when I came up, she was there ahead of me, clinging to the side of the canoe and laughing.

"Almost I would not be denied. But not for nothing was she a princess. She rested her hand on my arm and compelled me to listen. We should play a game, she said, enter into a competition for which should get the more squid, the biggest squid, and the smallest squid. Since the wagers were kisses, you can well imagine I went down on the first next dive with soul aflame.

"I got no squid. Never again in all my life have I dived for squid. Perhaps we were five fathoms down and exploring the face of the reefwall for lurking places of our prey, when it happened. I had found a likely lair and just proved it empty, when I felt or sensed the nearness of something inimical. I turned. There it was, alongside of me, and no mere fish-shark. Fully a dozen feet in length, with the unmistakable phosphorescent cat's eye gleaming like a drowning star, I knew it for what it was, a tiger shark.

"Not ten feet to the right, probing a coral fissure with her squid stick, was the Princess, and the tiger shark was heading directly for her. My totality of thought was precipitated to consciousness in a single all-embracing flash. The man-eater must be deflected from her, and what was I, except a mad lover who would gladly fight and die, or more gladly fight and live, for his beloved? Remember, she was the woman wonderful, and I was aflame for her.

"Knowing fully the peril of my act, I thrust the blunt-sharp end of my squid-stick into the side of the shark, much as one would attract a passing acquaintance with a thumb-nudge in the ribs. And the man-eater turned on me. You know the South Seas, and you know that the tiger shark, like the bald-face grizzly of Alaska, never gives trail. The combat, fathoms deep under the sea, was on—if by combat may be named such a one-sided struggle.

"The Princess unaware, caught her squid and rose to the surface. The man-eater rushed me. I fended him off with both hands on his nose above his thousand-toothed open mouth, so that he backed me against the sharp coral. The scars are there to this day. Whenever I tried to rise, he rushed me, and I could not remain down there indefinitely without air. Whenever he rushed me, I fended him off with my hands on his nose. And I would have escaped unharmed, except for the slip of my right hand. Into his mouth it went to the elbow. His jaws closed, just below the elbow. You know how a shark's teeth are. Once in they cannot be released. They must go through to complete the bite, but they cannot go through heavy bone. So, from just below the elbow he stripped the bone clean to the articulation of the wrist-joint, where his teeth met and my good right hand became his for an appetizer.

"But while he was doing this, I drove the thumb of my left hand, to the hilt into his eye-orifice and popped out his eye. This did not stop him. The meat had maddened him. He pursued the gushing stump of my wrist. Half a dozen times I fended with my intact arm. Then he got the poor mangled arm again, closed down, and stripped the meat off the bone from the shoulder down to the elbow-joint, where his teeth met and he was free of his second mouthful of me. But, at the same time, with my good arm, I thumbed out his remaining eye."

Percival Delaney shrugged his shoulders, ere he resumed.

"From above, those in the canoe had beheld the entire happening and were loud in praise of my deed. To this day they still sing the song of me, and tell the tale of me. And the Princess." His pause was brief but significant. "The Princess married me. . . . Oh, well-a-day and lack-a-day, the whirligig of time and fortune, the topsyturviness of luck, the wooden shoe going up and the polished heel descending a French gunboat, a conquered island kingdom of Oceania, to-day ruled over by a peasant-born, unlettered, colonial gendarme, and . . . "

140

He completed the sentence and the tale by burying his face in the down-tilted mouth of the condensed milk can and by gurgling the corrosive drink down his throat in thirsty gulps.

After an appropriate pause, Chauncey Delarouse, otherwise Whiskers, took up the tale.

"Far be it from me to boast of no matter what place of birth I have descended from to sit here by this fire with such as . . . as chance along. I may say, however, that I, too, was once a considerable figure of a man. I may add that it was horses, plus parents too indulgent, that exiled me out over the world. I may still wonder to query: 'Are Dover's cliffs still white?'"

"Huh!" Bruce Cadogan Cavendish sneered. "Next you'll be asking: 'How fares the old Lord Warden?'"

"And I took every liberty, and vainly, with a constitution that was iron," Whiskers hurried on. "Here I am with my three score and ten behind me, and back on that long road have I buried many a youngster that was as rare and devilish as I, but who could not stand the pace. I knew the worst too young. And now I know the worst too old. But there was a time, alas all too short, when I knew, the best.

"I, too, kiss my hand to the Princess of my heart. She was truly a princess, Polynesian, a thousand miles and more away to the eastward and the south from Delaney's Isle of Love. The natives of all around that part of the South Seas called it the Jolly Island. Their own name, the name of the people who dwelt thereon, translates delicately and justly into 'The Island of Tranquil Laughter.' On the chart you will find the erroneous name given to it by the old navigators to be Manatomana. The seafaring gentry the round ocean around called it the Adamless Eden. And the missionaries for a time called it God's Witness—so great had been their success at converting the inhabitants. As for me, it was, and ever shall be, Paradise.

"It was my Paradise, for it was there my Princess lived. John Asibeli Tungi was king. He was full-blooded native, descended out of the oldest and highest chief-stock that traced back to Manua which was the primeval sea home of the race. Also was he known as John the Apostate. He lived a long life and apostasized frequently. First converted by the Catholics, he threw down the idols, broke the tabus, cleaned out the native priests, executed a few of the recalcitrant ones, and sent all his subjects to church.

"Next he fell for the traders, who developed in him a champagne thirst, and he shipped off the Catholic priests to New Zealand. The great majority of his subjects always followed his lead, and, having no religion at all, ensued the time of the Great

Licentiousness, when by all South Seas missionaries his island, in sermons, was spoken of as Babylon.

"But the traders ruined his digestion with too much champagne, and after several years he fell for the Gospel according to the Methodists, sent his people to church, and cleaned up the beach and the trading crowd so spick and span that he would not permit them to smoke a pipe out of doors on Sunday, and, fined one of the chief traders one hundred gold sovereigns for washing his schooner's decks on the Sabbath morn.

"That was the time of the Blue Laws, but perhaps it was too rigorous for King John. Off he packed the Methodists, one fine day, exiled several hundred of his people to Samoa for sticking to Methodism, and, of all things, invented a religion of his own, with himself the figure-head of worship. In this he was aided and abetted by a renegade Fijian. This lasted five years. Maybe he grew tired of being God, or maybe it was because the Fijian decamped with the six thousand pounds in the royal treasury; but at any rate the Second Reformed Wesleyans got him, and his entire kingdom went Wesleyan. The pioneer Wesleyan missionary he actually made prime minister, and what he did to the trading crowd was a caution. Why, in the end, King John's kingdom was blacklisted and boycotted by the traders till the revenues diminished to zero, the people went bankrupt, and King John couldn't borrow a shilling from his most powerful chief.

"By this time he was getting old, and philosophic, and tolerant, and spiritually atavistic. He fired out the Second Reformed Wesleyans, called back the exiles from Samoa, invited in the traders, held a general love-feast, took the lid off, proclaimed religious liberty and high tariff, and as for himself went back to the worship of his ancestors, dug up the idols, reinstated a few octogenarian priests, and observed the tabus. All of which was lovely for the traders, and prosperity reigned. Of course, most of his subjects followed him back into heathen worship. Yet quite a sprinkling of Catholics, Methodists and Wesleyans remained true to their beliefs and managed to maintain a few squalid, one-horse churches. But King John didn't mind, any more than did he the high times of the traders along the beach. Everything went, so long as the taxes were paid. Even when his wife, Queen Mamare, elected to become a Baptist, and invited in a little, weazened, sweet-spirited, club-footed Baptist missionary, King John did not object. All he insisted on was that these wandering religions should be self-supporting and not feed a pennyworth's out of the royal coffers.

"And now the threads of my recital draw together in the paragon of female exquisiteness—my Princess."

Whiskers paused, placed carefully on the ground his half-full condensed milk can with which he had been absently toying, and kissed the fingers of his one hand audibly aloft.

"She was the daughter of Queen Mamare. She was the woman wonderful. Unlike the Diana type of Polynesian, she was almost ethereal. She was ethereal, sublimated by purity, as shy and modest as a violet, as fragile-slender as a lily, and her eyes, luminous and shrinking tender, were as asphodels on the sward of heaven. She was all flower, and fire, and dew. Hers was the sweetness of the mountain rose, the gentleness of the dove. And she was all of good as well as all of beauty, devout in her belief in her mother's worship, which was the worship introduced by Ebenezer Naismith, the Baptist missionary. But make no mistake. She was no mere sweet spirit ripe for the bosom of Abraham. All of exquisite deliciousness of woman was she. She was woman, all woman, to the last sensitive quivering atom of her—

"And I? I was a wastrel of the beach. The wildest was not so wild as I, the keenest not so keen, of all that wild, keen trading crowd. It was esteemed I played the stiffest hand of poker. I was the only living man, white, brown, or black, who dared run the Kuni-kuni Passage in the dark. And on a black night I have done it under reefs in a gale of wind. Well, anyway, I had a bad reputation on a beach where there were no good reputations. I was reckless, dangerous, stopped at nothing in fight or frolic; and the trading captains used to bring boiler-sheeted prodigies from the vilest holes of the South Pacific to try and drink me under the table. I remember one, a calcined Scotchman from the New Hebrides. It was a great drinking. He died of it, and we laded him aboard ship, pickled in a cask of trade rum, and sent him back to his own place. A sample, a fair sample, of the antic tricks we cut up on the beach of Manatomana.

"And of all unthinkable things, what did I up and do, one day, but look upon the Princess to find her good and to fall in love with her. It was the real thing. I was as mad as a March hare, and after that I got only madder. I reformed. Think of that! Think of what a slip of a woman can do to a busy, roving man!—By the Lord Harry, it's true. I reformed. I went to church. Hear me! I became converted. I cleared my soul before God and kept my hands—I had two then—off the ribald crew of the beach when it laughed at this, my latest antic, and wanted to know what was my game.

"I tell you I reformed, and gave myself in passion and sincerity to a religious experience that has made me tolerant of all religion ever since. I discharged my best captain for immorality. So did I my cook, and a better never boiled water in Manatomana. For the same reason I discharged my chief clerk. And for the first time in the history of trading my schooners to the westward carried Bibles in their stock. I built a little anchorite bungalow up town on a mango-lined street squarely alongside the little house occupied by Ebenezer Naismith. And I made him my pal and comrade, and found him a veritable honey pot of sweetnesses and goodnesses. And he was a man, through and through a man. And he died long after like a man, which I would like to tell you about, were the tale of it not so deservedly long.

"It was the Princess, more than the missionary, who was responsible for my expressing my faith in works, and especially in that crowning work, the New Church, Our Church, the Queen-mother's church.

"'Our poor church,' she said to me, one night after prayer-meeting. I had been converted only a fortnight. 'It is so small its congregation can never grow. And the roof leaks. And King John, my hard-hearted father, will not contribute a penny. Yet he has a big balance in the treasury. And Manatomana is not poor. Much money is made and squandered, I know. I hear the gossip of the wild ways of the beach. Less than a month ago you lost more in one night, gambling at cards, than the cost of the upkeep of our poor church for a year.'

"And I told her it was true, but that it was before I had seen the light. (I'd had an infernal run of bad luck.) I told her I had not tasted liquor since, nor turned a card. I told her that the roof would be repaired at once, by Christian carpenters selected by her from the congregation. But she was filled with the thought of a great revival that Ebenezer Naismith could preach—she was a dear saint—and she spoke of a great church, saying:

"'You are rich. You have many schooners, and traders in far islands, and I have heard of a great contract you have signed to recruit labour for the German plantations of Upolu. They say, next to Sweitzer, you are the richest trader here. I should love to see some use of all this money placed to the glory of God. It would be a noble thing to do, and I should be proud to know the man who would do it.'

"I told her that Ebenezer Naismith would preach the revival, and that I would build a church great enough in which to house it.

"'As big as the Catholic church?' she asked.

"This was the ruined cathedral, built at the time when the entire population was converted, and it was a large order; but I was afire with love, and I told her that the church I would build would be even bigger.

"'But it will take money,' I explained. 'And it takes time to make money.'

"'You have much,' she said. 'Some say you have more money than my father, the King.

"'I have more credit,' I explained. 'But you do not understand money. It takes money to have credit. So, with the money I have, and the credit I have, I will work to make more money and credit, and the church shall be built.'

"Work! I was a surprise to myself. It is an amazement, the amount of time a man finds on his hands after he's given up carousing, and gambling, and all the time-eating diversions of the beach. And I didn't waste a second of all my new-found time. Instead I worked it overtime. I did the work of half a dozen men. I became a driver. My captains made faster runs than ever and earned bigger bonuses, as did my supercargoes, who saw to it that my schooners did not loaf and dawdle along the way. And I saw to it that my supercargoes did see to it.

"And good! By the Lord Harry I was so good it hurt. My conscience got so expansive and fine-strung it lamed me across the shoulders to carry it around with me. Why, I even went back over my accounts and paid Sweitzer fifty quid I'd jiggered him out of in a deal in Fiji three years before. And I compounded the interest as well.

"Work! I planted sugar cane—the first commercial planting on Manatomana. I ran in cargoes of kinky-heads from Malaita, which is in the Solomons, till I had twelve hundred of the blackbirds putting in cane. And I sent a schooner clear to Hawaii to bring back a dismantled sugar mill and a German who said he knew the field-end of cane. And he did, and he charged me three hundred dollars screw a month, and I took hold of the mill-end. I installed the mill myself, with the help of several mechanics I brought up from Queensland.

"Of course there was a rival. His name was Motomoe. He was the very highest chief blood next to King John's. He was full native, a strapping, handsome man, with a glowering way of showing his dislikes. He certainly glowered at me when I began hanging around the palace. He went back in my history and circulated the blackest tales about me. The worst of it was that most of them were true. He even made a voyage to Apia to find things out—as if he couldn't find a plenty right there on the beach of Manatomana! And he sneered at my failing for religion, and at my going to prayer-meeting, and, most of all, at my sugar-planting. He challenged me to fight, and I kept off of him. He threatened me, and I learned in the nick of time

145

of his plan to have me knocked on the head. You see, he wanted the Princess just as much as I did, and I wanted her more.

"She used to play the piano. So did I, once. But I never let her know after I'd heard her play the first time. And she thought her playing was wonderful, the dear, fond girl! You know the sort, the mechanical one-two-three tum-tum-tum school-girl stuff. And now I'll tell you something funnier. Her playing was wonderful to me. The gates of heaven opened to me when she played. I can see myself now, worn out and dog-tired after the long day, lying on the mats of the palace veranda and gazing upon her at the piano, myself in a perfect idiocy of bliss. Why, this idea she had of her fine playing was the one flaw in her deliciousness of perfection, and I loved her for it. It kind of brought her within my human reach. Why, when she played her one-two-three, tum-tum-tum, I was in the seventh heaven of bliss. My weariness fell from me. I loved her, and my love for her was clean as flame, clean as my love for God. And do you know, into my fond lover's fancy continually intruded the thought that God in most ways must look like her.

"—That's right, Bruce Cadogan Cavendish, sneer as you like. But I tell you that's love that I've been describing. That's all. It's love. It's the realest, purest, finest thing that can happen to a man. And I know what I'm talking about. It happened to me."

Whiskers, his beady squirrel's eye glittering from out his ruined eyebrow like a live coal in a jungle ambush, broke off long enough to down a sedative draught from his condensed milk can and to mix another.

"The cane," he resumed, wiping his prodigious mat of face hair with the back of his hand. "It matured in sixteen months in that climate, and I was ready, just ready and no more, with the mill for the grinding. Naturally, it did not all mature at once, but I had planted in such succession that I could grind for nine months steadily, while more was being planted and the ratoons were springing up.

"I had my troubles the first several days. If it wasn't one thing the matter with the mill, it was another. On the fourth day, Ferguson, my engineer, had to shut down several hours in order to remedy his own troubles. I was bothered by the feeder. After having the niggers (who had been feeding the cane) pour cream of lime on the rollers to keep everything sweet, I sent them out to join the cane-cutting squads. So I was all alone at that end, just as Ferguson started up the mill, just as I discovered what was the matter with the feed-rollers, and just as Motomoe strolled up.

"He stood there, in Norfolk jacket, pigskin puttees, and all the rest of the fashionable get-up out of a bandbox, sneering at me covered with filth and grease to the eyebrows and looking like a navvy. And, the rollers now white from the lime, I'd just seen what was wrong. The rollers were not in plumb. One side crushed the cane well, but the other side was too open. I shoved my fingers in on that side. The big, toothed cogs on the rollers did not touch my fingers. And yet, suddenly, they did. With the grip of ten thousand devils, my finger-tips were caught, drawn in, and pulped to—well, just pulp. And, like a slick of cane, I had started on my way. There was no stopping me. Ten thousand horses could not have pulled me back. There was nothing to stop me. Hand, arm, shoulder, head, and chest, down to the toes of me, I was doomed to feed through.

"It did hurt. It hurt so much it did not hurt me at all. Quite detached, almost may I say, I looked on my hand being ground up, knuckle by knuckle, joint by joint, the back of the hand, the wrist, the forearm, all in order slowly and inevitably feeding in. O engineer hoist by thine own petard! O sugar-maker crushed by thine own cane-crusher!

"Motomoe sprang forward involuntarily, and the sneer was chased from his face by an expression of solicitude. Then the beauty of the situation dawned on him, and he chuckled and grinned. No, I didn't expect anything of him. Hadn't he tried to knock me on the head? What could he do anyway? He didn't know anything about engines.

"I yelled at the top of my lungs to Ferguson to shut off the engine, but the roar of the machinery drowned my voice. And there I stood, up to the elbow and feeding right on in. Yes, it did hurt. There were some astonishing twinges when special nerves were shredded and dragged out by the roots. But I remember that I was surprised at the time that it did not hurt worse.

"Motomoe made a movement that attracted my attention. At the same time he growled out loud, as if he hated himself, 'I'm a fool.' What he had done was to pick up a cane-knife—you know the kind, as big as a machete and as heavy. And I was grateful to him in advance for putting me out of my misery. There wasn't any sense in slowly feeding in till my head was crushed, and already my arm was pulped half way from elbow to shoulder, and the pulping was going right on. So I was grateful, as I bent my head to the blow.

"'Get your head out of the way, you idiot!' he barked at me.

"And then I understood and obeyed. I was a big man, and he took two hacks to do it; but he hacked my arm off just outside the shoulder and dragged me back and laid me down on the cane.

"Yes, the sugar paid—enormously; and I built for the Princess the church of her saintly dream, and . . . she married me."

He partly assuaged his thirst, and uttered his final word.

"Alackaday! Shuttlecock and battle-dore. And this at, the end of it all, lined with boilerplate that even alcohol will not corrode and that only alcohol will tickle. Yet have I lived, and I kiss my hand to the dear dust of my Princess long asleep in the great mausoleum of King John that looks across the Vale of Manona to the alien flag that floats over the bungalow of the British Government House. . . ."

Fatty pledged him sympathetically, and sympathetically drank out of his own small can. Bruce Cadogan Cavendish glared into the fire with implacable bitterness. He was a man who preferred to drink by himself. Across the thin lips that composed the cruel slash of his mouth played twitches of mockery that caught Fatty's eye. And Fatty, making sure first that his rock-chunk was within reach, challenged.

"Well, how about yourself, Bruce Cadogan Cavendish? It's your turn."

The other lifted bleak eyes that bored into Fatty's until he physically betrayed uncomfortableness.

"I've lived a hard life," Slim grated harshly. "What do I know about love passages?"

"No man of your build and make-up could have escaped them," Fatty wheedled.

"And what of it?" Slim snarled. "It's no reason for a gentleman to boast of amorous triumphs."

"Oh, go on, be a good fellow," Fatty urged. "The night's still young. We've still some drink left. Delarouse and I have contributed our share. It isn't often that three real ones like us get together for a telling. Surely you've got at least one adventure in love you aren't ashamed to tell about—"

Bruce Cadogan Cavendish pulled forth his iron quoit and seemed to debate whether or not he should brain the other. He sighed, and put back the quoit.

"Very well, if you will have it," he surrendered with manifest reluctance. "Like you two, I have had a remarkable constitution. And right now, speaking of armour-plate lining, I could drink the both of you down when you were at your prime. Like you two, my beginnings were far distant and different. That I am marked with the hall-mark of gentlehood there is no discussion . . . unless either of you care to discuss the matter now . . . "

His one hand slipped into his pocket and clutched the quoit. Neither of his auditors spoke nor betrayed any awareness of his menace.

"It occurred a thousand miles to the westward of Manatomana, on the island of Tagalag," he continued abruptly, with an air of saturnine disappointment in that there had been no

148

discussion. "But first I must tell you of how I got to Tagalag. For reasons I shall not mention, by paths of descent I shall not describe, in the crown of my manhood and the prime of my devilishness in which Oxford renegades and racing younger sons had nothing on me, I found myself master and owner of a schooner so well known that she shall remain historically nameless. I was running blackbird labour from the west South Pacific and the Coral Sea to the plantations of Hawaii and the nitrate mines of Chili—"

"It was you who cleaned out the entire population of—" Fatty exploded, ere he could check his speech.

The one hand of Bruce Cadogan Cavendish flashed pocketward and flashed back with the quoit balanced ripe for business.

"Proceed," Fatty sighed. "I . . . I have quite forgotten what I was going to say."

"Beastly funny country over that way," the narrator drawled with perfect casualness. "You've read this Sea Wolf stuff—"

"You weren't the Sea Wolf," Whiskers broke in with involuntary positiveness.

"No, sir," was the snarling answer. "The Sea Wolf's dead, isn't he? And I'm still alive, aren't I?"

"Of course, of course," Whiskers conceded. "He suffocated head-first in the mud off a wharf in Victoria a couple of years back."

"As I was saying—and I don't like interruptions," Bruce Cadogan Cavendish proceeded, "it's a beastly funny country over that way. I was at Taki-Tiki, a low island that politically belongs to the Solomons, but that geologically doesn't at all, for the Solomons are high islands. Ethnographically it belongs to Polynesia, Melanesia, and Micronesia, because all the breeds of the South Pacific have gravitated to it by canoe-drift and intricately, degeneratively, and amazingly interbred. The scum of the scrapings of the bottom of the human pit, biologically speaking, resides in Taka-Tiki. And I know the bottom and whereof I speak.

"It was a beastly funny time of it I had, diving out shell, fishing beche-de-mer, trading hoop-iron and hatchets for copra and ivory-nuts, running niggers and all the rest of it. Why, even in Fiji the Lotu was having a hard time of it and the chiefs still eating long-pig. To the westward it was fierce—funny little black kinky-heads, man-eaters the last Jack of them, and the jackpot fat and spilling over with wealth—"

"Jack-pots?" Fatty queried. At sight of an irritable movement, he added: "You see, I never got over to the West like Delarouse and you."

"They're all head-hunters. Heads are valuable, especially a

149

white man's head. They decorate the canoe-houses and devil-devil houses with them. Each village runs a jack-pot, and everybody antes. Whoever brings in a white man's head takes the pot. If there aren't openers for a long time, the pot grows to tremendous proportions. Beastly funny, isn't it?

"I know. Didn't a Holland mate die on me of blackwater? And didn't I win a pot myself? It was this way. We were lying at Lango-lui at the time. I never let on, and arranged the affair with Johnny, my boat-steerer. He was a kinky-head himself from Port Moresby. He cut the dead mate's head off and sneaked ashore in the night, while I whanged away with my rifle as if I were trying to get him. He opened the pot with the mate's head, and got it, too. Of course, next day I sent in a landing boat, with two covering boats, and fetched him off with the loot."

"How big was the pot?" Whiskers asked. "I heard of a pot at Orla worth eighty quid."

"To commence with," Slim answered, "there were forty fat pigs, each worth a fathom of prime shell-money, and shell-money worth a quid a fathom. That was two hundred dollars right there. There were ninety-eight fathoms of shell-money, which is pretty close to five hundred in itself. And there were twenty-two gold sovereigns. I split it four ways: one-fourth to Johnny, one-fourth to the ship, one-fourth to me as owner, and one-fourth to me as skipper. Johnny never complained. He'd never had so much wealth all at one time in his life. Besides, I gave him a couple of the mate's old shirts. And I fancy the mate's head is still there decorating the canoe-house."

"Not exactly Christian burial of a Christian," Whiskers observed.

"But a lucrative burial," Slim retorted. "I had to feed the rest of the mate over-side to the sharks for nothing. Think of feeding an eight-hundred-dollar head along with it. It would have been criminal waste and stark lunacy.

"Well, anyway, it was all beastly funny, over there to the westward. And, without telling you the scrape I got into at Taki-Tiki, except that I sailed away with two hundred kinky-heads for Queensland labour, and for my manner of collecting them had two British ships of war combing the Pacific for me, I changed my course and ran to the westward thinking to dispose of the lot to the Spanish plantations on Bangar.

"Typhoon season. We caught it. The Merry Mist was my schooner's name, and I had thought she was stoutly built until she hit that typhoon. I never saw such seas. They pounded that stout craft to pieces, literally so. The sticks were jerked out of her, deckhouses splintered to match-wood, rails ripped off, and, after the worst had passed, the covering boards began to go. We just managed to repair what was left of one boat and keep the schooner afloat only till the sea went down barely enough to get away. And we outfitted that boat in a hurry. The carpenter and I were the last, and we had to jump for it as he went down. There were only four of us—"

"Lost all the niggers?" Whiskers inquired.

"Some of them swam for some time," Slim replied. "But I don't fancy they made the land. We were ten days' in doing it. And we had a spanking breeze most of the way. And what do you think we had in the boat with us? Cases of square-face gin and cases of dynamite. Funny, wasn't it? Well, it got funnier later on. Oh, there was a small beaker of water, a little salt horse, and some salt-water-soaked sea biscuit—enough to keep us alive to Tagalag.

"Now Tagalag is the disappointingest island I've ever beheld. It shows up out of the sea so as you can make its fall twenty miles off. It is a volcano cone thrust up out of deep sea, with a segment of the crater wall broken out. This gives sea entrance to the crater itself, and makes a fine sheltered harbour. And that's all. Nothing lives there. The outside and the inside of the crater are too steep. At one place, inside, is a patch of about a thousand coconut palms. And that's all, as I said, saving a few insects. No four-legged thing, even a rat, inhabits the place. And it's funny, most awful funny, with all those coconuts, not even a coconut crab. The only meat-food living was schools of mullet in the harbour—fattest, finest, biggest mullet I ever laid eyes on.

"And the four of us landed on the little beach and set up housekeeping among the coconuts with a larder full of dynamite and square-face. Why don't you laugh? It's funny, I tell you. Try it some time.—Holland gin and straight coconut diet. I've never been able to look a confectioner's window in the face since. Now I'm not strong on religion like Chauncey Delarouse there, but I have some primitive ideas; and my concept of hell is an illimitable coconut plantation, stocked with cases of square-face and populated by ship-wrecked mariners. Funny? It must make the devil scream.

"You know, straight coconut is what the agriculturists call an unbalanced ration. It certainly unbalanced our digestions. We got so that whenever hunger took an extra bite at us, we took another drink of gin. After a couple of weeks of it, Olaf, a squarehead sailor, got an idea. It came when he was full of gin, and we, being in the same fix, just watched him shove a cap and short fuse into a stick of dynamite and stroll down toward the boat.

"It dawned on me that he was going to shoot fish if there were

151

any about; but the sun was beastly hot, and I just reclined there and hoped he'd have luck.

"About half an hour after he disappeared we heard the explosion. But he didn't come back. We waited till the cool of sunset, and down on the beach found what had become of him. The boat was there all right, grounded by the prevailing breeze, but there was no Olaf. He would never have to eat coconut again. We went back, shakier than ever, and cracked another square-face.

"The next day the cook announced that he would rather take his chance with dynamite than continue trying to exist on coconut, and that, though he didn't know anything about dynamite, he knew a sight too much about coconut. So we bit the detonator down for him, shoved in a fuse, and picked him a good fire-stick, while he jolted up with a couple more stiff ones of gin.

"It was the same programme as the day before. After a while we heard the explosion and at twilight went down to the boat, from which we scraped enough of the cook for a funeral.

"The carpenter and I stuck it out two days more, then we drew straws for it and it was his turn. We parted with harsh words; for he wanted to take a square-face along to refresh himself by the way, while I was set against running any chance of wasting the gin. Besides, he had more than he could carry then, and he wobbled and staggered as he walked.

"Same thing, only there was a whole lot of him left for me to bury, because he'd prepared only half a stick. I managed to last it out till next day, when, after duly fortifying myself, I got sufficient courage to tackle the dynamite. I used only a third of a stick—you know, short fuse, with the end split so as to hold the head of a safety match. That's where I mended my predecessors' methods. Not using the match-head, they'd too-long fuses. Therefore, when they spotted a school of mullet; and lighted the fuse, they had to hold the dynamite till the fuse burned short before they threw it. If they threw it too soon, it wouldn't go off the instant it hit the water, while the splash of it would frighten the mullet away. Funny stuff dynamite. At any rate, I still maintain mine was the safer method.

"I picked up a school of mullet before I'd been rowing five minutes. Fine big fat ones they were, and I could smell them over the fire. When I stood up, fire-stick in one hand, dynamite stick in the other, my knees were knocking together. Maybe it was the gin, or the anxiousness, or the weakness and the hunger, and maybe it was the result of all of them, but at any rate I was all of a shake. Twice I failed to touch the fire-stick to the dynamite. Then I did, heard the match-head splutter, and let her go.

"Now I don't know what happened to the others, but I know

152

what I did. I got turned about. Did you ever stem a strawberry and throw the strawberry away and pop the stem into your mouth? That's what I did. I threw the fire-stick into the water after the mullet and held on to the dynamite. And my arm went off with the stick when it went off. . . . "

Slim investigated the tomato-can for water to mix himself a drink, but found it empty. He stood up.

"Heigh ho," he yawned, and started down the path to the river.

In several minutes he was back. He mixed the due quantity of river slush with the alcohol, took a long, solitary drink, and stared with bitter moodiness into the fire.

"Yes, but . . . " Fatty suggested. "What happened then?"

"Oh," sad Slim. "Then the princess married me, of course."

"But you were the only person left, and there wasn't any princess . . . " Whiskers cried out abruptly, and then let his voice trail away to embarrassed silence.

Slim stared unblinkingly into the fire.

Percival Delaney and Chauncey Delarouse looked at each other. Quietly, in solemn silence, each with his one arm aided the one arm of the other in rolling and tying his bundle. And in silence, bundles slung on shoulders, they went away out of the circle of firelight. Not until they reached the top of the railroad embankment did they speak.

"No gentleman would have done it," said Whiskers.

"No gentleman would have done it," Fatty agreed.

THE END

153

www.ingramcontent.com/pod-product-compliance
Lightning Source LLC
Chambersburg PA
CBHW011512170626
46810CB00009B/3331